CW01666015

A.N.Porter

PHANTOM WEDDING

First published in paperback by
Michael Terence Publishing in 2024
www.mtp.agency

Revised Edition (2)

ISBN 9781800947139

Michael Terence
Publishing

She felt connected to the flat the moment she stepped across the threshold.

Connected?

Or entangled?

At that moment she wasn't analysing the feeling in her chest. She felt her heart thumping and put it down to excitement. Of course. What else? Patsy didn't think the Housing Association would ever offer her something so cute and stylish. She'd been on the waiting list for nearly a year and had almost given up hope.

She was impatient at the best of times. Waiting for the kettle to boil for her morning coffee vexed her beyond words. She would get one of those posh taps installed over the kitchen sink one of these days – when she had money to burn – the ones that give you boiling hot water at the flick of the wrist. But for now, she wanted to spend all her savings on making this flat her own.

She tried not to run around the place like an excited child at Christmas. She was trying to play it cool in front of the Housing Association bloke – she'd been to performing arts school as a kid, but this was going to be the hardest acting she had ever had to do. She peered out of the living room window. There was a sizable garden wrapping around the little block of eight apartments and a little stream which curved around the lawn heading off under a bridge over which the train tracks ran.

'That is Rainbow Brook,' said the housing guy over her shoulder.

'Rainbow Brook,' Patsy echoed. It sounded so rural. She imagined she was living in a cottage in a village in the Cotswolds, not a third floor flat on the edges of London's urban sprawl, which would one day soon, no longer be the edges, but the midst of a megacity, if all those cranes piercing the skyline were anything to go by.

The flat was at the dead end of a little road of other low-rise blocks. Her Beetle would have its very own parking spot – no more car wars like outside her flat in Cricklewood, where the streets were a free-for-all in so many ways.

She turned from the window and started decorating the plain colourless living room in her mind. Wood vinyl on the floor perhaps, three bright almond white painted walls and a feature wall in a bold chocolate coloured print with a leather sofa to match. There were two bedrooms, so finally she could have friends to stay, and a *compact* kitchen (as the housing officer called it), but she would make it work for her when her pots and pans and spice rack were in place.

The housing officer said something else, but she was so lost in interior designing she didn't catch what he said. She assumed it was something like, 'Check out the bathroom!' So, she wandered down the short narrow hallway and looked in at the bath where she imagined many a night soaking, with mellow tunes on the radio and candles glowing all around. The tiling was still in good condition. The flats could only have been thirty years old at most and this one looked as if it had barely been lived in.

'Why did the last tenants move out?' she called out to the officer, wondering why anyone would want to give up this little hidden gem when affordable assured tenancies were so rare and one as nice as this was almost impossible to find in London.

The officer said something behind her, but it couldn't be in reply to her question because it was in another language, an incomprehensible one. Perhaps he was on the phone to someone at the office, or more likely his wife or mum at home asking him what time he'd be back for dinner. It might have been Polish that he spoke. There were many Polish people in London these days, many of them in the housing trade, Patsy thought, but it was a flicker of a thought. She didn't really care because at that moment she was obsessed with the idea of ripping out that white porcelain wash basin and putting in a hand beaten copper one – she'd seen it on Pinterest, and it transformed a bathroom.

She floated back to the living room and looked down at the brook which flowed beside the car park and down to the main road. Standing on the grassy bank was a very tall, skinny old man, probably a homeless one, Patsy thought, judging by the vast distance between his frayed red trousers and his battered brown shoes and the holes in his purple pinstriped suit jacket. His hair was smoky grey and stuck out from beneath a yellow hat which was too pointed to be a bucket hat like the ravers wore at the summer festivals in Finsbury Park, but it wasn't quite as tall as the kind of hat that Gandalf would wear, Patsy thought with a smile as she thought about her fiancé's favourite films of Middle Earth. She couldn't wait to tell Ben about this place. She couldn't wait to share it with him. She couldn't wait to—

Her thoughts popped as the man on the riverbank turned sharply and looked up at her as if he knew she was watching him. He locked eyes with her and shook his head slowly and deliberately. His face was like a ploughed field, packed with folds as if he'd spent his whole life telling people bad things. His skin was pale as if he rarely went outside and his cheeks and slender nose were red as if he drank a lot. Clearly a pissed homeless man, Patsy thought tearing her eyes from his bloodshot ones and backing into the living room out of sight.

The housing officer said something over her shoulder again and it made her jump this time. It was so loud and so aggressive. It had a robot-like echo, whatever foreign language he was speaking, to Patsy's ear it was abrasive, and one she'd never heard before.

'I'm sorry,' Patsy said as politely as she could, 'I don't understand…'

Her voice trailed off when she saw that no one was standing next to her. No one was even standing in the room for that matter. She felt the blood rush to her face and her heart began to pound uncontrollably, she was about to head to the bedroom to find out where the officer had gone, when there was a knock at the front door, stunned, she hurriedly flung it open.

Her heart sank, because it was perhaps the last person in the world that she wanted to be standing on the other side of that door.

It was the housing officer.

'Sorry about that,' he chirped in a pure thick authentic cockney English accent, not a hint of a foreign tongue about him. 'I just had to step out for five minutes to take a call.'

'That's all right,' Patsy said hearing her own voice tremble ever so slightly.

'What do you think of the place?' he grinned. 'Wicked, innit?'

She chose to ignore it, this feeling of dread. The thumping of her heart and the blood rushing through her veins. She told herself it was the pure excitement of it all. Her head was all over the place with plans for the future and a feeling of having won the lottery with this place. She wasn't thinking clearly. She had imagined the voice because she had assumed that the housing officer was still in the room while she dreamed about wallpaper and soft furnishings. So, when he'd said, 'Wicked, innit?' She'd replied, 'Yes. It's perfect.'

The officer had handed her the keys and wished her well and now she stood outside the front door, *her* front door on the little landing between her flat and the only other one on the top floor of the block.

'The penthouse,' she whispered and grinned as she put out her hand to stroke the door as if it were her cat, Nelson. She was thinking how she would freshen the paintwork up here with a nice coat of eggshell blue perhaps, when she felt a sharp stabbing in her index finger. She pulled her hand from the door and examined her finger for a splinter. But there was nothing there. Perhaps it wasn't from the wooden door then, she thought. Perhaps it was some kind of electric shock. Static, she told herself confidently, as if she knew about stuff like that.

She heard a click behind her and turned to see a shadow lingering behind the frosted glass of her neighbour's door. She thought for a moment about going to introduce herself. The shadow too seemed to be pondering its next move. But something told Patsy it wasn't the time, so she skipped off down the stairs to be met on the second-floor landing by a young woman who was struggling to find door keys in her bag while trying to keep hold of a little girl. The girl was far more interested, it seemed, in trying to throw herself down the stairs than going inside the flat.

'Come here, you!' the woman snapped in a rough North London accent, nearly tripping over the pushchair which was falling over backwards under the weight of all the shopping bags hanging off it. 'Sorry about this,' the woman said as she nearly knocked Patsy over in a bid to catch her daughter who moved in her arms now like a slippery fish. 'Watch the lady!' she said, her pale white skin growing redder with frustration by the second.

'It's all right,' Patsy smiled. 'Do you need a hand?'

The woman looked at Patsy in shock. Perhaps she wasn't used to being offered help, Patsy thought, or perhaps it was the colour of Patsy's skin. She hadn't picked up any racist vibes from the woman. She had been perfectly nice so far, so she told herself not to be so paranoid.

Patsy didn't wait for an answer to her offer of help. She righted the pushchair, 'Shall I take her while you get yourself inside?'

The woman looked unsure still, but as her daughter continued to thrash about in her arms, she huffed and said, 'Hell yeah! You can take her for the rest of the day if you like.'

Patsy laughed, although the woman didn't look like she was joking at all, and she handed over the child, who became instantly still in Patsy's arms. The woman, despite still digging deep in her bag, noticed the change.

'Bleeding hell. You've got the magic touch, you have. Got kids yourself I bet.'

'Actually, I don't,' Patsy said. 'But my fiancé and I are going to start trying soon. After we're married of course.'

The woman looked her up and down. 'Where you from?' she said examining Patsy through narrow eyes.

'North London born and bred,' Patsy smiled.

'Really? mixed girl from North London? You sound a bit posh for that.'

Patsy sighed inwardly. '*Anyone would seem posh compared to you,*' was what she wanted to say, but she stopped herself. She didn't think it was the wisest move to make, given the woman was living right below her. So, she smiled. 'Well, I went to private school, and my mother speaks like royalty! But I don't consider myself to be posh. I'm from North London. Moving into the flat above you actually.'

'Really?' the woman squeaked. 'Ah, thank gosh for that.'

Patsy thought for a moment her neighbour was happy that Patsy was moving in, but she quickly realised she was celebrating finding her keys.

'Yeah, so we'll be neighbours. I'm Patsy, by the way,' she said as the woman shoved the pushchair inside a cluttered hallway that desperately needed a lick of paint.

'Patsy By The Way?' the woman said taking her child back with an enormous sigh. 'That's a funny name.'

'No, not Patsy By The Way… my name's…'

'I know, you silly moo. I'm just messing with you.' The woman smiled for the first time and Patsy tried not to stare at her brown teeth and the teenage acne still clinging to this twentysomething's face. She ran a hand through her greasy hair and said, 'I'm Lauren. But most people call me Loz.'

'Nice to meet you, Loz.'

'Well, you can't be any worse than that last couple that lived up there. Always screaming and shouting. Sounded like a massacre was going on up there half the time.'

That sense of dread tried to worm its way back into Patsy's gut, but she dismissed it. 'Really?'

'Yeah,' Loz shrugged. 'Now, I better get this one cleaned up and get myself out these leggings. Since I put some weight on, they're riding right up, cutting the blood supply off to my fanny.'

Patsy felt her face getting hot.

'Not that that's a bad thing. It might stop any more of these little bastards popping out. See you around then!'

Loz slammed the door and Patsy turned toward the stairs. She found Loz to be a little crude but comical. Patsy found herself smiling and thinking to herself that despite being worlds apart, she and Loz would probably get along famously.

Most of the family came to help her decorate. She billed it as a *painting party*. She knew that they wouldn't be able to resist the *party* part – her family were fun and full of life, and there was no denying that they knew how to have a good time. They weren't so impressed, however, when they realised just how significant the *painting* part would be.

'So, when does the party start?' her little brother Vernon huffed, throwing himself on one of the sofas.

'Mind!' Patsy said even though it was covered with a dust sheet. 'That's new and you've got paint all over you.'

'Um! If it hadn't been for me lugging these things up the stairs…'

'And me!' their dad chimed in.

'…you would have no sofas at all.' Vernon kissed his teeth long and loud.

'Don't do that!' his mother sighed. 'You sound so common when you do that.'

'Oh f…' Vernon stopped himself, but it was too late.

'And no cussing either!' Rose added.

Patsy watched her mother. She held a paint roller, but she wasn't painting. She appeared to be listening to something and it wasn't Vernon's language. Her eyes were darting around as if she was tracing things all around her. It wasn't an unusual sight to Patsy. Her mother was always *off with the fairies*, as Luca liked to describe it.

'She is right, you know,' Luca chimed in again to help chastise his son. 'Listen to your mother. You think you are one of these… um… lane persons, but you are not, and you do not want to be.'

Patsy and Vernon looked at each other for a moment, then cracked up.

'Lane person?' Patsy laughed.

'Dad, it's a roadman, not a lane person. For f…' he stopped himself again.

'Road man, lane person, street urchin, what is the difference, eh?' he said slapping his roller on the wall as he began painting again.

Patsy and Vernon loved to wind their father up. He was born in Sicily, and still had a strong Italian accent and was not well versed in the slang of his children, much like most parents on the planet. Rose gave her children a warning glare, but both the kids could see the grin she was doing her best to smother. Patsy knew her mother was just happy to see her kids having fun together, even if it was at the expense of her long-suffering husband. Fun in the family was usually at the expense of one family member or another – it was just the way families worked.

'Man's bare jokes, fam,' Vernon said, curling up with laughter on the sofa, and making sure he used as much slang as possible to irritate his dad further. It worked.

'There he goes again!' Luca sighed. 'Why did we bother sending them to good schools?'

'Them?' Patsy squawked. 'Don't drag me into this. I speak properly.'

'I speak properly,' Vernon pantomimed a Royal.

Patsy threatened to throw her paintbrush at him. 'Get up and do some work!'

'Me? I've been working my fingers to the bone. Look at that brush!' he said nodding at the weapon Patsy was brandishing at him. 'There's not a drop of paint on it. You've spent the whole time telling everyone else what to do, poncing about like a princess.'

'I have not,' Patsy snapped, stifling a grin because Vernon was spot on.

It was very easy for her to act helpless when her parents were around. They were so good at looking after their kids it was tempting to let them do everything, especially when you were still in your twenties, as Patsy and Vernon were, although pushing thirty Patsy had a childlike innocence and immaturity that seemed to lead people to do things for her. Patsy was the very spoilt typical princess of the family, and it irritated her siblings no end. Their British-Jamaican mother had become a very successful entrepreneur in her own right in the health and beauty Industry. Now in her late fifties, Rose had been an ambassador for her own products merely by how stunning she always looked. She had started with a stall in Camden Market called Forgotten Melodies it had sold all kinds of homemade homeopathic therapeutic soaps, creams, crystals, jewellery, and books. Additionally, she had run a herbal despatch business where she would mail out to customers remedial herbs – like her Jamaican mother she was a natural herbalist, able to rustle up a herbal remedy to cure just about anything known to mankind. She had then invested her wealth wisely and wanted her children to aspire to be the best that they could; always encouraging them to dream big and to realise those dreams. She was ostentatious and vivacious, buying herself and them fancy clothes and jewellery, Rose was very warm and kind. Although Patsy sometimes found it a challenge living up to the way everyone idealised Rose's beauty with her kissed by the sun golden complexion and her perfect features, and accomplishments, she felt that perhaps she could just never be that beautiful, who on earth could be?

Patsy had come up against colourism in the black community that even though she was mixed race, her complexion although caramel had that of a brown Indian-esque tone, whilst her mother was extremely fair skinned for a black woman, and at times passed for white. Patsy had found that people were almost disturbed by this making menacing comments to her as a child that left her feeling alienated. It didn't help that her siblings were also extremely fair which increased that alienation.

'Someone needs to supervise,' Patsy grinned.

'And make the coffee,' Luca hinted.

'OK, OK, who wants tea or coffee?' Patsy laughed, but she stopped abruptly as the living room door opened slowly by itself.

Her heart started racing; she had no idea why…

…until she looked down and saw Nelson sauntering in. Then she beamed, as she always did whenever she saw her cat. A beautiful slender rare red point Siamese cat. He looked more like a puma than a domestic animal, but loved nothing more than curling up on Patsy's lap whenever she watched the TV and stretching out with her arm around him in bed. Ben complained; said he felt like a gooseberry; that Patsy was more in love with Nelson than him. She knew he was joking – sort of.

'Not in here, baby!' she said scooping Nelson up in her arms. 'We don't want you walking in the paint, do we?'

Vernon mocked the way she cooed at the cat, so Pasty gave him the finger as she took Nelson out to the kitchen to make the coffee.

She put the kettle on and gave Nelson one of his favourite treats. He gratefully curled himself around her legs in the hope of more.

'That's enough for now, baby,' she said. 'We don't want you getting fat, do we?'

Nelson jumped up onto the counter enticing Patsy to stroke him and when she felt how soft his fur was and was reminded of the way he loved her, she said, 'OK. One more.'

But before she could give him the treat, his hackles stood up, he hissed, baring his razor-sharp teeth, and backed into the corner swiping at the air with his paw. Patsy instinctively put out her hand to reassure him and he scratched her with his claws.

She yelped. 'Nelson, what the…?'

Then a voice like some kind of supersonic wind roared past her ear and was gone in an instant. But no matter how brief it was it made her want to duck just as she did when a fighter jet roared across the skies of North London. Nelson bolted from the room, and she tried to continue with the coffee, but the teaspoon rattled against the cup like wind chimes in a storm, her hand was trembling so much. And no matter how brief it was, she recognised the voice. It was the same voice that had shouted in her ear the day the housing officer had shown her round. But this time the voice was even angrier. The language was still incomprehensible to her, but she had no doubt it wasn't welcoming her here.

When Ben got home that night, she didn't say anything about the voice. Because there was nothing to say. She knew it was just her imagination, or some kind of draught rushing through the flat. It was a new home to her with all the creaks and sighs and rumbles that every home has. It was just that she didn't know them yet. However, she knew that they would one day be as familiar to her as the sound of Ben's gentle snoring on one side of her and Nelson's purring on the other, which massaged her torso as he pressed against her under the duvet.

She shivered. Summer was just about hanging on, but all the windows were open to let the paint fumes out and the temperature had dropped in the early hours. She slipped out of bed trying not to wake either of her bedfellows. Ben continued to sleep like a log, but as soon as she stirred, Nelson shot off the bed to find another place in the flat to nestle. Patsy sighed. She felt bad for disturbing the cat, but what could she do? She went into the living room to see if closing the windows was an option yet.

She stood in the dark and took a sniff. The smell of paint was still present, but not dangerously so, she reckoned. She felt Nelson pushing his face against her bare leg and reached down to give him a stroke. He purred his thanks.

'Let's close these windows now, ey, baby?' she said straightening up.

Streetlight from the road was casting a glow round the side of the building where the windows opened over the brook. And as she focused on one of the panes, she saw a face.

It was a fleeting moment because she yelped, a short sharp sound and found herself instinctively running to the window to shut the person out. But before she'd even taken a step the face was gone.

When she got to the window she looked out. There was no one there.

'Of course,' she muttered to herself.

How could there be? She was on the third floor of a block of flats with sheer brick walls down all sides. There was no way someone could have got up here and looked in the window.

Was there?

She looked down to the riverbank. It brought back the memory of the old man she had seen there the first time she had visited. The memory collided with the present in her sleepy mind and for a moment she thought it was that old face she had seen at her window. Or thought she had seen. Whatever, she knew the face was familiar. And she knew it was a pale white face. But she didn't believe it could be the old man's face. No, it was more familiar to her than that, she thought. And besides, what did he do, shimmy up the wall like a rock climber? He could barely walk without the stick he'd had in his hand, she recalled.

She looked to the side of the window along the wall. There was a drainpipe stretching down from the roof all the way to the ground. Someone – a very athletic and probably not very heavy someone – could possibly shin their way up it, but could they then reach her window from there? She guessed not.

Nevertheless, she closed the windows and locked them. Even if the paint fumes had been potent, she would have still locked the windows right then.

As she turned back into the room, she caught sight of the photo on top of the TV. It was of her and Ben. Ben worked in construction, so he spent a lot of time outdoors, but no matter how tanned he got he always looked pale next to Patsy and her caramel brown skin.

She examined the photo and thought about opening the window again to test her theory that the photo had somehow been reflected and magnified in the window and that it was Ben's face she had seen. But she didn't want to open it again to find out if that was true – or perhaps she didn't want to open it again because she feared that it would *not* be true. She reassured herself, of the most probable explanation. A trick of the light, a reflection, it made sense.

Nothing else did.

She went around the flat closing all the windows then crept back into bed, wrapping herself around Ben – not just to warm herself up, but to bring her a sense of security.

Ben moaned sweetly at her touch and pressed her hand to his chest. They stayed that way for a while and Patsy was just about to drop off when she felt the bed tilt.

Then she felt the breath on the back of her neck.

And then the whiskers tickling her ear.

'Hello, baby,' she said, turning over to see Nelson's red eyes flashing at her through the dark.

She allowed him to bury himself in her armpit while she stroked him with her free arm.

She heard Ben tut loudly as she unwrapped herself from him. She felt a pang of guilt, but Nelson's fur was too irresistible, too comforting. It was exactly what she needed it seemed.

She was asleep in seconds.

She was woken in the morning, not by her alarm telling her to go to work, but before that, by a damp feeling on the sheet next to her. In the grogginess of waking, she thought for a moment that she had spilled something. Some water which she always made sure was on the nightstand in case she got thirsty in the night? But she would have remembered doing that, wouldn't she? Then she worried that she might have wet the bed. Not that she had done that since she was a child, but perhaps she had some infection that had caused her to be incontinent, or maybe in a deep dream state she had dreamt that she was on the loo. She told herself to calm down, it was probably a heavy period, she had come on early without warning.

But as she pulled back the duvet to look and her brain started to wake up properly, she remembered that her last period was only two weeks ago.

And there would never be this much…

…blood.

The late summer sun was already seeping through the curtains and so it wasn't hard to see what had happened. When she screamed Ben sat bolt upright.

'What the f…?' he followed Patsy's gaze to her side of the bed and the corpse of Nelson that lay there, his body sliced open from neck to groin and his entrails swimming about in a pool of his blood, which Patsy was now thrashing about in as she tried to get away from it.

She didn't know whether to be disgusted by the goo on her skin or devastated by the death of her beloved pet. Either way she sobbed her heart out.

'Oh god!' she cried as she leapt from the bed and paced up and down the room, her hands on her head not wanting to look at the awful sight of her mutilated cat, but her eyes being drawn towards it with a strange magnetism. 'My baby! My baby!'

Ben had leapt out of the bed too and stood helplessly shouting, 'What happened? What did you do?'

'Me?' she shrieked as Ben's words registered. 'Do you think *I* would have done this to him?'

'Well… who did it then?' Ben shouted. 'Someone's been in here while we slept and done this?'

'I don't know!' Patsy bellowed in frustration.

All she did know was that Nelson had not simply died. He had been murdered.

'Look, go!' Ben said in softer tones. 'Go and get cleaned up and I'll… deal with this.'

Patsy nodded; glad someone was taking control. She hurried to the bathroom. As she left the bedroom she heard Ben sigh, 'Gross,' and she hated him for saying that about her beautiful cat.

She stood in the bath and washed herself, watching the blood spiral down the plughole through the prism of her tears, the roar of the shower masking her sobs which continued to come uncontrollably.

She took her time deliberately. She felt bad for leaving Ben with the… remains, but she didn't think she could handle witnessing that scene again. She heard him cursing and huffing and she heard the sound of plastic bags being tied up. She heard the washing machine door slamming and the water beginning to pump into it.

'You OK, babe?' Ben's voice at the bathroom door made her jump and she suddenly felt guilty for being in there for so long.

'Yes, coming,' she said looking at her bloodshot eyes and wet cheeks in the mirror.

'I'm just going down to the garden,' Ben said softly at the door. 'I'll dig a little hole and we can give him a little funeral, yeah?'

As she stood in the garden and Ben heaped the last shovelful of earth over the plastic bag that was now Nelson's coffin, Patsy felt guilty again, this time for the hate she had felt when Ben had been grossed out by the situation. Of course, it was gross. And he had dealt with everything so well, bless him. He had taken control, he knew exactly what to do, as if…

She shook from her head the ridiculous turn her thoughts were taking and put her arm around her fiancé's waist as he straightened up.

'Do you… um… want to say a few words?' he stuttered. 'I'm not sure how this works.'

'Let's just each of us say a little prayer for him silently,' Patsy said.

A bathroom window clicked as someone opened it on the second floor of the block.

Ben nodded up at it. 'Then we should get inside before someone wonders what the hell we're doing out here.'

They held a moment's silence, during which Patsy said her goodbyes. Then after, as they both shuffled about awkwardly on the grass, Ben whispered, 'You, OK?'

Patsy nodded and he ushered her inside.

As they passed Loz's door it opened as if she'd been waiting to hear their footsteps.

'You all right, mate?' she asked, dressed in nothing but a Mickey Mouse nightshirt that was struggling to cover her thighs. 'This your fella?'

'Yeah,' Patsy said. 'Ben, Lauren, Lauren, Ben.'

'Nice to meet you,' Ben said. 'I'll go and finish cleaning up.'

As he went Patsy saw Loz looking him up and down. 'Wow! Good looking bloke.'

Patsy immediately felt protective and wanted to tell Loz to put more clothes on next time she came out on the landing, until her neighbour hissed:

'I heard all the commotion this morning. Is he beating you?'

'What?' Patsy said, frowning as she tried to process Loz's words.

'Coz, I've been there, mate. Trust me, I know how it is. It took me long enough, but I finally got the police involved and got rid of the little prick. So, if you need help, I know…'

'Beating? Me?' And when the penny dropped Patsy quickly added, 'No, no, gosh, no, he doesn't… he doesn't beat me. He's… he's not like that.'

'So, what was all the noise about this morning then?' Loz said sounding a little disappointed that she was wrong. 'Sounded like a horror movie up there. I thought, bloody hell they're just as bad as the last lot.'

'Oh, sorry,' Patsy sighed. 'I was really upset. My cat… died. We just found him. I couldn't stop crying, sorry if I disturbed you…'

'Oh, mate,' Loz said with a genuine concern. 'Sorry to hear that.'

'We just buried him in the garden. I hope that's allowed.'

Loz shrugged. 'I don't give a monkey's; I don't suppose anyone else will. Perhaps put a little cross or something there so the gardener doesn't dig it up though.'

Patsy took a deep breath at the thought. 'Oh gosh, yeah. I'll do that.'

Loz examined Patsy's face. 'You all right though? You look wrung out. I s'pose you really loved that cat, ey?'

Patsy nodded. 'Yeah. I really did.' And before Loz could examine her anymore, Patsy made her excuses. 'I better go and… got to get to work,' she said heading for the stairs.

'All right, mate. Take care,' said Loz and before she slammed the door, Patsy heard her grumble, 'Oh… oh… crap… What have you done now, you little terror!'

Ben and Patsy went about their morning routines as if nothing had happened. *Almost* as if nothing had happened. The autopilot of their lives drove them to get ready for work as usual – can't be late, don't want to get in trouble with the boss. Occasionally, as she brushed her teeth or moisturised her face, Patsy caught her breath when the thought of Nelson leapt into her mind as quickly as he used to leap onto the kitchen counter to ask for food. Then she would have to do all she could to stop the tears otherwise she would have had to reapply her make-up for the umpteenth time that morning.

'I've got to go,' Ben said poking his head around the bathroom door as Patsy did her mascara yet again.

'Hey,' she said, stopping him in his tracks. 'Someone was in our home last night.'

'You sure?' Ben frowned.

'Well, how else did that happen to poor Nelson?' Patsy snapped.

'I know, I know,' Ben sighed, 'but… there was no sign of forced entry. So how did they get in?'

Patsy dropped her eyes to the floor.

'What?' Ben said, sensing there was something she wasn't telling him.

'I saw someone… well, I thought I saw someone at the window in the middle of the night.'

'What window?'

'The living room window,' Patsy said feeling her face getting hot.

'Our living room window on the third floor?' Ben said with a healthy dose of sarcasm. He looked at his watch impatiently.

'Yeah, I know that's virtually impossible… and I would have put it down to a trick of the light or something, but now this happened to Nelson, perhaps I really did see someone there.'

She could see Ben was doubtful, so she added:

'And there's been other things. Noises. Voices. I don't know. As if someone is trying to play tricks on me, trying to scare me.'

'Who the hell would try and do that to you?' Ben said, his brow becoming more furrowed by the second.

Patsy almost said it. She almost told Ben exactly who she thought could have done this, but she couldn't bring herself to do so. She was afraid Ben would lose it if she told him. She thought he would think she had encouraged it… Him.

So, she simply shrugged like a naughty schoolgirl.

'Someone who wanted this place for themselves?' Ben offered. 'Someone who's not happy about us living here.'

Patsy shrugged again. 'Do you think we should call the police?' she asked.

Ben thought for a moment. Patsy could see him weighing up the pros and cons. Of course, they should call the police, but Ben was a proud man. A man's man. He was about as blokey as it's possible for a bloke to get. He was strong and protective and fit as… But behind closed doors he could be tender with her too. She watched as he saw his masculinity being threatened by the idea of letting the police take charge of the situation.

'Old Bill will be of no use,' he grumbled. 'Don't worry. Let's just make sure the place is all locked up from now on and if anyone tries to come back tonight, they'll have me and a baseball bat to deal with.'

'But you can't stay up all night on guard,' Patsy said putting a hand on his chunky forearms.

'Watch me!' he said with a half-smile before kissing her and heading out the door, calling out as he went, 'Make sure every door and window is closed and locked all right?'

'All right,' she said, looking at her own reflection sheepishly.

'You never told him?' JJ asked as she made the coffees.

'No,' Patsy whined, leaning on the kitchenette counter watching JJ pour and stir. 'I thought he would get angry.'

'Well, what's wrong with that?' JJ asked. 'He could go round and give Zack a good kicking.'

'Oh, I wouldn't have minded that, I suppose,' Patsy muttered, 'but I thought he might get angry with *me*. Think I'd led Zack on.'

JJ looked at Patsy over the top of her round glasses. She had a twinkle in her eyes.

'What?' Patsy hissed so the rest of the office couldn't hear. 'I did not lead him on!'

'You sure?' JJ grinned mischievously. 'Here!' she said handing Patsy her coffee.

'Yes, I'm bloody well sure,' Patsy said taking comfort in the warmth of the cup. 'You know I wouldn't have led him on. He was nuts. And more importantly he wasn't my type at all.'

'So, if he was hot, you might have led him on?' JJ chuckled as they went back to their desks.

'Maybe,' Patsy grinned, and they both giggled.

Patsy was glad that she had a friend like JJ who made her smile even in the darkest times. She had been friends with JJ for years and loved her edgy fashion style her politically empowered activist mindset along with her big heart, JJ truly cared about family and friends and was always there for the good times and the bad. Not like some fair-weather industry friends, who were only there for the guest list and celebrity hook-ups. But as Patsy sat at her laptop now and got back to the press release, she was editing; her mind kept wandering to Nelson and the awful way he met his end. But before the tears could come again, she would think of Zack and anger would replace the sadness.

The day she moved into her flat in Cricklewood he was there. He had the studio opposite. As her dad and Patsy had lugged boxes of her stuff from their cars up the stairs to the second floor, he had popped his head out of his door, smoothing down his greasy mop of greying hair and offered to lend a hand.

Patsy had said, 'No, we're fine, thanks,' even though she would have loved a hand, but it was the polite British thing to do, wasn't it.

'We?' muttered Zack stabbing at his glasses with his index finger and peering about with his magnified pale green eyes to see who might be helping Patsy.

'Yeah, my dad,' Patsy smiled, nodding towards the stairs.

Zack had looked relieved then, but Patsy hadn't really thought about it at the time.

'Right. No husband helping you today? I suppose he's at work,' Zack had laughed awkwardly.

Patsy had echoed his awkward laugh as she said, 'No, no, I'm single, no husband.' It would be another week or so until she met Ben at a club in Soho and another six months before things got really serious.

Zack had grinned through his unkempt beard then and Patsy had noticed how brown his teeth were. That and the stench of stale smoke now reaching her from across the hallway told her that her new neighbour was a very heavy smoker.

'Can I help?' he asked, edging out like a crab from behind his door.

Patsy thought for a moment. He seems harmless enough. And it's good to be friendly with the neighbours. So… 'Erm, only if it's no trouble. You must have better things to do,' she smiled.

'Um… no. No, I don't actually,' he said looking momentarily embarrassed.

'Let me dump this,' Patsy said quickly to fill the silence, 'and I'll show you where we're parked.'

'You found a parking space round here?' Zack said. 'Bloody hell. Well done you!'

Her dad had laughed and joked with Zack that morning, but then her dad could get on with anyone. And when the boxes were all inside, she felt she had to offer Zack a cup of tea or something. It was the polite thing to do. She hated herself for being so polite sometimes.

Zack had been so grateful. His eyes lit up as she handed him the cup, as if she was handing him a small box with a wedding ring in it. As he drank, she had the time to examine him. He wore a grey hoody under his anorak and his green corduroy trousers had seen better days. As he gripped her mug, she noticed his long nails had crescents of dirt under them and his beard had crumbs in it. Since she hadn't yet offered him a biscuit, those crumbs must have been there for hours. She couldn't see herself hanging out with Zack. She hated to judge people on appearance, but appearance was everything in the circles she moved in, mainly because she was an ex-model that worked in PR, specifically with pop stars. She looked like a pop star herself and was often mistaken for the artiste. Part of her job was to trot around after top-ten selling R&B singing sensation Tia Sash and make sure she was always looking her best, always saying the right things, and that her social media was always portraying her in the best light. Patsy spoke the language of Instagram better than anyone. Most of her working life was about appearance. And yet the moment that thought about Zack had passed through her mind she scolded herself. He had been nothing but friendly and helpful. Isn't that exactly what you need from a neighbour? And so, she found herself smiling at him and saying, 'When I finally get all this stuff unpacked, you'll have to come round for dinner.'

'Really?' his eyes shimmering as if he might cry with joy at any minute.

'Sure. Why not?'

'I'll help you unpack if you like,' he said resembling a spaniel with its tongue hanging out.

'No, no, it's fine,' Patsy said and this time she wasn't just being polite. She didn't want a stranger going through her stuff, no matter how friendly he seemed.

He hung around clutching his tea until Patsy's dad said he had to go, then Zack finally got the hint that it was time for him to leave too.

The next morning, she saw an envelope had been slid under her door. She opened it to find it was a card that said *Good luck in your new home!* with an image of a key and a heart shaped keyring hanging from a nail on a wooden front door. It was from Zack.

She told herself it was a nice thing for someone to do. But she couldn't help feeling it was a bit creepy too. Even so, she did invite him for that dinner, and they made small talk easily enough. Patsy was good at that. It helped with her job. If Zack told her about something she had no interest in whatsoever, she would find something nice to say about it.

'Star Trek. Completely obsessed by it, me. Watched every episode there's ever been, at least three times.'

'Oh?' Patsy said. She couldn't think of anything more tedious, but said, 'I used to watch that with my brother when we were kids.'

'Really?' his grin bursting through his beard. 'Like two peas in a pod, aren't we?'

Nelson meowed as he wandered through the room at that moment and Zack's eyes sparkled.

'Ooh, what's his name? Or is it a she?'

'It's a he and his name is Nelson,' Patsy said smiling at her baby boy.

'What, after Horatio Nelson? Has he only got one eye or something?' Zack sniggered at himself as he examined Nelson's eyes.

'No, no,' Patsy laughed.

Zack went to scoop up Nelson in his arms but the cat's heckles went up and he hissed at Zack before darting out of the room. Patsy had never seen her cat react like that to anyone. She made an excuse to shield Zack from embarrassment.

'He'll be fine when he gets to know you.'

'Yeah?' Zack breathed heavily. 'I love cats. But I couldn't eat a whole one,' he joked lamely.

After that night, she would notice Zack's door closing whenever she opened hers, as if he was eternally loitering outside her flat. His smoky stench was always by her door even if he was not, telling her that he had been there moments before. He started to invite her to conventions or exhibitions, usually of some nerdy sci-fi thing and when she made excuses, he started slipping notes under her door asking banal but benign questions with hearts drawn on them. She didn't respond and did all she could to avoid him, but that was hard to do when he lived two strides away from her.

One summer evening she was looking out of her second-floor bedroom window over the gardens of Cricklewood when she heard, 'Oh, Juliet! Juliet!'

She looked down to see Zack in the alleyway between the gardens.

'This is where you sigh and go *Romeo, Romeo, wherefore art though Romeo?*' he called up at her with a grin. 'Here I am Juliet!'

She didn't know what to do or say, so she laughed awkwardly and pretended her phone was ringing, gesturing at it and ducking inside to take the imaginary call.

When she invited friends or family round that summer, he'd be there in the alleyway calling out, 'Juliet! Juliet!' So eventually she had to keep the windows closed and everyone complained about being too hot. She didn't say why she was making everyone sweat, but JJ noticed there was something up and soon got it out of Patsy.

Then as summer turned to autumn, so Zack's silly obsession turned icy and dark. The benign notes under the door stopped saying things like; *What's your favourite colour?* and became malignant: *I like the way you dance around the kitchen when you cook*. Or, *What colour are your knickers?*

But the straw that broke the camel's back was when he wrote, *what would be your preferred way to die?*

She showed the scrap of paper to her sister. JJ would have been supportive, but she would have tried to see the funny side and Patsy didn't know that there was a funny side anymore. With Kim, she was bound to get a no-nonsense objective point of view. Patsy's big sister rarely saw the funny side of anything and would not spare your feelings if she thought you were being an idiot. She would tell you, plain and simple:

'You fool!'

'What?' Patsy said as Kim tossed the scrap of paper back at her.

'Why did you wait for it to get to this?' Kim said snappily, tossing her long-lemonade braids, about as if she was trying to whip her little sister with them. Patsy could not understand why she wore her hair like that, after all it wasn't like she needed extensions with her naturally long thick wavy hair near touching her waist. It was like something from a hair commercial.

'I don't... I didn't...' Patsy stuttered.

'The guy is clearly unhinged,' Kim said scowling at Patsy's front door as if, with X-ray vision, she could see him loitering on the other side. 'Did you call the police?'

Patsy shook her head.

'Did you tell Ben?'

'Not yet.'

'Why not?'

'Coz if he goes round and thumps Zack, it'll be Zack calling the police on us.'

Kim sighed and took out her mobile.

Pasty tried to stop her. 'If Zack knows we called the police, he might get annoyed and do something.'

'We will see about that...' Kim said dialling.

The police were not very helpful. They didn't even go to Zack's apartment. They just sat drinking Patsy's tea and making her feel awful.

They raised their eyebrows at the messages she did have and raised their eyebrows when she told them she'd thrown the others away, as if she was lying, as if there had never been any other messages.

'What did you think I was going to do, make a scrap book?' she snapped eventually. 'It's not like I was happy to get them.'

That did her no favours with the officers. They left shortly after that, telling her to call again if he tried to make contact.

If Kim had been there, she may have given the officers so much lip, Patsy thought worriedly, but luckily Kim had to rush back to work before the police had arrived. She worked for a Wildlife TV programme. She was a researcher, but the bosses were beginning to let her try some TV presenting. She had her sights set on being the main presenter on the programme one day. She loved animals, Science, and anything logical and mathematical. She had no time for anything romantic or wishy-washy. She was the astronomy to Patsy's astrology.

'Right, then the housing association need to rehouse you,' Kim said when she called Patsy after her shift. 'Get on the phone to them first thing in the morning!'

Patsy was grateful for the push that her big sister had given her, but once again, she came up against a dead end. The housing association said that they didn't have anywhere else available for her; that there was a long waiting list of other people in real need.

'And are you not in real need?' Kim said, kissing her teeth loudly. 'Give me the number, I'll have a word with them!'

Patsy made some excuse, afraid that Kim would cause her to be removed from the housing list altogether.

So, Kim announced, 'We'll go and see the local MP then.'

Patsy curled up with embarrassment as Kim made her case to the member of parliament for Camden Central Council, Liberal democrat MP; a sincere empathetic well-spoken elderly white lady with a colourful shabby chic attire; who seemed very sympathetic to their cause unlike the housing association or the police. She wrote one letter to the Housing Association regarding the fear and harassment, it took a few weeks and phone calls, but the MP emphatically delivered on her promise. Patsy was offered a flat on the top floor of the little block by the picturesque Rainbow Brook on Factory Way – a hidden oasis of calm in North London's colourful multicultural urban quarter.

The night after Nelson was killed, Ben did the washing up then sat in the living room with his baseball bat at his side. He fell asleep in seconds.

Patsy watched him as he began to snore. They had never lived together in Cricklewood. It was too early in their relationship for that. But when she was offered this flat in Factory Way, they were more secure, and she invited him to move in with her. He jumped at the chance. Patsy hoped it wasn't just because he couldn't wait to get out of his mum's house where he still lived at the ripe old age of thirty-two. He reassured her that, that wasn't the case and said that he never thought he would be able to live with a girlfriend, until he met Patsy. So, this girlfriend very quickly became his fiancé and their pillow talk soon turned to thoughts of making the second bedroom a nursery.

'Babe,' she said nudging him gently.

Nothing.

So, she poked him harder. 'Babe.'

He jerked as if a bolt of electricity had passed through him, he grabbed the baseball bat and made to swing it at Patsy.

'Ben! It's me!'

Ben let the bat fall to the floor. 'Oh! I'm sorry, babe,' he said breathlessly. 'I thought… what did you do to me? I thought I was being electrocuted or something.'

'You must have been dreaming,' she smiled, though inwardly she frowned at the memory of putting her hand on the front door the day she first looked around and the similar sense of an electric shock she had felt then. 'Come to bed.'

'But I need to…' Ben said blinking around the room.

'What, fall asleep here instead?' Patsy mocked him gently. 'Just come to bed. I'll feel safer if you're next to me than all the way in here.'

Ben liked the sound of that and followed her out to the bedroom. But before they left the living room, Patsy turned and said, 'Bring the baseball bat.'

It must have been a few hours later that her eyes slowly opened as she registered a sound. Ben was by her side, breathing heavily, but the sound was coming from under the bed.

She smiled to herself and closed her eyes again, which were still heavy with sleep. As she started to fall back into the dream world she'd just emerged from, her mind chattered away to itself:

I know that sound. That crispy sound. The sound of all the magazines and envelopes and packaging I keep under the bed. The sound of little feet padding slowly over the packaging. Not feet of course, but paws. Pressing at the jiffy bags, kneading them like they would knead my thighs when I was watching TV. The sound of Nelson making a temporary nest out of all my rubbish under the bed.

It had always been a comforting sound to Patsy. She knew his routine. He would spend a bit of time under the bed before jumping up onto the duvet and purring loudly in her ear, just as he was doing right now. Then Patsy, without really waking up or opening her eyes would lift the cover so he could nestle by her side, just as he was doing right now.

The only trouble is, her mind chattered as she was about to slip back into her dreams, *Nelson was murdered last night. He's buried in the back garden. So, who – or what – is that curled up under the duvet with you now?*

Her eyes snapped open and she froze.

The room was still dark. She couldn't see a thing, so her hand slowly snaked its way out from under the duvet and found the lamp on the nightstand. Her fingers moved around it like a spider's legs until one of them felt the switch. Then, she intended to flick on the light and at the same time throw back the covers, but as soon as she flicked on the lamp she was faced with Nelson. But not the baby boy she knew and loved. This Nelson had clearly been buried in a plastic bag for a day. Its tongue lolled stupidly from its mouth, entrails hung from the gash in its body and maggots crawled around one empty socket in its face, the eye having been feasted upon.

Patsy was still frozen with fear and shock. A small part of her wanted to celebrate Nelson's resurrection and hurry him to a vet for an operation, but the greater part of her knew he was not back from the dead at all.

He was still very much dead.

As soon as this registered, after a second which seemed like an hour, she screamed and threw back the duvet to throw this monstrous Nelson off the bed.

Ben woke choking on his own snores and grabbed the bat before his eyes were even open. 'What? What?' he shouted. 'What is it?'

He stood by the bed, brandishing his weapon and looking down at Patsy, who sat upright staring wide-eyed at the corner of the room, to where Nelson had catapulted. They both breathed heavily, and Patsy pointed to the corner.

'What?' Ben repeated. 'WHAT?' he demanded.

Eventually Patsy managed a squeak. 'It was Nelson.'

'Nelson?' Ben grumbled. 'The cat?' He lowered the bat.

Patsy nodded; her eyes glued to the shadowy recess of the room.

'Your *dead* cat Nelson?' Ben said, his relief soaked with sarcasm. 'And where is it now?'

Patsy shook her head.

'Patsy?' Ben said quietly. 'Is he still here?'

Patsy found the strength to move. But she wouldn't put her feet on the floor at first. She hung over the bed and looked underneath it at the magazines and packaging there. No sign of Nelson. She looked around the room. Up on the wardrobe, under the chair. Then finally she stepped gingerly out of bed and looked around the other side of it where Ben was still standing.

'No. He's… it…' She couldn't call it a he. It wasn't her baby boy anymore. 'It's gone.' She sat on the edge of the bed, and flopped down, exhausted.

Ben sighed and sat next to her. 'Babe. You know Nelson wasn't here, don't you. You must have dreamed about him.'

Patsy shook her head. 'It wasn't a dream. It was there. On the bed. Looking at me. Its eye was…' She shuddered and allowed Ben to hug her.

'You're grieving. It's to be expected,' he cooed.

They rocked together for a moment, until a thought occurred to Patsy. She bolted upright and even though she could see the bedroom door was still shut, she ran to it, yanked it open and started hurrying round the flat, turning the lights on and looking in every place she could think of for the thing that had been Nelson. She was terrified of finding it, but even more driven to prove to Ben it wasn't a figment of her imagination or part of a nightmare. She could recall the stench of its breath under her nose, hear the wet crackle of the maggots on its rotting fur. It was real. She knew it. She was certain. But where the hell did it go?

Ben eventually stopped her from turning the sofa upside down and wrapped his arms around her. She felt his tight embrace, felt his muscular arms lock around her and she felt caged, it was not like a hug. She struggled for a moment, but he was too strong and eventually she melted into a miserable mess of tears.

'It wasn't a dream. It wasn't. It was real,' she sobbed.

'OK, OK,' Ben said soothingly, but she knew he didn't believe her. 'Let's get you a nice cuppa, then we'll try and get some sleep, ey?'

He lowered her into the armchair and nipped out to put the kettle on. She heard the tinkling of cups and teaspoons. She felt like vomiting. She had no desire to drink anything. And as the kettle rumbled away, she looked at the window and saw nothing but the reflection of the living room brightly lit. She felt the need to switch off the light, so after wiping her eyes, she did just that.

Now it was easier to see outside and more importantly, she knew it was harder to see inside, because she had a feeling she was being watched.

She stepped cautiously towards the window, but not too close. Just close enough to see down to the road. She thought she saw some movement by the riverbank, so she sprang forward into full view of whoever was down there. She still wasn't sure, so she opened the window and stuck out her head.

'What are you doing?' said a voice over her shoulder.

She jumped so violently that she thought she might fall out of the window for a moment. But when she realised it was Ben behind her holding a steaming mug of tea, she relaxed.

'I thought I saw…' Her voice trailed off. She could see the doubt in Ben's eyes.

'What?' he said, his face contorted with concern.

'Nothing,' she smiled and took the tea.

She waited until Ben was in the toilet and then poured the tea down the sink. She allowed him to take her back to bed, she enjoyed being in his warm embrace for a few minutes, but when he had drifted off to sleep again and his arms loosened around her, she slipped out of bed. She looked at her phone. It said 4:01AM. She took it to use as a torch and crept out of the room. In the hallway, she pulled a coat over her nightshirt, slipped on some flat shoes, and went out onto the landing.

The moment she closed her front door she turned to see light coming through the glass of her neighbour's. She had no idea who lived there still. She hadn't had the nerve to go and knock on the door to introduce herself. Something told her she wouldn't be welcome. She saw the shadow of someone shrinking away from the glass and it reminded her of the way the spectre of Zack always seemed to be lurking outside her flat in Cricklewood even though she never saw him there.

She crept down the stairs and, as she passed Loz's flat, she saw a light under her door too.

'Doesn't anyone sleep in this place?' she muttered to herself.

She descended the next flight of stairs and stepped out into the night. As soon as she did, an enormous roar made her drop the phone.

It was just a freight train hurtling towards London.

'Oh damn!' she said as she retrieved her phone from the ground hoping the screen wasn't broken. It seemed OK, so she turned to her right, to the river and followed it round to the back garden.

If the thing on her bed had been a dream, then Nelson's grave would be undisturbed, she had reasoned. And although she did not want to find anything but a small mound of packed down dirt in the flower bed, if she did, then she would have to consider the idea that she was going nuts.

'No, no, it's OK,' she muttered to herself, her torchlight sweeping back and forth across the lawn as she walked. 'You're grieving. You've never lost anyone close to you in your whole life. You have no idea what that's like. But you've seen enough movies and read enough books.

It messes you up, that's for sure. And perhaps that's what you're going through right now having lost Nelson. The madness of grief. Yes, yes, that must be it,' she told herself as her torch found its destination: the mound of dirt in the flower bed…

…Except this mound of dirt was not packed down. It was loose, freshly tossed aside and it stood by a hole, the small hole that Ben had dug yesterday morning. And in the bottom of that shallow grave was a shopping bag, ripped to shreds by something with claws and soaked in claret coloured blood.

‘OMG it’s definitely Zack,’ JJ hissed, enjoying the thought a bit too much for Patsy’s liking. ‘He’s pissed at you for leaving Cricklewood. He’s hunted you down and now he’s trying to make your new life with Ben a misery. It’s so obvious. He’s jealous so he’s trying to terrorise you.’

‘I know I know,’ Patsy said staring at her laptop screen where the analytics for Tia Sash’s socials swam before her eyes, an incomprehensible kaleidoscope of figures to her anxious brain. ‘I know it’s the most rational explanation. But what about Nelson’s corpse, standing there on my bed, looking at me like a monster? How did Zack do that?’

‘How did he get in and kill Nelson in the first place?’ JJ whispered in Patsy’s ear as she perched on her desk. ‘I don’t know, but clearly where there’s a will there’s a way. And Zack clearly has a will. Or should I call him Romeo?’ she snorted.

JJ, in her own annoyingly facetious way, was making a good case for Zack being the cause of all these horrific events, but the very same words she spoke told Patsy that there was no realistic way that he could have made them happen.

‘Um, Patsy!’ came the voice of her boss from the other side of the office.

Patsy snapped out of her thoughts and peered over the top of her cubicle.

‘I have Tia’s manager on the line. She’s about to start an interview for *Today’s The Day* and you’re supposed to be there making sure they don’t try to trip her up like last time.’

Pasty’s eyes darted at the clock in the corner of her screen. ‘Oh crap!’ she gasped before poking her head up again and calling out, ‘On my way!’

When Patsy skidded onto the studio floor at the nation’s most watched daytime TV magazine show, the floor manager was running around like a headless chicken.

‘Where is she?’ he growled at a hapless runner.

‘She won’t come out of her dressing room until her PR person arrives,’ the young spotty man said with a quivering voice.

‘That’s me!’ Patsy piped up. ‘I’m here.’

The floor manager looked at her with a mixture of relief and contempt. 'Well, she's supposed to be on that sofa and ready to go the moment that chef finishes his puff pastry.'

'How long do we have?' Patsy asked, trying to look composed.

'Three minutes.'

'Which way?' Patsy said to the runner, no longer looking composed.

'I'll show you.'

The runner lived up to his job title and legged it down the corridors of the studio complex with Patsy doing her best to keep up in her two-inch kitten heels.

'In here,' he said breathlessly as they came to a door with Tia's name on it.

'Thanks,' Patsy said knocking loudly and calling out, 'Tia! It's Patsy.'

The door flew open and Tia Sash, looking like a B-list pop star, in a pastel pink trouser suit with a faux leather jacket, dragged Patsy into the room, rudely slamming the door on the runner.

'Who styled you today, Tia?'

'The studio's stylist… Don't get me started, I know – not my normal style.'

'We've got two minutes,' Patsy said. 'You look great. What's up?'

'Just check my hair!' Tia said sitting at the dressing table.

Patsy did as she was told and ran her fingers lightly through Tia's mass of corkscrew curls. 'It looks great.'

'Don't let them start talking about money again,' Tia whined.

'I won't.'

'Don't let them talk about the stuff between me and Greg.'

'I won't,' Patsy said rolling her eyes at the thought of Tia's bulldog of a manager. Patsy knew full well that Greg Yale was making millions from Tia and that Tia had still hardly seen a penny from her platinum record sales. Tia's family had encouraged her to take him to court, but she had tried a different, more private approach. There had been scenes, arguments, and of course the press had got wind of it. But Tia was too scared to walk away from the man who had made her.

There was a frantic knock at the door. 'We need you now. Right now… please,' the runner called out.

Patsy could hear in his voice the fear that his job and career in TV was slipping through his sweaty fingers, so she ushered Tia from the room, and they walked as quickly as Tia's strut would allow them to the studio and the sofa where everyone's favourite presenting duo and celebrity couple Russ and Gina were soon to join her after they'd finished bantering with the resident chef Phillippo.

'What do you think of my sausage in your hole?' Phillippo said in a thick French accent.

Russ nearly spat his mouthful of puff pastry toad in the hole across the kitchen.

'Ooh!' Gina said in a loud shrill voice. 'Naughty, naughty, Phillippo.'

'What?' Phillippo said, playing up to the cameras. 'I'm talking about my recipe.'

'Yes, but we call it toad in the hole,' Russ said wiping his mouth.

'Well,' Phillippo said, '*You* might call it toad in the hole, but this is my special French twist on the dish and so I have renamed it Sausage In Your Hole. Besides, where is the toad? There is nothing like a frog in this dish. You British have some crazy names for things. Makes no sense.'

Patsy watched as the floor manager signalled to them to wind up this nonsense and get on with the next segment. She looked over at Tia who was examining her hair anxiously in the monitor.

Russ said, 'Well, it's very tasty whatever it's called.'

'And,' Gina added, like the well-oiled machine they were together, 'you can find the recipe and many others on our website at the usual address. Thank you, Phillippo.'

'Yes thanks, Phillippo, but we have to leave you now because…'

The pair scurried to the other side of the studio where Tia sat.

'We are super *super* excited to have none other than the princess of Pop and R&B herself, Tia Sash in the studio, everyone!'

The crew and Patsy applauded loudly, and Tia turned on her dazzling smile. Russ and Gina fawned all over her and asked her questions about her latest single and video. But as Tia talked about a gruelling night shoot and what it was like to be covered in honey, Patsy was distracted by a gentle meow from the back of the studio.

'Keep the cats back there,' the floor manager mumbled into his headset. 'We don't need them in place for five minutes yet.'

Patsy followed the floor manager's gaze to the loading bay where the runners were bringing in three cages. In each was a cat. Her jaw dropped when she noticed one of them was a red point Siamese. Sphinx-like, with a luxurious off-white coat adorned with beautiful vivid reddish points just as Nelson had been, its red eyes flashed in the studio lights. Patsy couldn't believe what she was seeing. Red point Siamese cats were extremely rare, in fact – they were the rarest of the Siamese breed as it is difficult to breed out the tabby lines to achieve the clean pure colour of the coat, she learnt later that this was the point: the segment after Tia's interview was about rare breeds of cat – but that wasn't what shocked her so much. This one was the spitting image of Nelson, and its eyes were locked on Patsy's as if it recognised her.

Patsy felt her skin tighten and her stomach flood with something molten. Her feet took her across the studio floor towards the cat, as if the cat's eyes were reeling her in. Somewhere behind her she heard Russ – asking Tia something about money troubles and a legal case against Greg her manager, but Patsy couldn't tear herself away from the cat.

'Where's the cat handler?' she heard the runner ask his fellow gofer.

'It's that bloke?'

'Which bloke?'

'The old geezer,' whispered the gofer. 'With the yellow hat. The one who looks homeless.'

This snapped Patsy out of her trance for a moment and she followed the runners' gaze to the geezer in question, chatting idly to one of the crew by the loading doors.

Patsy's phone started buzzing incessantly in her pocket, text after text was coming in, but she couldn't tear her attention away from the old man. It looked exactly like the man who had stared up at her from the banks of Rainbow Brook. Her mouth began to feel dry. She felt compelled to go and say something to him, but she didn't know what she would say, she just knew she had to approach him. The text messages stopped, and someone tried to call her instead. She had forgotten to turn off her ringtone, so a tinny version of Tia's latest single jangled out from her pocket. This snapped her back to reality, and she hurriedly fished out her phone and clicked it to silent mode. As she did so she saw it was Greg Yale calling her. She also saw about ten different text messages, also from Greg. Each was more frantic and angrier than the last. She read the most recent one which said, 'SHUT THE INTERVIEW DOWN NOW YOU STUPID COW!'

She gasped and hurried back to the line of cameras all trained on Tia who was looking like a deer in headlights, babbling away as she tried to make light of Russ and Gina's probing questions. Questions Patsy had been told to stop them asking.

'Come on!' Russ goaded Tia. 'Why would you stay with a manager who cons you out of most of your earnings? Is there something more between you than manager and client?'

Patsy ran up to the gallery. As she entered, she heard the director say:

'Camera one, stay close on Tia. This is bloody gold dust.'

'Those questions are not appropriate,' Patsy shouted. 'Stop them now or I will drag her off set while the cameras are still rolling!'

The director and engineer looked at each other for a drawn-out moment, silently debating Patsy's words. Patsy saw their eyes sparkle in the lights of the wall of screens. What she had threatened to do was too irresistible to them. The publicity for their show would be so good. So, they ignored Patsy and told Russ and Gina to keep probing.

'Did you lose your job?' Kim whispered as she and Patsy stood up with the rest of the congregation to sing the next hymn.

Patsy chose now, in the middle of the Sunday service, to tell Kim about what had happened at the TV studio with Tia Sash. She felt protected that way. Otherwise, she was sure Kim would have flown off the handle and berated her little sister for such careless work.

'Not exactly,' Patsy said.

'What's that supposed to mean?' Kim tutted loudly enough so that the old lady in front of them turned to see if the tut was directed at her.

Patsy and Kim both smiled sweetly at the old lady, as they had been programmed to do to their elders since they were kids and pretended to sing along with the hymn. When the old lady had turned back to the front, Patsy continued:

'I still work for the company, but they took me off looking after Tia directly.'

'Why did you not stop the interview earlier?' Kim asked with an irritation that Patsy fully expected.

Patsy tried to find the words. 'It's silly really…'

'I know that,' Kim grumbled sarcastically, 'but why?'

'I saw a cat. And an old man,' Patsy added as if that would make everything perfectly clear.

Kim side eyed her sister.

'The cat looked just like Nelson. And the old man who was handling it looked just like a bloke I've seen hanging around the flats.'

'What are you saying?'

'I'm saying that this old bloke might have something to do with what happened to Nelson.'

'I thought you were convinced it was Zack who was doing all this?' Kim muttered.

'I was. Well, JJ was, and she got me thinking, but now this happened at the studio…'

'What happened?' Kim growled. 'Nothing happened. You saw a cat that looked like Nelson and a man that looked like someone else. There are millions of cats that look like Nelson and a million old men that look the same. As much as I hate to admit it, JJ is right. We know Zack is deranged. We know he's obsessed with you. He has motive. It's the logical conclusion.'

'But the shopping bag. It had been ripped to shreds by claws. Cat's claws,' Patsy mumbled.

'Or long nails,' Kim suggested.

'What?' Patsy frowned.

'I never forget when you described Zack to me, that first time you met him. The glasses, the anorak, the greasy hair, the dirty beard, and the long dirty nails around your coffee cup. They are the claws you're looking for, Patsy. Not Nelson's. Nelson was mutilated. Things don't come back from the dead. It just isn't possible.'

Patsy looked up at the altar and the crucifix hanging above it. 'Don't they?'

'Oh please!' Kim said kissing her teeth.

'Then why are you here every Sunday?' Patsy hissed.

'So, I don't get an earful from Mum and Dad of course,' Kim said rolling her eyes at her own inability to stand up to her parents on this point. 'Have you called the police about him?'

'Who?'

'Zack.'

'No.'

'Have you even told Ben yet?'

'About what?'

'*Zack!*'

'No,' Patsy huffed. 'And Ben didn't want to call the police about Nelson anyway.'

'Oh my G…' Kim said exasperated.

The old lady in front turned around again, to abruptly stop Kim from saying the Lord's name taken in vain.

Patsy and Kim smiled sweetly again until, slowly, she turned back around.

Kim began to berate Ben's machoism, but Patsy stopped her abruptly: 'Shh! Mum's watching.'

Kim followed Patsy's gaze up to the altar from where their mother Rose, in her preacher's robes, led the service and glared at her two girls for disturbing the congregation.

Family tradition had it that after the Sunday service it was all round to Mum and Dad's for Sunday dinner. It was non-negotiable except for a medical emergency – or work in Ben's case today, but since he wasn't officially family yet, Rose and Luca were not so insistent on his attendance anyway. However, for Patsy, it was clear that no medical excuse was going to wash today; evidently in good health, there was no way Patsy could slip out after church and avoid the inevitable interrogation from her mum about whatever it was that was so important it would permit her daughters to disturb the word of the Lord. Entrepreneurial even in matters of God, after selling her successful beauty business aged 50, Rose Conti had founded her own church from home. She had inherited her entrepreneurial drive from her Jamaican father who had come to England to seek his fortune, on arrival had been disappointed that he was more successful in Jamaica than his new English friends. He quite quickly took off to seek his fortune in the USA instead after brandishing England as too '*backwards*!' Rose establishing a church was unexpected to other family members, but it hadn't surprised Patsy at all, when Rose had announced that she was giving up her entrepreneurial life to become a preacher. She was always the God-fearing matriarch of the family, a compassionate woman that everyone looked up to. She was the 'problem fixer' that all friends and family would reach out to when things went wrong. It made perfect sense that she would become a preacher. As a schoolgirl, Patsy knew that Sundays meant the living room was transformed with rows of green folding chairs and congregants coming and going all day. Now, at least, Rose ministered from a church building down the street, which was decorated of course in true *Rose fashion* - for everything about her was fashionable and chic, it had been transformed from a run-down mediocre shell, to a pristine, interior–designed establishment with bright modern décor, mini creche, café and manicured gardens – it even had a music centre with a basement recording studio where the choir would rehearse and produce their podcast.

'It's nothing,' Patsy said when the questions came thick and fast. 'Pass the rice and peas, Vernon!' she added trying to distract her mother.

But Rose knew every trick in the book when it came to her children. She took the bowl of rice from her son and held onto it like bait. '*Nothing* doesn't warrant a conversation in the middle of the twenty-third psalm. So?'

'It's just a little trouble at work,' Patsy said, feeling her face flush.

'She got fired,' Kim cut in.

'Fired?!' Vernon, Luca and Rose all exclaimed in unison.

'No!' Patsy said glaring at Kim. 'I wasn't fired. I'm just not working directly with Tia anymore.'

'But you still work for the company?' Luca said.

'Yes.'

'Thank God,' he said, crossing himself.

'But why are you not working with that... girl anymore?' Rose said – she had never been able to bring herself to describe Tia as a singer or seen anything Tia had ever done as art. Rose always thought that Patsy should not be working for a popstar, as she should be the *popstar* with her beautiful voice and looks, Rose thought she was wasted – she should be taking the mic. She had invested in her dancing and singing – why was Patsy content to sit behind a desk and run around after Tia like a gofer?

'She didn't stop an interview on daytime TV from going wrong. Very wrong,' Kim groaned.

Rose sighed. 'Well, I'm not sure I would mourn the loss of *that* job.' She handed over the rice and peas at last.

'No, but it's the reason she was distracted that's the issue here,' Kim said pompously.

'Thanks, Kim,' Patsy sneered at her sister.

'What do you mean?' Rose probed.

'She has a stalker,' Kim said.

'What?' Luca looked at Patsy, anxiously.

'I'm not sure,' Patsy said. 'There's been some strange things happening in the flat. Voices and... Nelson...'

'...was killed,' Kim interrupted, yet again.

'Killed?' Rose grimaced.

Patsy nodded. 'And then he came back as if from the dead.'

'Who?' Luca said, confused.

'Nelson.'

'That's where the stalker comes in,' Kim said. 'Someone has been messing with the cat's corpse, trying to freak her out and it's working, clearly.'

'Do you know who this stalker is?' Patsy's father asked with great concern.

'Yes,' Kim said.

'We're *not* sure,' Patsy corrected, pushing some chicken around her plate with a fork.

'Hmm,' Rose said sagely. 'And I'm not sure there's a stalker at all.'

Patsy looked up. And everyone looked at Rose when she added:

'At least, not a living one.'

Back in the flat that night, Patsy stood in the living room listening. But she could hear nothing.

'It's like Piccadilly Circus in there,' her mother had said at dinner when everyone had demanded that she clarify what she meant by *no living stalker*. 'Your flat. It's full of voices. Full of lost souls.'

Kim had of course rolled her eyes and thrown her fork onto her plate with a loud clang to let everyone know she thought her mother was talking absolute rubbish. But Patsy had recalled Rose at the painting party, roller in hand, appearing to listen to something, her eyes moving as if she was tracing things all around her. *Off with the fairies*, as Luca liked to describe it.

'Are you saying it's haunted?' Vernon had grinned, eyes sparkling with mischief.

'Haunted,' his mother had grimaced. 'Such a tabloid word. Let's say there's just a lot of spiritual traffic passing through. You've heard it yourself,' she'd told Pasty knowingly. 'You said you'd heard voices.'

'Angry voices yes,' Patsy had said, her own voice trembling. 'And then what happened to Nelson… Are these spirits dangerous? What should I do about it, Mum?'

'You should call the bloody police,' Kim had said.

'Kimberly!' Luca scolded her then, not for doubting her mother, but for swearing.

'Look,' she went on, 'you remember the bloke that lived opposite her in Cricklewood. Zack. He's a creep. He was obsessed with her. Stalking her. That's why she moved out.'

'Why didn't we know about this?' Luca asked Patsy.

'I didn't want to worry you,' she'd sighed, looking daggers at Kim for upsetting her father.

'So, this man is causing you problems in your new place?'

'Obviously,' Kim had said, and the conversation had turned to Patsy keeping serious information like this from her parents, while Rose sat quietly staring at her youngest daughter.

Now Patsy stood in the flat listening intently, her mother's stare imprinted on her memory; a stare which said: '*We need to talk, but not now.*'

She took out her phone and texted her.

When can you come?

The response was typically brief and to the point.

Tomorrow. 3PM.

Patsy listened some more. Nothing but the sound of Loz's daughter running around causing havoc no doubt for her poor mother. Up and down the corridor she heard the little feet scamper with surprising heaviness. A naughty giggle or two occasionally reached Patsy's ears from the little terror, but apart from that, her own flat was calm.

She put on Netflix and watched her current favourite sitcom while Ben was still out – he'd made it quite clear how much he hated it. She had some chocolate too, comforting herself with both her visual and gastronomic guilty pleasures. Occasionally a breeze would ruffle the curtains, or the gutters would creak outside as the temperature changed. Her heart would stop for a moment, she would imagine Nelson wondering in or the old man's face at the window, but then she would bury herself in her comfort viewing and try to forget it all.

When her phone rang, she flinched before she saw it was Ben calling.

'Hey babe,' she said, trying to sound cool.

'Hey. Do you mind picking me up from the station? I'm knackered. Can't be bothered to walk back.'

'Sure,' she said, happy that he would be back soon. 'What time do you arrive?'

'About ten minutes I reckon.'

'Oh, right. I'll come now then.'

'Thanks babes. Love ya.'

'Love you too.' She hung up and looked at herself in the mirror. She was in her chilling out clothes, but at least not in her pyjamas yet. She could get away with what she was wearing just to pick up Ben. She slipped on some flat shoes and opened the front door.

The smell of cigarette smoke hit her immediately.

Her eyes darted instinctively to the flat opposite, just as they used to in Cricklewood. She saw a shadow shrink away from the frosted glass and her heart started racing. She stood there for a moment, thoughts racing through her head like clouds in a windy sky. *It can't be him. It's not him. Mum told me what was happening here... But do I want to believe her? What's worse? Zack stalking me or my flat being...?* She couldn't say the word; that 'tabloid' word Vernon had used. She didn't really believe in the supernatural. Not in *that* way. She believed in God. Her mother was a pastor. She loved her mum, and she never doubted her mother's sanity. No, it was the ghosts and the ghouls that she didn't believe in. Or didn't want to believe in.

She shook all these clouds from her mind and went downstairs, taking another look at the neighbour's door as she descended, but there was no movement there now.

'People smoke,' she told herself. 'It's not unusual, unfortunately. That smell means nothing.'

As she went outside into the cold autumnal air, the light was fading fast. It took her a moment to realise that it was Loz standing by the white mailboxes which were fixed in rows to the wall. And it was not just the light that made recognising her slow; it was the fact that Patsy had assumed Loz was in her flat on the second floor, since she could still hear her daughter running around throughout the Netflix show.

'Oh, all right, Patsy?' Loz said. 'Just getting the mail in. I always hope for something exciting but it's just a load of junk as usual.'

'A load of it,' Patsy observed as Loz pulled reams of flyers and bills from her mailbox.

'Oh yeah. That's coz I've been away for a few days, visiting my mum. It soon builds up, don't it?'

'Yeah,' Patsy said enjoying the lightness of the conversation with Loz until a thought struck her. 'You've been away?'

'Yeah. Southend. Weather was cold of course so we couldn't really enjoy the beach.'

'But...' Patsy wasn't sure how to address the subject.

'What?' Loz examined Patsy's face, seeing something was up.

'When did you get back?'

'Right now. Just got off the train.'

'Have you been inside yet?'

'No. Why?'

'Do you…?' *Of course, she doesn't leave her daughter on her own for days. That would be insane*, Patsy scolded herself. She tried a different angle. 'So, who looks after the little one while you're away?'

'Mindy?' Loz frowned.

Patsy nodded.

'No one,' Loz snorted, as if it was a ridiculous idea. 'She comes with me.'

'Oh,' Patsy said, involuntarily clutching her car keys, so they dug into the palm of her hand. 'It's just… Where is Mindy now then?'

'Oh, she's here somewhere. Can't keep still for a minute that one. Mindy!' Loz called out. 'Probably round the back garden, getting covered in dirt. Mindy! Come on! We're going upstairs. We're having spaghetti hoops for tea.' Loz noticed Patsy's troubled face again. 'You all right, girl?'

'Yeah, it's just… weird. I could have sworn I heard Mindy running about in your flat this evening. Like for the last couple of hours.'

'No, mate. Impossible. Like I said. We've just got back.'

'I thought I heard her giggling too.'

Loz was distracted now. 'Where is the little gremlin?'

She set off across the car park and around the side of the block to the garden behind. Patsy felt compelled to follow her.

'Mindy!' Loz called out with a dash of concern now. 'Where are you?'

Patsy was suddenly concerned for the little girl too and they both hurried into the garden to find Mindy sitting cross legged on the lawn, just as Loz had suspected – covered in dirt.

But when Patsy saw just why Mindy was covered in dirt, she wanted to vomit.

Mindy was sitting right where Nelson had been buried. She had dug with her fingers into the soil and found the plastic bag that Patsy had buried there when she'd found the grave empty. Mindy had tied the blood-soaked ribbons of the lacerated bag around her neck, like some kind of macabre scarf and she was talking quietly to the hole as if someone was in there.

'No, that's not your home. You can come home with me if you like. It will be warmer inside. I will make you a nice bed.'

'What's she done now?' Loz sighed.

As she and Patsy approached the flower bed, they saw the corpse of Nelson, looking more putrid than ever in the bottom of the hole. And very much dead.'

'Oh my God, is that your cat?' Loz said. 'Come here, you're a nightmare!' she said, apologetically, scooping up her daughter. 'I'm so sorry, Patsy, mate. I don't know why she would've done this.'

Patsy was speechless.

'Right, you, upstairs now! We're going to have a bath before you get any bleeding spaghetti hoops. Sorry again, mate,' Loz called out as she made for the car park again. 'I'll get this one cleaned up and then… do you need help with that?' she said nodding at the corpse.

Patsy wasn't even looking at Loz – her eyes were fixed on Nelson – but she knew what Loz was referring to. She just shook her head. Then eventually said, 'It's OK. I'll sort it.'

But Loz was already gone.

Lauren had told Mindy to take off whatever that filthy thing was around her neck. But Mindy screamed so loudly when Loz tried to take it off, that her mother allowed her to keep it on for now.

'Just while I get the bath ready, then it's going in the bleeding bin.'

Mindy sat on her bed examining the dirt beneath her fingernails. Each nail had a crescent of earth beneath it and they each looked like black moons to Mindy. She heard the water thundering into the bath like a storm. She heard her Mum muttering to herself, swearing and tutting, like she always did. She heard the tone of water in the bath getting lower and she knew that that meant the water was getting deeper and it would soon be time to get in. And that meant her mother would take her necklace away from her. Her beautiful princess necklace, of green and white and claret – emeralds and diamonds and rubies. But she wasn't going to give her mother, the wicked witch, the pleasure of stealing it from her. Mindy would take it off herself and put it somewhere only she could find it.

She reached up to the handle of the plastic bag, which she had stretched over her neck, and tried to pull it back over her head. But it wasn't as easy to get off as it had been to get it on. She tried to stretch it some more, but at that moment she heard a voice rush past her ear. An angry voice in a language she didn't understand.

And she felt the handle get tighter; so much tighter that it began to cut into the skin on her neck.

She jammed her fingers between the handle and her neck, but the plastic tightened so much that it cut into her little digits like a wire through cheese and forced them to press against her own windpipe. She started to panic. She tried to scream, but by now the handle was so tight she couldn't make any noise, but a horrible rasp.

The rasp became a gurgle. Her vision became cloudy. She felt a wetness as her fingers bled, the bright fresh blood trickling down her neck to mix with the old crusty clots of Nelson's on the bag. What new and shiny rubies were here now!

When Lauren came in, she was marching with all the impatience of an exhausted mother. But the moment she saw her child slumped on the bed with the plastic bag cutting deep into her throat and her eyes as bloodshot as her own the last time her husband had tried to strangle her, Lauren's legs went to jelly and she fell onto the bed, clawing at the bag until it fell away from her daughter's lifeless body.

In bed that night, Patsy clung on to Ben.

'How was Sunday dinner?' he asked as he started to doze off.

'Oh, the usual drama.'

'Urgh!'

'Mum thinks there might be something...' She chose her words carefully, knowing Ben would find the whole idea of something supernatural nonsense. '...something spiritual going on in the flat, with Nelson and that.'

Ben snorted derisively. Patsy had expected that, but it still annoyed her.

'She's coming over tomorrow afternoon to... take a look.'

'What, is she bringing, a crucifix and holy water?' Ben giggled.

'Ben! Mum's just trying to help. In her own way.'

Ben turned over and patted the baseball bat which leant against the headboard. 'This is the only help we need.'

Patsy thought for a moment. She wanted to bite back at Ben for dissing her mother and her spiritual practice, but before she could think of something cutting enough, she heard Ben snoring.

When her eyes snapped open, it was still dark. She guessed she hadn't been asleep for very long. She looked at the alarm clock. 1:11AM. She sighed. She hoped this didn't mean she'd have trouble getting back to sleep. She examined her senses for a moment. Did she need to go to the toilet? Is that why she woke? No. No need to get up. She closed her eyes again and told herself to get some sleep. She lay that way for a minute, maybe two, before she thought she heard something, someone in the room. Her eyes sprang open again and she looked towards the door. As her eyes strained into the darkness, she thought... no, she was *sure* she saw a shape, like that of a man standing there. She could feel Ben beside her, so it couldn't be him, but she was so frozen with fear that she couldn't even move a finger to prod Ben awake. The figure looked as if he was wearing a heavy dark coat with his collar turned up and a large hat with a wide brim. This tall, dark shadow walked... no, *glided* noiselessly across the room toward her and stopped at the foot of the bed, looming over her.

Her skin was clammy now. She was petrified. She felt the mattress tilt as the figure sat on the end of the bed. She felt it shift and spread itself along her body. She felt the weight of it as it lay itself upon her, as if it were about to take advantage of her. She felt such an awful sense of revulsion and terror that she began to pray.

'God,' she said inwardly, 'Save me. Save me from this evil. I will go to church every Sunday for the rest of my life if you stop this—'

She felt its breath on her face. Then she heard it speak.

'The child will die,' it whispered. 'The child will die.'

Then the breath on her face ceased, the weight lifted from her body, the air cleared, and she knew it was gone. She was able to move, and she wrapped herself around Ben, who muttered something in his sleep like, 'I'm good enough now the cat is gone, ey.'

She didn't mention anything to Ben in the morning. She knew he wouldn't believe a word of it. Instead, she went to work as usual – well, not quite as usual, since she wasn't working for Tia anymore and everyone in the office kept giving her looks like *How could you cock up so badly?* Then at 2:30PM she left, having already made some excuse about a doctor's appointment to her boss that morning. But her appointment was not with her doctor, of course, but at home with her mother.

Rose stood in the middle of the living room just as she had done at the painting party, but now there wasn't a roller in her hand but a cup of tea.

She took a slurp. 'It's a busy place.'

'Spirits you mean?' Patsy asked genuinely interested.

Her mother held up her hand for quiet. 'And not just in here, I imagine.'

She walked into the bedroom. Patsy followed her. Ben's clothes were still on the floor from last night. She grabbed them and threw them in the washing basket before her mum could pass comment. Patsy hated that Ben was messy it caused them to bicker, but yet he continued to drop items on the floor.

But Rose's only comment was on the unseen entities, not the laundry. 'Here too.'

'This is where I've seen the most stuff and…' Patsy was silenced again by Rose's hand, so she sat on the bed while her mother continued to listen.

'Hmm,' Rose mused. 'It's a wonder you get any sleep in here at all.'

'Can you do something?' Patsy asked.

Her mother looked down at her as if she was disappointed that her daughter would even need to ask and said, 'Of course I can do something. I didn't come all this way for the tea. Too strong, by the way.'

Rose handed her half-drunk cuppa to her daughter and marched back to the living room. Patsy dumped the tea in the kitchen sink and found her mum pulling a large gold crucifix on a chain from her big canvas shopping bag. She put it over her head and arranged it neatly on her chest like armour. Then she delved in the bag again and pulled out a plastic four-litre milk bottle, with a white label - HOLY WATER printed on it in comic sans font. It wasn't quite the ornate chalice Patsy expected such a sacred liquid to be contained in, but she didn't dare quibble over such details with her mum. If it was good enough for Reverend Rose, it was good enough for her.

Rose opened the bottle and began sprinkling the holy water around the room. As soon as she did so Patsy heard the voice, the angry voice, and its incomprehensible language raging at her as it rushed around the room. She gasped.

'You hear it?' Rose asked her.

Patsy nodded, ducking each time the voice roared past her ear.

Her mother looked ever so slightly pleased with herself. Then she declared, 'In the name of Jesus Christ our God and Lord, we cast you out of here. We come against you with the blood of Jesus! We confidently undertake to repulse the acts and deceits of the devil.'

With that, the windows began to shake as if something was trying to get in – or perhaps get out. Patsy heard more voices now, some calling out as if in pain, some cussing in languages she unfortunately understood well enough.

Rose went on, 'God arises; his enemies are scattered and those who hate Him flee before Him. As smoke is driven away so are they driven; as wax melts before the fire, so the wicked perish at the presence of God. Come!' Rose ordered her daughter and marched into her bedroom.

Patsy didn't need to be told twice. She wanted to stay close to her mother. As they went out into the hallway, Patsy's nose filled with the stench of smoke – cigarette smoke – just as she had smelt on the landing last night before going to pick up Ben before she and Loz had found Mindy digging up Nelson.

There was a knocking at the door now. More than a knocking. Someone was hammering a fist on it frantically. Patsy went to open it, but her mother stopped her.

'No one is there. Don't worry.'

Then the letter box flipped open with a desperate clang and Patsy felt the air being sucked out of the flat through the little opening.

Rose tugged on her daughter's sleeve, and they went into Patsy's bedroom. She watched in awe as Rose threw handfuls of holy water around the room. The cacophony of voices became a terrible orchestra of screams now, blood curdling, as if the water burnt whatever was there. Rose tossed a little water under the bed and the magazines and envelopes shot out across the room like leaves in a storm and Patsy could've sworn she heard the cry of Nelson.

'We drive you from us, whoever you may be,' Rose announced. 'Unclean spirits, all satanic powers, all infernal unwanted entities, all wicked legions, assemblies and sects,' the reverend roared over the noise. 'For we wrestle not against flesh and blood, but against principalities, against powers, against the rulers of the darkness of this world, against spiritual wickedness in high places,' she declared, quoting from her favourite book of the Bible, Ephesians.

And then the room, the entire flat, fell silent.

The two women looked at each other breathlessly for a moment before Rose quickly composed herself in front of her daughter and said, 'I think a cuppa is in order. But not so weak this time.'

'How's it going?' JJ asked perched on Patsy's desk. 'At home I mean with Zack and that.'

'Oh, it's all sorted,' Patsy chirped.

And it was. The flat was peaceful after Rose had finished her *clearance* as she preferred to call it. Patsy was sure now that whatever had been causing her so much distress was gone. She felt lighter and so did the atmosphere at home. But she didn't feel able to explain just how that had come to be to JJ. 'It wasn't Zack after all,' she lied. It was… someone else. They wanted the flat or something. They were trying to scare us out.'

'They?' JJ probed. 'What, were they non-binary?'

'Pardon?' Patsy said, trying to get back to her work.

'You said *they* this and *they* that. Was it a bloke or a woman or…?'

'Oh…' She had to think quickly. 'Some woman. A right nutter by all accounts. I didn't see her. The police picked her up pretty, quickly.'

'So, it was nothing to do with Zack?' JJ asked, failing to disguise an air of disappointment.

Patsy shook her head.

'Well, that's good I suppose, coz there's enough drama kicking off here.'

'What do you mean?' Patsy knew she had no hope of getting her work done until JJ had got out all the gossip.

'Since that disastrous interview on *Today's the Day*, the tabloids have swooped on Tia and Greg like the bloody vultures that they are. They've been printing all sorts of rubbish, and, just as they planned, it's caused Greg to get defensive and opened up old wounds between the two of them. Tia's thinking of giving him the boot for real this time and apparently, she's considering taking him to court as well.'

'Who says?'

'Lola, your replacement. And I guess she knows better than most.'

'Oh damn,' Patsy whispered despairingly. 'What did I do?'

'It's not your fault,' JJ reassured her. 'It would have kicked off sooner or later with that tosser. You just hurried it along. Did Tia a favour really, innit.'

Kim called round to Patsy's place after work. She had heard on the family grapevine about the *exorcism.*

'She prefers the term clearance.' Patsy enjoyed correcting her big sister for a change. But her enjoyment didn't last for long.

'Clearance? It's not a bloody DFS bank holiday sale,' Kim shook her head, exasperated by her little sister's tendency to romanticise life, she found it pretentious, yet humorous. There was 5 years between them, but Kim was a practical, logical, cynic; old beyond her years and often found her sister mildly irritating, but she loved her dearly. 'Call it what you like, it doesn't stop it being ridiculous.'

Patsy was irritated now. 'What's ridiculous about it?'

Kim didn't reply, she just scratched at the rim of the mug her tea was in with a long shellac fingernail – sky blue to match her eyeshadow – as if there was some dirt there, and so irritated Patsy even more.

'Are you calling what our mother does and what our mother believes in ridiculous? Well, Kim?'

'Not ridiculous then,' Kim pouted, looking around the kitchen in a manner that was strangely reminiscent of her mother at the painting party. 'But foolish.'

'Oh, everything's foolish to you, if it's not your way of doing things.' Patsy snapped.

'It's foolish coz it's dangerous.'

'What are you talking about?' Pasty said noticing a softening in her sister's demeanour.

Kim grumbled, 'Messing with things you don't understand.'

'But I thought you didn't believe in all that stuff,' Patsy said, feeling like she was about to get one up on Kim. 'So how can it be dangerous?' Unusually Kim didn't have an answer and Patsy felt vindicated. 'Anyway,' she went on, 'it worked.'

'What did?'

'The clearance. It's sorted now. There's no more trouble, no more weird goings-on.'

'It's not sorted,' Kim stated with a sense of sadness that Patsy wasn't used to seeing in her big sister.

'It is, I'm telling you. I know, I live here,' Patsy insisted, 'So you see it wasn't Zack at all. Lucky, we didn't get him into trouble unnecessarily, wasn't it.'

Kim looked around the room again, shook her head and dumped her mug in the sink. Patsy thought her sister might be about to cry. But before she could be sure, Kim was on her way out of the front door. 'I'll see you later,' she huffed.

'Kim!' Patsy called after her. 'It wasn't Zack.'

The front door slammed, and Kim was gone.

Patsy sighed and went to the living room with her unfinished tea. She slumped onto the sofa and turned on the TV. The evening news was on, and Tia Sash was making headlines. She was taking her former manager Greg Yale to court over earnings she claims he owed her. Millions of pounds worth. And she was even accusing him of sexual assault too.

'*Former* manager,' Patsy said to herself. 'My gosh. It's all-out war now then.' She felt a heady mixture of guilt and triumph for Tia finally breaking the chains Greg had put on her. 'Unless the judge sides with Greg,' she thought.

The sound of Mindy running up and down Lauren's flat downstairs interrupted her gloomy thoughts. It was a welcome interruption. She didn't mind. It was a damn sight better than the roar of ghouls and visitations by phantom cats and shadowy figures. Unlike all those dead things, Mindy was the epitome of life. Yes, she could exhaust her poor mother sometimes, but she was just a ball of energy, innocence, and vitality. Patsy thought about how life would be with her own child running around this flat. She smiled broadly.

The news had moved on to the next item – Inflation levels. Clearly not as important as Tia Sash's finances. Patsy turned off the TV – she'd had enough news for one day. She sat enjoying the sound of Mindy for a moment. Mindy and her friend by the sound of it. Because there were two girls giggling and chattering below. Two sets of little feet running up and down. And the sound of a ball now against the wall. A two-beat rhythm as the ball must have been thrown, hit the wall, bounced on the floor, and been caught again.

Patsy's brow furrowed as this rhythm seemed weirdly close now. It seemed to be behind her, not below. It seemed as if the girls were playing in the hallway of *her* flat, not Lauren's. But that was impossible of course. Nevertheless, Patsy felt compelled to investigate, but just as she stood to do so, there was a knock at her front door.

'Kim,' Patsy said to herself. 'Come to apologise no doubt. She didn't use the buzzer so she must have been brooding on the stairs all this time.'

She opened the door and Greg Yale was standing there, looking more than a little angry.

Greg was a boulder of a bloke. He didn't so much stand in the doorway as obstruct it. Patsy gulped like a cartoon character when she recognised him.

'Can I come in?' he barked through his thick strawberry blonde beard which seemed to muffle the words enough so that it took Patsy a moment to work out what he said. 'Well?' he said butting the air with his head.

Patsy's reply was to back down the hallway to the living room, the only space big enough to accommodate Tia's ex-manager.

Standing at 6'3 he was tall enough to have to duck to get inside and wide enough to have to turn sideways a little, to get in without catching his expensive classic single breasted Burberry suit on the doorframe. He reminded Patsy of a Viking. He wore a long white silk scarf around his tree trunk of a neck and his white skin with faint craters on each cheek, from what looked like what was a bad case of acne during adolescence, was tanned from countless days in the south of France, thanks to Tia's earnings, no doubt, Patsy thought bitterly despite fear being her overriding emotion right now.

'Can I get you… a drink?' she stuttered.

Greg looked around the room as if he'd never seen anything like it in his life; never seen anything so small and so ordinary. He looked at the sofa and the armchair as if he was considering sitting down. Patsy prayed he wouldn't for fear he might break anything he sat in – not because he was so huge (well, not just), but because he looked like the kind of person who would throw himself into any seat, he sat in. And yet she heard her own voice saying involuntarily:

'Would you like to sit down?'

She hated the sound of her simpering voice, but he had the kind of presence that made you simper.

'No, but I'll have a whiskey if you've got one,' he said as if that was a tall order for the likes of Patsy, who he evidently considered a peasant, by his tone.

'Yes, I have actually,' she said with a bit too much pride as she hurried to the kitchen and poured a glass of JD with trembling hands.

Just as she was about to return to the living room, she poured herself a quick shot and downed it. The burn in her throat was like the slap of a coach around a boxer's face. She was ready to fight. Kind of.

'Here,' she said in a firmer tone now the whiskey was moving through her body.

He took it and sniffed it. Then took a sip. 'Ah!' he hissed to himself, as if it was the worst whiskey he'd ever been given, but he still downed it in an instant. 'Right,' he said handing her the glass back, 'enough of the niceties. I just came here to tell you…'

'How did you know where I live?' The thought popped out of Patsy's mouth before she'd had a chance to check it.

'I'm Greg Fu-ck-ing Yale,' he said as if she was stupid, 'And you work for the PR company that I basically fund, so it wasn't hard. Which brings me back to my point before you rudely interrupted me.'

'Oh,' Patsy said feeling like she was back at school.

'Why couldn't you interrupt Russ and Gina the way you just interrupted me, ey?'

Patsy opened her mouth to respond, but Greg wasn't waiting for a reply.

'You really messed up that day, you know. And you're lucky you still work for Fliproc Media at all.'

'Look, I know I…' Patsy began, but Greg was not finished.

'Shut up. I'm talking!' he barked.

Patsy shrank instinctively, but the whiskey in her veins told her not to let him berate her.

Greg went on, 'I came here to tell you in person – as if I've got time to waste on girls like you…'

'Women.'

'Ey?'

'Women like you,' Patsy said bravely. 'I'm a woman not a girl.'

Greg was caught off guard momentarily, but he quickly recovered – he spent his life arguing with people. 'I couldn't give a monkey's what you call yourself. Woman or girl, you're a little bitch…' He took a step towards her, and she tried to stand her ground, but he was too close; he seemed to radiate heat like a bonfire and Patsy was compelled to take a step back. '...and you will stand up in court next week when my legal team summon you and you will tell the world that Tia told you she was going to make up this crap about me assaulting her to get money out of me.'

'But she didn't. She never spoke to me about...'

'I know that you dumb thicko! But if you don't get up in court and say it, you will be fired from Fliproc Media and you will never work anywhere in this business ever again, Capiche?'

'You don't get to decide who's fired from the company,' she said, her eyes pooling with tears.

'Don't I?' Greg smiled a smile full of white veneer teeth. 'Who do you think had you removed from the Tia roster? Your boss?'

Patsy was speechless.

'Your boss is my bitch, like everyone else in this fake industry and the sooner you realise it the better.'

The glass in Patsy's hand twisted from her grasp and floated in the air between her and Greg. Patsy would have been shocked had she not experienced equally strange things in this flat before. She was just surprised because she thought her mother had cleared the place. Greg, however, was totally gobsmacked.

'What the fu...?' he began.

His sentence was cut short as the 8 cm tall mouth-blown crystal tumbler glass zoomed through the air and whacked him on his Viking-esque long patchy balding head. The solid crystal spirit tumbler didn't smash on his head or on the floor where it landed, but it sent Greg reeling, it stayed suspended unrealistically in time and space.

'Jeeeeeezzzz,' he gasped grabbing at his head, which was already bulging with a bruise.

The armchair slid along the floor at great speed and rammed into Greg's shins sending him crashing to the floor like a felled oak. Patsy let out a yelp, but she didn't know whether to be frightened or secretly pleased. The windows began to rattle violently just as they did when Rose had performed her clearance, one of them was yanked open by an invisible force and the air rushed through the flat. On that air rode the sound of children screaming and shouting. Patsy thought for a moment of Mindy and her friend below and she even had the most bizarre concern that all this noise might be disturbing Loz. But that was all forgotten when Greg's enormous iceberg of a body levitated and shot across the room heading for the open window. Whatever these entities were capable of there was no way Greg Yale was going to fit through that window in one piece, despite it being the biggest in the room. But it seemed that the entities didn't care about such details, or perhaps that was the point. Greg shot feet first through the window, but his torso jammed in the frame like a cork in a bottle for a moment. He looked back at Patsy with an expression of sheer terror, the likes of which no one had ever seen on Greg Yale. Patsy was clinging to the sofa watching with a grim fascination.

'Help me!' he shrieked.

Then the room was filled with the sound of cracking. Patsy thought it was the PVC window frame giving way, but it wasn't. It was the sound of Greg Yale's hips snapping, his ribs being crushed and his shoulder blades splitting as whatever was pulling him through the window succeeded.

And then – just like that, he was gone.

The noises were silenced, the furniture still and the windows no longer quaking.

Pasty rushed to the window to look out and see what had become of Tia's former manager and, no doubt, former human. But there was no sign of him. She looked at the window frame, expecting Greg's guts to be smeared there, but it was as clean as ever. She looked out again and a figure caught her eye this time, down by the brook. But it wasn't Greg. It was the old man. The same very tall, skinny man she had seen there the day she had been given the keys to the flat, in the same frayed red trousers, battered brown shoes and purple pinstriped suit jacket full of holes. The same smoky grey hair stuck out from beneath his yellow hat and the same bloodshot eyes locked with hers as he shook his head slowly and deliberately again. It was dusk now and the furrows in his face looked deeper than ever in the shadows, but his pale skin shone like a moon.

'Hey!' Patsy called out. 'Wait there!'

She didn't know how, but she felt that this man had something to do with all the bizarre goings-on in her flat. She needed to know right now, so she ducked inside, found some shoes, and headed downstairs.

When she ran from the building she flinched as a commuter train roared out of town taking hundreds of workers from the city back to their suburban homes, but it didn't slow her down. She quickly crossed the car park to the riverbank and wasn't really surprised to find that the old man was gone.

She looked around and listened for a while. The sound of ducks on the brook caught her attention. She suddenly felt the need to check the river for Greg's body. She went up and down the water's edge trying to work out by looking up at her window where the body might have landed, but after a while she gave up, with a strong feeling that wherever the body was, it wasn't in this realm anymore.

Then another thought struck her. How did Greg come here? He must have driven. He wouldn't lower himself to come by public transport, which means his car must still be here and if his car was here then eventually it would be traced, and a connection made with Patsy. She turned back to the car park. It was obvious which car was Greg's. The black Tesla stood out proudly against the other budget cars, including her yellow second-hand Volkswagen Beetle, which she endearingly called 'Lolly.'

'Oh no!' Patsy whispered to herself.

She approached the car carefully wondering for a moment if Greg had a driver who was waiting for him in there. It wouldn't surprise her. Greg had delusions of grandeur. She peered inside. It was empty. She breathed a sigh of relief, but the relief was quickly replaced by fear. This car could not stay here. It would lead the police here. It would lead them to her. She wondered if Greg had somehow left his car keys behind in her flat. Then she wondered if a Tesla even needed a key. She was about to try the door when she stopped herself. Fingerprints... She could feel herself getting hot, her forehead starting to bead with sweat even though it was cold autumn evening.

'What do I do?' she asked herself agitatedly. 'What do I...?'

The Tesla, almost silently, began to reverse out of its parking space. Patsy sprang back out of its way and watched as it shot off down the road and out of her life, she sighed with relief. She had heard that Tesla's could drive themselves, but she wasn't sure if this was what was happening now or if it was being driven by one of her ghoulish guests. Either way, she didn't feel fear as she had done in the past about these entities. Perhaps they weren't the same ones. But this time she felt they had been protecting her from Greg and she went back upstairs almost with a spring in her step.

On her way downstairs the next morning, Patsy bumped into Loz coming out of her flat. When Loz clocked Patsy, she almost hid behind her front door, but their eyes had met, it was too late to hide. Patsy registered all this in a few steps. She also registered how rough Loz looked. Dark circles under her eyes – darker than usual. Her skin looked patchy and red in places as if she'd been rubbing at it nervously. She looked like she hadn't eaten a good meal in a few days either. Mindy on the other hand was as bright and energetic as always. She bowled out of the flat so fast, Loz didn't even try to stop her. The little one, began hopping down the stairs. Patsy watched her go for a moment before turning back to Loz.

'Hey. Are you OK?'

'Never better,' Loz said with a huge dose of sarcasm, which made Patsy think it was OK to say:

'I don't want to be rude or anything, but you're not looking too well. Are you feeling OK? Anything I can do?'

Loz looked detachedly, into the middle distance for a moment, as if she was searching for an answer to Patsy's question. She puffed her cheeks and blew out the air despairingly. 'Nah,' she said in a raspy tone. 'Nothing anyone can do. I mean… yeah… I feel like crap. Must be coming down with something. I was just on my way to the corner shop for some… medicine.'

'Well, I can go for you if you want,' Patsy said taking a quick look at the time on her phone. 'I'm not late for work… yet,' she grinned.

'Nah, it's OK,' Loz sighed.

'No really, it's fine. What medicine do you need?'

'Twenty Marlboro Gold Superkings and a bottle of the cheapest gin.'

'Oh,' Patsy stopped in her tracks. She peered over the banister to see where Mindy had got to. She was getting to the ground floor fast, but Patsy knew she wouldn't be able to open the main door, so she relaxed a little and turned her attention back to Loz.

'It's OK, really,' Loz insisted weakly. 'I need the fresh air.' She squinted as if her head hurt, or as if she was anticipating the sunlight, which she clearly hadn't seen for days. She shut her door and hitched her shopping bag over her shoulder to show Patsy she was fit and able.

'OK,' Patsy said. 'I'll give you a lift?'

'I just said I need the fresh air,' Loz snapped unapologetically. 'I won't get that sitting in a car now will I.'

Patsy felt she was in the way now, so she made her excuses and went on ahead. But when she got to the front door Mindy had her nose pressed against the glass as if she was a prisoner waiting to escape, so Patsy waited for Loz to catch her up. She smiled at Mindy while they stood there listening to Loz dragging her feet along the cold grey lino covered landings and stomping listlessly down each stair. Mindy pressed her lips to the glass and blew so her mouth inflated comically and made a farting sound. She looked up at Patsy and grinned. Patsy grinned back as Loz reached the ground floor.

'Did she have a friend over last night?' Patsy asked, turning to Loz.

'Ey?' Loz said groggily.

'Mindy. Did she have a friend over last night? I thought I heard two little gremlins running up and down the corridor and playing ball against your wall. Not just one, as usual,' she smiled down at the little gremlin in question.

Loz looked startled and stuttered. She looked as if she might vomit at any second, but eventually she managed, 'Yeah… yeah. A friend over last night. Keeping me up all night with their nonsense. That's why I feel so bloody rough. Yeah, that's it.'

'Ah, well, nice she has some playmates, though,' Patsy smiled.

'Yeah,' Loz said a little more brightly. 'I s'pose it is. She has playmates,' she added, almost to herself.

There was an awkward pause, which Patsy ended with, 'Right, well, I better get off to work. See you two later.' She opened the door and Mindy bolted. As usual Loz didn't seem that bothered. 'Last chance for a lift!' Patsy sang, trying to lighten the heavy atmosphere.

'I'm good. You go!' Loz said, her face still stony.

Patsy got the message and walked to her car. She looked about the car park as she got into her Beetle. No sign of the Tesla.

Last night seemed like a bit of a bad dream to her now, but strangely, she hadn't slept so well in a while. She watched Mindy standing on the riverbank, picking violet-blue Lobelia flowers, and tossing them into the stream. She smiled, even though her heart was in her mouth at how close Mindy was to the edge. She looked around to see that Loz was nearby, and did not seem disturbed by this at all, so she set off to work. She looked in the rearview mirror as she drove off. It looked as if Loz had forgotten Mindy as she slouched down the road alone, but after a long tense moment for Patsy, she saw Mindy race into view after her mother, so Patsy accelerated away.

That week was pleasantly uneventful for Patsy. Work was just the usual: editing press releases, booking interviews and appearances. Home was quiet and Ben's baseball bat found its way back into the back of the wardrobe again. She never discussed her mother's visit with him, and he never asked. In his mind, he was the protector of the household and he had succeeded in doing his job.

But when she arrived in the office on Friday, the place was buzzing. Most of the staff were glued to the TV on the wall and those who were pretending to still work hard at their desks had the news channels open on their laptops.

'What's going on?' she said, sidling up to JJ by the TV.

'Greg Yale,' JJ said, her mouth full of croissant. 'He disappeared.'

Patsy felt the blood drain from her body. 'How do you mean?'

'His car – he had a Tesla – was found parked on the edge of a cliff in Kent. They reckon he topped himself.'

'Have they found a body?' Patsy said a bit too eagerly.

JJ shook her head and swallowed her mouthful. 'Not yet. But they reckon he threw himself off there into the sea,' she said pointing at the images of the Kent cliff on the screen. 'That or he *staged* it to look like suicide and he's done a runner to avoid the court case. Dead or alive there is one hell of a manhunt on to find him.'

'Hell of a manhunt,' Patsy whispered to herself.

'What are you doing tonight?' JJ said.

'What? Why?' Patsy said still distracted by the screen.

'Let's go out. Celebrate.'

'Celebrate what?'

'Ding dong, the wicked witch is dead!' JJ grinned at Patsy, but Patsy's eyes were still glued to the screen.

It wasn't unusual for Patsy to have a hangover on a Saturday morning. She liked the routine of having a long lie-in, cuddling up to Ben, having some morning sex, then catching up with the news – or rather the gossip – on her socials.

This morning they had both started kissing still half asleep when the sun was barely up. He hadn't used a condom; she allowed it. She was ready to get pregnant. She wanted to be a mother one day very soon. And she knew Ben was into it too – as far as a man is ever into it. Then they had rolled over and fallen asleep again. Her head was banging after raving all night with JJ. They had used the company membership to have a few liveners at Oxford House on The Strand before using a connection to gain entry at the Hertford Avenue Club into *VIP*, of course.

'Well, if it's good enough for Stormzy and Little Mix it's good enough for JJ and Patsy,' JJ had winked as they pushed past the queue outside. JJ recalled the time they saw Leigh-Anne Pinnock in VIP – JJ was a big fan identifying especially with her activism and the way she advocates for various racial issues.

But Patsy's lie-in was short-lived. Mindy and her visiting pal were making such a lively noise, in her fragile state it sounded to Patsy as if they were in her flat, not downstairs. That ball being thrown against the wall again. Thump, thump… thump thump. Annoying bloody kids. She wondered if she should have made Ben wear a condom after all. She turned her pillow over, enjoyed the cooler side of the Egyptian cotton and tried to drift off again.

But the giggling from the girls was getting louder and louder now, and even more annoying. Patsy couldn't sleep. She couldn't take anymore. It sounded now as if they were in the bedroom with her, a few feet away. It was bizarre, but Patsy felt the compelling need to peek over the top of the duvet just to check they weren't.

She was stunned. Dumbfounded by what she saw. She caught her breath and froze under the duvet.

Sitting at her desk were two girls, but they weren't Mindy and her friend. They were five or six years of age, dressed in long white smock-like dresses, done up at the neck. The dresses were not clean but smudged with sooty patches. Their hair was equally in need of a good wash and one of them had a big floppy yellow bow on the left side of her straw-like blonde hair. The other had slightly shinier frizz-like curly hair. Patsy recognised it as a black girl's hair – the natural curls greased down in a bob hair cut which ended high up on her neck. The two girls were turned away from Patsy, beavering away at something as they chattered. Patsy's heart was thumping like the ball that had been against the wall of her hallway – and she knew then that it had been her hallway and not Loz's – but, despite her fear, she sat up a little more to take a closer look, as quietly as she could, as she didn't want to draw attention to herself - now was not the time to see their faces. One was drawing a picture with coloured chalk. Patsy didn't own any coloured chalk. The other was playing some kind of board game. Patsy didn't own any board games. The board was mostly decorated with the image of a union jack flag. It seemed to be a game about the British Monarchy. There was a large crown-shaped design in the centre with a cartoon image of a king and queen sitting on their thrones. A trail snaked its way from the crown to other images on each side and corner of the board. It was hard for Patsy to make out all the images from this distance, but she wasn't prepared to get any closer. She saw Buckingham Palace, Windsor Castle, Kensington Palace, and Balmoral Castle. The box for the game which sat alongside the blonde girl confirmed this. It said *Royal Palaces.* She looked at the picture in the centre again. It was a king being crowned, but it wasn't King Charles the III. This king had a large greying beard, and the game was clearly a hundred years old at least, you could tell from the style of the images.

Her arm quivered as she held herself upright on the bed. She instinctively shifted in case it was the awkward position that was making her arm spasm, but she soon realised both hands were trembling too. The blonde girl began to turn her head. Afraid to be seen by them,

Patsy lay flat and pulled the duvet over her head. Her breathing was fast, she was burning up under the duvet, she could barely get enough oxygen into her lungs. She wanted to throw back the covers and gasp, but she daren't move or make a sound.

Her eyes reeled around in her head as she tried to focus on the sounds in the room. She could barely hear anything over the sound of the blood thumping through her ears. Eventually she pulled the duvet down, ever so slowly, until her eyes and nose were free. The room was brighter now as the morning wore on. There was no sound from the girls. Patsy dared to peer over at the desk at last.

They were gone.

But they had left something behind.

Patsy got out of bed and, on unsteady legs, she stepped slowly towards the desk. The board game was gone, but the picture that the blonde girl had been drawing in chalk was still there. It was a basic drawing, the kind you would expect from a child of that age, but what it depicted was clear enough. There was a building, a big black building with red, yellow, and orange flames coming from it on all sides. There were faces looking out from the windows of the building, with downturned mouths. Patsy inhaled sharply as she realised, they were trapped there, in the fire. And there was a woman standing outside the building. Patsy knew it was a woman because she had a big pregnant belly and even a little stick baby could be seen in the womb, so she knew it wasn't just a badly drawn fat person. But the most disturbing thing about this whole scene, was that the woman herself was on fire and the flames were coming from her womb. She reached out to pick up the picture. Her hands were still trembling. She didn't know why she was even reaching out, but she suspected she might screw up the picture and flush it down the toilet. Just as her fingertips touched the edges of the paper…

'What do you think you're doing?' a voice growled over her shoulder.

She yelped and spun round to see Ben laughing at her. He grabbed her and hugged her.

'Sorry,' he said as she punched him with relieved playfulness. 'I couldn't resist.'

He kissed her repeatedly as she relaxed into his arms.

'You scared the crap out of me!' she smiled.

'That was kind of the point,' he grinned. 'What were you doing anyway?'

Patsy thought for a moment. She wondered if she should even tell him about what she had seen. She knew he wouldn't believe her. But the picture. That was right here. It wasn't a matter of belief. It was physical evidence.

'Look,' she said, turning to the picture.

There was nothing but a pile of ash on the desk.

'What's that?' Ben frowned at it.

'Ben,' Patsy said her heart racing again, 'that was a picture, a child's drawing a few seconds ago. That's what I was looking at when you came up behind me.'

'What child? What picture?' Ben said poking at the ashes. 'And why did you burn it?'

'I didn't burn it,' she said suddenly raising her voice in pitch and volume.

'All right, all right,' Ben said putting his hands up. 'Calm down.'

Patsy tried to begin to explain, but she couldn't find the words.

'Are you saying someone's been in here again?' Ben offered eventually.

'No,' she mumbled. 'Well, not in the way…' and she gave up with an enormous sigh.

'Are you still drunk?' Ben smiled, trying to lighten the atmosphere. 'You were hammered when you got back last night – or should I say, this morning!'

She slumped back on the bed.

'Get a bit more rest,' Ben said. 'I'll go and buy us some breakfast, ey?'

'Sounds good,' she yawned.

As soon as she heard Ben leave the flat, she called her mother. She didn't even say hello, but went straight in with, 'They're back.'

'Who?' her mother said, expecting a more traditional greeting.

'The entities, spirits, whatever they are.'

'Oh,' her mother said. 'Are you sure?'

'I'm not sure they're the same ones. That angry bloke thing hasn't been back, but now there's two children playing ball in my hallway and sitting at my desk in the early hours.'

'Children?'

Patsy thought about mentioning Greg Yale's departure through the window too, but she didn't think it wise to do so on the phone. She hadn't told another soul about Greg. She thought it best not to get anyone else messed up in it. Besides, people, no matter how much you trust them, have a tendency to tell at least one other person such great gossip and before you know it…

'Yes,' she said into the phone.

Her mother made thoughtful sounds down the line, then said, 'Perhaps it's not the place for you after all.'

'What do you mean?'

'I mean, perhaps you should move out.'

The thought had never occurred to Patsy. She loved this flat, its location, its serene, beautiful brook with its array of quacking ducks, was a hidden gem, an oasis in a metropolis. She loved the space and, most important of all, it was an assured tenancy. Places like this were gold dust. There was no way she was going to give it up, no way she was going to be driven out, even by this coterie of ghosts and she told her mum as much.

'But you can't live in fear,' Rose said with more concern now.

Patsy thought about the fear she felt this morning on seeing the girls in her room and the unsettling picture they had left behind. But she also realised that, so far, they had never been aggressive to her, not in the way that the other shadowy entity had. She also thought of the way she had felt protected when Greg had been removed from the flat as he threatened her. She couldn't tell her mother about Greg, so she said, 'I'm not sure.'

'About what?'

'About… about fear. The kids are a bit annoying, playing ball games at all hours, but otherwise… they're not aggressive.'

'Well, that's good,' her mother said coolly. 'Let's hope it stays that way.'

'But can't you come and shoo them off again?' Patsy asked.

There was a pause, the sound of her mother breathing heavily. 'Well, I'm not sure it will make much difference. I am better with evil entities. With real spiritual warfare,' she said rather too grandly for Patsy's liking. 'It doesn't sound like these ones are wishing you harm. And such spirits are around all of us, all the time. It's just that you are able to see them. Like me. It's a gift.'

'Or a curse,' Patsy muttered, aversely.

'I wondered when one of you kids would start seeing. You took your time.'

'Took my time?'

'Well, I was seeing when I was a child.'

'My gosh,' Patsy yawned. 'How exhausting for you.'

'No more than being a mother,' Rose said with a wry chuckle.

'Thanks mother,' Patsy said sardonically. 'Well, in that case I'm going to go and have some breakfast.'

'Breakfast?' her mother groaned, 'it's nearly lunchtime.'

'Yes, thanks for reminding me. I had a late night.'

'Don't be late tomorrow for dinner!'

'I never am,' Patsy sighed.

Her mother hung up.

'OK, bye,' Patsy said with more sarcasm into the dead phone, rolling her eyes, before she flaked out on the bed again, starfish style.

Ben returned moments later with coffee and pastries. He knew the way to Patsy's heart. He threw a couple of newspapers on the bed. His favourite tabloid and her favourite lifestyle magazine. But she didn't pick up the magazine. Her attention was grabbed by the headline on the front page of *The Daily Celeb News*:

TIA SASH HAD YALE BUMPED OFF

Tia Sash's court case accusing her former manager Greg Yale of raping her took an unexpected turn last night when Tia was questioned by police over Greg Yale's disappearance. The music mogul's Tesla car was found abandoned on a cliff top in Kent on Thursday and at first it was thought he had committed suicide – or faked his own death – to avoid a guilty verdict in the rape case Tia had brought against him.

Earlier this week the model, singer and actress had recounted in court at The Old Bailey the moment he allegedly assaulted her. During Wednesday's testimony, Sash told the court that she felt helpless and treated like an 'object' when Yale showed up to her hotel room in London when she was first being courted by record companies.

'I was panicking with fear,' the *Treat Me Right* singer told the court. 'I was kind of hysterical through tears.'

Sash said she was physically afraid of the music industry heavy weight. She felt powerless because he was a 'big guy', adding, 'He's big. He's broad. He's overweight. He's domineering.'

Tia, who said she only weighed 9 stone at the time, said she has been the victim of sexual assault in the past and feared being beaten if she didn't follow Yale's demands for sex.

She stated that she was a powerless singer at the time trying to make her way in the business. She said Yale asked her to 'touch him' but she refused before he then referred to 'a load of A-List pop stars' whose careers he 'supposedly made'.

The court heard that his voice moved from 'pleading, to aggressive and demanding', as he forced her onto the bed leaving her 'shaking' before he 'forcibly assaulted her'.

Tia's lawyer Mark Hawthorn Esq. told the court: 'Ms Sash feared that he could crush her career if she reported what he had done to her.'

'You OK, babe?' Ben was right next to her, but his voice sounded distant. She was lost in thought. She felt so sorry for Tia and the sexual abuse she'd had to endure in her life. Then there was the way Yale had ripped her off financially, and now this, being suspected of bumping him off, as *The Daily Celeb News* so sensationally put it. And to top it all, Patsy was the only person in the world who knew for a fact that Tia was innocent. But to help her out Patsy would have to tell the police that Yale was at her flat the night he went missing and some ghosts dragged Yale through her window and out into another spiritual realm. She had a feeling that wouldn't go down too well, and she would end up serving time.

'Do you think she did it?' Ben said, reading the article over her shoulder.

Patsy turned to him, slightly irritated. 'Of course not. I know her. There's no way she would do this. Or even ask anyone else to.'

Ben turned the pages of the newspaper as he spoke, looking for more sensational stories. 'Well, then the police will soon realise there's no evidence to suggest she did anything. They just have to go through the motions, you know,' Ben kissed her shoulder, seeing she was upset.

'I hope so,' Patsy mumbled noticing a four-inch ad in the back pages, which read:

GOLDIE PEACEHAVEN
Expert in spiritual house cleansing.
If spirit entities are causing you
stress at home,
Goldie can help.

Akashic Connection courses, Akashic Readings,
Space Clearing and Earth Energy Dowsing.
Call Goldie NOW!

'Got you an apple Danish thingy,' Ben said waving the pastry under her nose.

She took it and stuffed it in her mouth, grateful for the sweet anaesthetic it brought.

‘It’s only for a week or so,’ she whispered to Ben in the kitchen as Vernon and his girlfriend Nina unpacked in the second bedroom.

‘Then why have they brought more stuff than I did when I moved in for good?’ Ben scowled.

‘That’s Nina probably. You know what girls are like. We need more stuff than men,’ Patsy tried to keep it light. ‘Half of it’s her makeup probably.’

‘Well, she needs it,’ Ben winked.

Patsy slapped his arm playfully. ‘Don’t be rude. She’s OK.’

‘Yeah,’ Ben giggled. ‘Great personality.’ He shut up abruptly as Vernon stuck his tightly barbered head around the door and chirped:

‘All right roomies?’

Ben smiled weakly.

‘Everything OK?’ Patsy asked her little brother, who was five years her junior - whom she adored. He always made her laugh with his comical nature, although sometimes led astray by his streetwise friends, overall, he was a good kid. Vernon stood out from the crowd for his looks and intelligence – excelling above each class that he was transferred to, no one could keep up with him.

‘Everything’s amazing,’ Vernon said. ‘Thanks so much for doing this. Otherwise, we would have had to stay with Mum and Dad and that would have done my head in.’

‘I feel you,’ Patsy said in sibling solidarity.

‘Don’t worry. We won’t get under your feet! It’s just until our new landlord sorts himself out anyway.’

‘Why didn’t you stay in your other place until then?’ Ben asked as diplomatically as he could.

‘Well, we’d have to sign for another six months at least, and we’ve had enough of that place. It’ll only be a few weeks, max.’

‘Oh? Patsy told me a week,’ Ben said, looking daggers at her.

‘Or so,’ Patsy corrected him.

‘Oh, sorry,’ Ben said, switching the kettle on, ‘I didn’t realise *or so* meant a month.’

‘Can we get one of those?’ Vernon said. ‘We’re bare thirsty in here.’

'Ey?' Ben said.

'Make them a cuppa too, Ben,' Patsy said.

'Cheers, mate,' Vernon said and bounced off back to the unpacking.

Ben took two more mugs from the cupboard and put them on the counter with enough force to underline his irritation. 'I'm not going to be his servant for the *next week or so*.'

'It's just a cup of tea,' Patsy hissed. 'Get on with it!'

They all watched TV together that evening. Patsy enjoyed having a busy household, she enjoyed having her little brother to stay. It reminded her of her childhood, more simpler times - when she, Kim and Vernon were kids and they all lived at home, laughing, and bickering. Ben spent most of the evening sighing in the corner as they all watched *UK's Got Talent* – Nina and Vernon's choice.

When Nina got up and announced, 'Right, I'm off to bed,' Ben could barely conceal his delight. He grabbed the remote and switched over to the sports channel.

'So early?' Pasty said a little disappointed.

'Well, I'm going to put on my face pack first. Do you want one? One of the paper ones. Easy.'

'No, I'm good thanks,' Patsy smiled.

'OK, whatevs. Come on, Vernon bear!' Nina sang.

Vernon jumped up dutifully, though his eyes were still fixed on the TV and the boxing match Ben had found.

'Vernon bear?' Ben snorted.

'Oh, shut up,' Vernon muttered.

Patsy smiled at her brother, who was slim, strikingly handsome, and short; well shorter than his 5'10 girlfriend.

'Don't you have pet names for each other?' Nina asked Patsy, puzzled.

'Um… I suppose,' she said.

'Yeah? What?'

Patsy thought for a moment longer. 'What do we say, Ben?'

'Babe,' he offered, eyes still on the TV.

'Erm not very original,' Nina said disdainfully pulling Vernon away to bed.

'Goodnight!' Patsy called after them.

'Night!' Vernon said.

'You call me *My Beautiful* really, but what is it to do with her?' Patsy muttered to Ben.

Ben stayed up to watch the end of the boxing. Patsy had gone off to bed an hour before. It was around two in the morning when his eyes snapped open, and he realised he'd fallen asleep in the armchair with the TV still babbling away to itself.

He cursed. He worried now, no matter how knackered he felt, that he would go to bed and lie there wide awake for ages. He wished he had spent the whole night asleep in the chair. But his neck was aching from the awkward position he had slumped into. He knew he had to get to bed. He switched off the TV and walked out of the living room, switching the lights off as he went. He stopped by the bathroom, decided he couldn't be bothered to brush his teeth, but he couldn't afford not to have a 'whizz' as he liked to call it. He went into the bathroom without turning on the light. The glare of the fluorescent bulb always made him wake up too much. He kept the door open a little to let the hallway light in, just enough so he didn't spray everywhere. Patsy was always having a go at him for that – and that was when the lights were on.

After he flushed and was heading for the bedroom, he heard some chatter from the living room. It sounded as if the TV was on again. He went back into the living room to see that the TV was indeed on again. But no one was in there watching. The lights were still off, and the TV sent a blue flicker around the room.

'What the…?'

He strode over to the set.

'Who the…?'

He looked around, listened to make sure no one was in the kitchen making a cuppa or something, about to come and watch the TV again. Nothing.

'I must be going mental,' he said to himself. 'Or I was still half asleep, so I didn't press the right button.'

He made sure he pressed the right button now. Stood for a moment to make sure it didn't come back on. Then, as he turned to leave the room, he noticed a face in the window.

'Jeez!' he yelped, startled.

His body flooded with adrenaline until he realised it was a reflection of his own face. He approached the window, as if to make sure it was really him. Some of the things Patsy had said recently got him thinking. But of course, there was no one out there, three floors up. He tutted at himself, and at Patsy for being so paranoid. Although, he had to admit, whoever massacred Nelson, must have been one sick person. 'Still,' he smiled to himself like a mischievous schoolboy, 'it saved me a job.'

He turned back into the room and as he made for the door in the near darkness, he rammed his foot into the armchair. He cussed and focused on the chair. Had it been moved? It wasn't that close to the TV usually, he was sure. He shoved it angrily out of the way, nursing his toes for a moment. Then he told himself to get to bed. He was too tired for all this nonsense. He would see to it tomorrow, assuming it was Vernon or Nina, meddling with stuff. That's why he hated having people in his space. His and Patsy's space. They had their routine and it worked well. He didn't like someone messing with it.

He stomped out of the living room, but his way was blocked. In a slow-motion second, he saw the large silhouette of a person in the doorway. He tried to focus on their face, but they were wearing a white mask, with holes cut for the mouth, nose, and eyes. The mask made the wearer blank and emotionless. Ben had seen all the *Halloween* films, and he was sure now he was living them for real.

'Fuuuuuuuuuck!' he bellowed, stumbling back into the living room.

His masked attacker screeched, an unearthly noise and slammed on the lights, blinding Ben for a moment as she shrieked, 'Oh come on, Ben, chill out!'

Ben blinked and focused on Nina towering over him.

Vernon and Patsy, having heard the commotion, had scrambled out of their beds and were at the doorway now.

'What are you doing?' Ben shouted at Nina.

'I just got up to use the toilet and wondered who was in here at this hour.'

'What is that on your face?'

'My face pack, what do you think?'

'You look like bloody Michael Myers,' he said jumping to his feet and trying to look composed.

'Who?' Nina must have frowned, but you couldn't tell under the mask.

Patsy and Vernon held it as long as they could, but were very soon, roaring with laughter.

'Oh, my days! I wish I'd been a fly on the wall for that one,' Vernon cackled.

'Vernon just shut it,' Ben muttered.

'Oh, don't worry, babe,' Patsy giggled, putting an arm around him. 'Come to bed. I'll look after you.'

'Ha, ha!' he sneered, trying not to laugh himself. 'Glad I'm keeping you all entertained.'

'The ghosts left you a nervous wreck, eh Ben?' Vernon grinned.

'What ghosts?' Ben said tramping off to bed.

Patsy told Vernon to shush.

'Why?' he shrugged, 'You and mum went on about it at dinner that time. Perhaps you should get her to come and do her voodoo on this place.'

Patsy didn't tell him that she already had. 'It's not voodoo,' she grumbled. 'She's a pastor Vern, not a witch doctor. Now, shall we all get back to bed?'

'Yes, please,' Nina said patting her mask to make sure it was still securely stuck to her face as she wandered back to the spare room.

Vernon couldn't resist one more jibe and he tapped on Ben's bedroom door as he went to his with Nina. 'One two, Freddy's coming for you,' he sang in a voice like a Muppet.

'Shut up!' Ben called out – by the sound of his voice his face was already buried in his pillow.

Patsy joined him and snuggled up to his warm body. They lay that way for a moment, listening to Vernon and Nina chatter indistinctly in the next room. Patsy felt Ben's body relaxing and knew he was starting to drop off. But before he could, there was a scratching sound, a childish impish giggle, then a louder tapping.

Patsy rolled over and grabbed her phone, turning on the torch and shining it at her desk.

Nothing.

The sounds stopped.

Patsy put her arms around Ben again, but as soon as she had the scratching and tapping began. Then a scratchy voice called out, 'Red Rum, Red Rum!'

'Shut up, Vernon!' Ben's shout came as such a shock to Patsy that she catapulted herself to the other side of the bed.

But she sighed with relief when she heard Vernon cackling on the other side of the wall and Nina telling him off.

She lay on her back listening for a while. Finally, the flat was still and silent. She smiled. It reminded her of home again. Being a kid and her parents trying to get them all to shut up at night.

She rolled over and hugged Ben. And as soon as she did, the scratching and tapping started. Ben didn't care anymore. He was already fast asleep.

'Exhausted from all the drama,' she thought wryly.

She rolled onto her back again and grabbed her phone. She couldn't be bothered to get up and she didn't want to shout and wake Ben, so she thought she'd text Vernon. But before she could type one word the noises had stopped.

She exhaled. Dumped her phone on the nightstand again and rolled over to spoon Ben. It was uncanny that the moment she touched him the noises started again, just as before. Almost as if

Vernon could see – which was a creepy thought and one she banished from her mind quickly. Even though the noises stopped the instant she moved away from Ben, she WhatsApped her brother anyway:

SHUT UP AND GO TO SLEEP!

Vernon didn't reply. She watched the screen for a minute. To see if the two little ticks turned blue. They didn't. But at least he was quiet now. So once again she put down the phone, feeling far too awake, but she put her arms around Ben again to try and…

Scratch, scratch, scratch… Tap, tap, tap.

She rolled away.

The noises stopped.

'No way,' she whispered. And rolled back to Ben to test the theory.

Scratch, scratch, scratch… Tap, tap, tap.

She rolled away.

The noises stopped.

Then she heard the sound of prankish giggles, but it wasn't her brother Vernon. There were two voices that sounded like children, it could only be the little girls who had sat at her desk playing. She peered over the duvet. Beaming her torch at the desk. They weren't there. But they were clearly somewhere nearby. It was odd because she didn't feel scared this time. She felt very annoyed. They were clearly playing, messing with Patsy and she wasn't amused. She wanted to sleep. There were three things that irritated her, anyone who messed with her food, her money or her sleep, this was a no-no.

She rolled over and put her arms lovingly around Ben. And, just as she expected, the tapping and scratching recommenced.

'Shush!' she hissed into the dark. 'I'm not having it, you lil' imps!'

There was more giggling, but it soon faded, and Patsy drifted off to dreamland.

Ben's eyes opened at 5:55AM. He must have sensed the person standing by the bed. He caught his breath, but he didn't make a sound or fly at the intruder in a rage. He knew it was Vernon playing around again. In the half light of the dawn, he could see he was wearing one of Nina's ridiculous face pack masks. Not surprisingly Vernon wasn't an expert in applying them, unlike Nina, so, it was twisted and stuck on so badly that it looked more like wet bandages than paper. He waited for Vernon to do something, but he just stood by the bed trying to look like a zombie or something. Ben bided his time, giving no indication he was awake yet, keeping his eyelids as near closed as possible. He gathered himself, took a deep breath, then jumped out of bed with a roar grabbing Vernon's mask which came off easily in Ben's hand. It was wet, but not with water. And it didn't feel like paper, but actually like the bandages he had imagined they could be. The bandages were wet with something oozing, like puss and one look at the face it came from confirmed that it probably was puss.

It wasn't Vernon. It was far too tall to be Vernon, Ben realised now. And it was a white man, Ben could tell from the neck, but not the face, because the face didn't have much skin left on it. It was raw with fourth-degree burns, every inch of it, down to the muscles and tendons, raging red with black charred edges.

Ben cried out and thought he might vomit. He pushed the figure away, but his hands met with no resistance, and he fell forward onto the floor. A light was flicked on, and Patsy was there with him.

'What is it? What did you see?' she said urgently, as if she knew exactly what he had seen.

'Nothing,' he shook her off, embarrassed. 'It was a dream. A nightmare. Bloody Vernon and Nina. If they hadn't freaked me out, I would have slept fine. Oh, look at the time! I could have had another hour in bed before work.'

Patsy watched him as he glanced furtively around the room, as if he was making sure that something wasn't there; something that, she had a feeling, really had been there moments ago.

In the kitchen the next morning everyone was subdued. Even Vernon, who usually bounced through life whatever time of day it was. He and Nina looked like they'd barely slept. Ben was still brooding after his 'nightmare' and Patsy was watching everyone anxiously.

'How was it?' she asked Nina.

'Mmm?' Nina said through a mouthful of cereal as she leaned against the counter.

'Your first night in our spare room. Sleep well?'

Nina threw a glance at Vernon.

'I suppose it was just weird,' Vernon offered, 'sleeping in a new place. You know. We'll get used to it.'

Nina must have inhaled some milk as she coughed and spluttered. Vernon gave her a loving pat on the back, but she shrugged him off.

'Well, I slept like shit, thanks to your attempt at pranking us all night.'

'All night?' Vernon said scornfully. 'It was once.' He chucked his porridge in the microwave. 'Anyway, I would've slept all right if…'

Nina threw him a look, slammed her bowl in the sink and went off to their room. Vernon followed and Patsy listened to him saying, 'What? You kept waking me up telling me there was some…'

The door of their room shut, and Patsy could eavesdrop no more.

On her way out to work she decided to knock on Loz's door. She hadn't seen her for ages, and she felt she'd been a bad neighbour for not checking up on her after she looked so ill last time.

'To be fair, you've had quite a bit on your plate,' Patsy said to herself wryly by way of an excuse.

She tapped Loz's door lightly. It was still early. She didn't want to wake her. But with a child Mindy's age, Patsy thought it was unlikely Loz could ever sleep past 8AM. She heard something topple over and then feet sliding listlessly along the lino. A huge sniff. And then the door opened.

Loz looked even worse than the last time Patsy had seen her. But what really struck Patsy was the stench coming out of the flat. It was like the smell of chicken that was past its sell by date, mixed with a reminder of her chemistry class at school. It was a smell like Formaldehyde. She thought it was emanating from Loz herself, which convinced her that Loz was heavily drinking these days so, as well as her concern for Loz, Patsy was worried for Mindy with her mother in this state.

'Gosh, Loz, you don't look well at all.'

'You're always great for my self-esteem, you, aincha,' Loz said trying to make a joke without a hint of a smile on her blotchy face.

'Sorry, but I'm worried about you.'

'I just need a drink… I mean, a coffee, then I'll be right as rain.'

'Mindy keeping you up at night?'

Loz's pale face became paler. She seemed thrown by the question. Her lips quivered as they tried to form an answer. But then Patsy's attention was grabbed by Mindy springing into view next to Loz and beaming up at Patsy.

Patsy looked down and smiled. Mindy, unlike her mum, was looking well, which relieved Patsy no end. Loz might not have been looking after herself, but she wasn't allowing Mindy to be neglected.

'You have to spend some time on yourself too,' Patsy said to Loz. 'You can't be any help to this one if you get sick. I don't mind looking after her once in a while to give you some time to recharge if you'd like.' Patsy couldn't help it. She just came out with it. She didn't think she had the time to look after Mindy and she wondered what Ben would say especially now with Vernon and Nina staying, but she would tell him that it was a good dress rehearsal for having a child. If they couldn't look after a toddler once a week for a couple of hours, how were they going to deal with a baby of their own twenty-four-seven?

'I want play with the girls,' Mindy managed to say in that endearingly unrefined way that toddlers do.

'Eh?' Patsy smiled at her.

'In your flat,' Mindy said pointing upstairs. 'The two girls.'

Patsy felt her face get hot and her stomach flip. She didn't know what to say. She was freaked out. And she didn't want Loz to be any more disturbed than she clearly was, so she just looked at Loz and shrugged.

'I'll think about it,' Loz sighed and began to close the door.

Patsy looked down at Mindy, who was grinning ear to ear.

'OK,' Patsy said, relieved to be allowed to rush off. But as she headed for the stairs Loz's voice stopped her.

'Oi. Pats.'

'Yes?' Patsy said sheepishly.

'Thanks, yeah? I really appreciate it… I'll be all right.'

Patsy nodded, smiled weakly and hurried off to work.

She couldn't get Mindy's words out of her head all day. How the hell did Mindy know about the girls? She recalled her mother's words on the phone.

'I wondered when one of you kids would start seeing. You took your time.'

'Took my time?'

'Well, I was seeing when I was a child.'

Perhaps Mindy was *seeing* too, as Rose liked to call it. Perhaps she was clairvoyant, like Rose was as a child. Perhaps this had something to do with why Loz was such a mess at the moment. Patsy knew all too well how exhausting it could be having uninvited guests of the spiritual kind in her home. But how would she broach the subject with Loz? If Loz had no idea what she was talking about, then Patsy would look bonkers, so then why would she let her look after her kid? And then when would Loz ever get the chance to get better?

Patsy's thoughts were interrupted, as they usually were, by JJ slamming her hands on Patsy's shoulders.

'W'sup, girl?'

'Are we in an American rom com now?' Patsy laughed, enjoying the distraction JJ provided.

'What do you mean?' JJ said.

'The accent, the, *'W'sup, girl?'*

JJ laughed too. 'I'd love to be in one of them rom coms. And I'd be perfect as the best friend role. They always give them to black girls, don't they?'

Patsy smiled, 'You're not wrong.'

'I'm never wrong,' JJ chirped. 'Coffee?'

As they made coffee in the kitchenette JJ regaled Patsy with the latest on Tia.

'The press are camped out, outside her house in Hampstead. Social media is a cess pit of lies about her.'

'I know,' Patsy said. It wasn't hard to see what was going on. Every time she opened her phone it delivered her up a feast of bad news about Tia. 'She needs someone to take control of her socials. What the hell is that new girl doing for her?'

'She needs *you* to take control of her socials,' JJ said mischievously.

'I know, but what can I do? I've been sacked.' Patsy felt guilty enough about not being able to give Tia an alibi, the least she could do was help her fend off this bad press.

'Well, since Greg ain't around anymore, talk to Maggie. She might give you the job back.'

'I don't know,' Patsy said looking sheepishly over at her boss's glass box of an office.

'Then call Tia directly. You have her number,' JJ said eyes sparkling.

Patsy's hands were shaking as she dialled, so she shook them as she waited for Tia to answer.

'She's not going to answer,' Patsy told herself as she sat in the toilet cubicle. 'Why would she want to talk to me, I screwed…'

'Patsy?' Tia sounded just like Loz looked this morning.

'Tia,' Patsy exhaled. 'Look, first I just wanted to apologise for…'

'I need a place to stay. Somewhere no one would ever guess.'

'Oh, OK, um…'

'Your place. Can I crash at your place for a few days. Just to put the press off the scent. They'd never believe I'd hang out in your area.'

Patsy would have been offended if she wasn't so pleased that Tia was talking to her. 'Sure, sure, and you need someone to sort out your socials. I can help you, Tia. Let me help you. I owe it to you.'

'Damn right you do. So, send me your address.'

'The only thing is I've got my brother and his girlfriend staying at the moment so it's a bit…'

She heard Tia cuss under her breath and was afraid she was losing her again.

'Anyway, it's fine,' Patsy went on quickly. 'I'll make it work. I'll send the location. I'll be home by six. OK?'

'K.'

Tia hung up.

When Vernon got home from work that evening, Patsy was in the kitchen cooking up a treat. He called out 'Wagwan, sis!' and went to throw himself on the sofa. But he froze in the doorway to the living room when he saw beautiful willowy legged pop star Tia Sash with her loose flowing corkscrew hair down to her waist there watching TV… Dressed up to the nines, in comparison to everyday folk. With her red Gucci Horsebit-detailed jacquard-knit wool mini dress and long black Yves Saint Laurent Auteuil boots, with gold-plated set back high heel. Which made her look much taller than her normal 5'7" height.

She didn't look up as he stared, jaw on the floor, for a moment before spinning round and marching to the kitchen.

'Sis?' he hissed.

'Yeah?' she said looking up from the garlic she was smashing up.

Vernon silently mouthed the next bit, his lips and tongue stretching around like those of a cartoon character. 'Tia Sash is in the living room.'

'What?' Patsy said enjoying Vernon's utter amazement.

'I said,' he bellowed, 'Tia Sash is in the living room.'

'I can't hear you,' she said stifling a grin and looking down at the garlic again.

Vernon scurried over to Patsy and said in her ear, 'What is Tia Sash doing watching TV in your living room?'

Patsy stopped herself from bursting out laughing and said quietly, 'I'm working for her again. And she's staying here for a few days.'

'Here? In your flat?'

'Yeah? So?'

'Where in your flat?'

'On the sofa. There's nowhere else at the moment, is there?'

'On the *sofa*?' he squeaked. 'But she's Tia '*Platinum selling*' Sash. She doesn't sleep on a sofa.'

'All right?'

Vernon almost collapsed at the sound of Tia's voice behind him.

'Tia, this is my little brother, Vernon,' Patsy said, pointing at him with the knife she was now chopping onions with.

'Not so little,' Vernon said with a nervous laugh, pulling himself up as tall as he could, although he was barely taller than Tia. 'Nice to meet you,' he stuttered, holding out his hand with ridiculous formality.

She smiled, quite used to this kind of fawning reaction, and shook his hand. 'I'm Tia.'

'I know,' Vernon blurted out. 'I mean, of course you are, everyone knows that.'

Patsy smiled as she watched her little brother's golden-brown skin going an unusual shade of red.

'So…' he said crossing his arms, uncrossing his arms, leaning against the counter, then standing up straight again, 'you're staying with us, I mean here, for a few days?'

'Yeah, hope I don't get in the way.'

'No, no, no, no, no, no, but… we can't have you sleeping on the sofa. You must sleep in my bed. I mean, sleep in the spare bed where I was sleeping, and I'll take the sofa.'

'It's OK,' Patsy said.

'Yeah, you're in there with your girlfriend, right?' Tia said. 'Where's she going to sleep.'

'Oh,' Vernon looked disappointed at the mention of Nina. 'Yeah, well, we can both sleep in the living room. You need your own space. I'll get some of our stuff out your way, so…'

He shimmied around Tia and went to the bedroom.

'Vernon!' Patsy caught up with him and found him tripping over his suitcases trying to get them out of the room.

'Chill, man,' Tia said over Patsy's shoulder. 'I'm good on the sofa. Honest.'

'But you… you're, you need to get your beauty sleep. I mean, not that you need it, not at all, you're beautiful, you're extremely beau…' he caught his breath, 'but what I mean is…'

'What *do* you mean?' Nina said her head appearing over the top over Tia's and Patsy's.

'Oh, Nina,' Vernon smiled a crooked smile. 'When did you get back?'

Tia and Patsy slunk off to the kitchen digging their nails into each other's arms to stop themselves roaring with laughter.

'I've heard of bringing your work home with you, but this is taking it a bit far, isn't it?' Ben laughed as he got into bed.

'I had no choice really,' Patsy whispered. 'I owed her after Gre…' she checked herself in an instant, '…after I screwed up that interview for her. And it really will be just a few days.'

'Of all the times,' Ben chuckled as he settled his head into the pillow. 'I mean, with Vernon and Michael Myers here.'

Patsy slapped him playfully, glad that he seemed to be taking this all with a sense of humour. But it's amazing what *celebrity* does to regular people, she thought to herself.

'Wait 'til I tell the blokes on site tomorrow,' Ben sighed. 'Tia Sash is sleeping on our sofa.' He grinned at the thought. Turned over and switched off the light.

She felt the bed tilt and caught her breath. She prayed it wasn't that entity, the figure in the heavy coat and wide brimmed hat. He… it hadn't returned since Rose did the clearance. She prised one eye open, dreading what she might see on the bed. There *was* a figure, but it was Ben standing by the bed. The mattress had shifted because he had got up, not because someone or something had crept onto it. She watched as Ben slid his feet along the carpet slowly in the dark, fumbling out of the room.

Patsy felt her body relax – it was only then that she realised just how tense she had been. She expected to hear the bathroom door squeak and the flush go as Ben took himself to the toilet, but the sound never came. She drifted off before she got the chance to hear it.

But when Tia screeched, Patsy was wide awake again and rushing to the living room. She slammed on the light and found Tia slapping Ben and cussing him out as he rolled around on the carpet.

'What's going on?' Patsy said instinctively putting herself between Tia and Ben. She looked at Ben for an answer, but he seemed dazed. She could tell from his eyes that he was barely awake.

'Your boyfriend is playing you,' she spat the words at Patsy. 'Coming in here and laying down next to me in nothing but his boxers. What the hell?'

'Hey, hey, hey,' Ben said blinking incessantly. 'I don't know what's going on. I just woke up with you punching me. How did I get here?'

'Oh, sleepwalking, were you?' Tia snorted derisively. 'Original.'

'Hang on! Hang on!' Patsy said holding up her hand to Tia while staring into Ben's eyes. 'What happened? Tell me!'

'I don't know. I just woke up here. And there was giggling. Little girls giggling.'

That was all Patsy needed to hear. She turned to Tia. 'Tia,' she said locking eyes with her. I don't know if I can explain this, but I guarantee Ben was not awake when he came in here. You have to trust me. He knows what you've been through. We both do. And he would never be so dumb as to try something like this right under my nose.'

'Ey, I wouldn't try something like this period. Anywhere,' Ben grumbled as he got up from the floor.

'All right, Ben, go back to bed!' Patsy demanded.

'I must have been sleepwalking, all right?' Ben said softly to Tia, who nodded at him, the slightest nod as he left.

'Tia,' Patsy said again now they were alone. 'You're going to think I'm nuts, but those girls Ben heard giggling.'

'I heard them too,' Tia confessed, interjecting.

'Really?' Patsy was gobsmacked.

'Are they, like, spirits?' Tia said without a hint of sarcasm.

Patsy's eyes bulged. She wasn't expecting that.

'I had a feeling when I first came here,' Tia said. 'They made Ben do that then?'

'Yeah,' Patsy said, looking over her shoulder to make sure Nina and Vernon were not there. 'I'm sure of it. They're mischievous. I think they might be trying to come between me and Ben. At first it was just noises and annoying sounds every time I got near him in bed. But this. This is going too far. I need to try and get rid of them, once and for all.'

'Yeah. You should if this is the kind off stunt that they pull. Little shits!' Tia said with the twinkle back in her eye.

Patsy let out a huge sigh of relief. 'I can't believe that you…'

'Believe?' Tia offered.

Patsy nodded.

'I've seen bare mad shit in my time, girl.'

Then a thought struck Patsy. If Tia was open to things of a spiritual nature, then Patsy could tell her everything.

'Well, that's good,' Patsy said carefully, 'because I know what happened to Greg.'

Tia's face dropped.

'I wish I'd been here to see that disgusting man's face,' Tia said with a joyless laugh, looking at the window, which Patsy had told her had been Greg's exit from the building and from this world. But very quickly her face was overcast again.

'What you thinking?' Patsy asked her. She was sitting on the sofa next to Tia, where she'd sat while she related the entire story of Greg's visit to the flat. Tia's bedding was pushed to one end in a big pile and Tia leant on it as if she needed the support now.

'With no body there's no way to prove I didn't do it. Or I didn't have someone else do it.'

'With no body,' Patsy tried to reassure her, 'there can be no accusation of murder.'

'There can be no *trial* for murder in a court of law,' Tia corrected her with surprising wisdom. 'But we both know that won't stop me being tried by social media. Until I'm in the ground.'

'That's what I'm here for,' Patsy said putting a reassuring hand on Tia's knee. 'I'm going to sort out the socials. Make sure everyone sees what we want them to see in their newsfeeds.'

'That's going to be a full-time job,' Tia sighed.

'I can do it. As long as Maggie lets me,' Patsy said a little manipulatively.

'Don't worry,' Tia frowned. 'She'll be paid enough. She'll let you.'

Patsy smiled, trying not to look too happy about getting her old job back. 'Now, let's try and get some sleep. We've got work to do tomorrow.'

Thump, thump… thump thump. Thump thump… thump thump.

Patsy's eyes snapped open. She looked at her phone. 5:55.

'Little Gremlins!' she huffed.

She listened for a while as the ball was thrown against the wall in the hallway. Then the giggling from the girls got louder, just as before, and she knew they were in the bedroom, a few feet away. She peered over the duvet. It was no surprise, but she felt her pulse begin to race. The girls were sitting at Patsy's desk, still in their long white smocks, done up at the neck, still smudged with sooty patches. Their hair was as dirty as before and the blonde girl still had the big floppy yellow bow on the side of her straw-like blonde hair. Patsy found herself focusing on the black girl's neck under her high bob cut as she nodded her head in time to the movement of her piece around the Royal board game. Tap, tap, tap, tap, tap, tap.

Patsy knew she had to have a showdown with them She had to warn them off. *Tell* them off. They were little girls, for goodness' sake. She was the adult. She was in charge here, she told herself. She wanted to shout at them, but that might freak Ben out. And he'd been freaked out enough for one night, not to mention Vernon and Nina in the next room, who somehow seemed to sleep through the whole Tia debacle. Patsy had a feeling, that, in fact, they'd heard it all, but Nina was keeping Vernon on a tight leash – there was no way she was going to let him go and see whatever drama Tia was causing in her nightwear in the living room.

Patsy sat up slowly, moved her half of the duvet aside and slid herself along the bed so she was perched on the end right behind the girls. She took a deep breath and then hissed at them:

'Listen to me, girls! Enough of this!'

The girls froze. The blonde girl stopped drawing. The black girl stopped playing. They fell silent. No more giggling or tapping, but they kept their eyes on their games.

'You need to go. No more noise, no more games! This is not your home. This is mine. Do you understand? I'm sorry, but I don't want you here. If you helped with that horrible man who came here,' she said referring to Greg, 'then I understand why you did it, but I don't want you to come between me and my boyfriend. I will hug him whenever I want to. And you will not drive us apart by making him do silly things like you did tonight. Do you understand?'

They didn't respond, but Patsy felt she was getting through. She took their silence as guilt, if not remorse. So, she went further.

'Look at me when I'm talking to you!' she demanded.

The girls dropped their heads a little further. Patsy was convinced they were starting to feel remorse now. She felt empowered to push them further.

'I said, look at me when I'm talking to you!'

The girls looked at each other as if to get the other's permission to turn. Then very slowly, they turned to face Patsy.

She slapped her hand over her mouth to quieten the gasp that came rushing from her lungs.

Both the girls had faces that were so severely burnt they were almost unrecognisable as faces.

Pasty found herself scrambling back to her pillow and yanking the duvet over her as if it were an armour that could protect her from such horror. But no matter how hard she scrunched up her eyes, no matter how hard she tried, she would never be able to rid her mind of that image. She lay there for a moment, listening, then, steeling herself, she threw back the duvet and stared into the dawn light that was bleaching the darkness further with every minute.

They were gone.

She lay there listening to the blood rushing through her ears for a moment, then curled herself around Ben. No sooner had she touched him:

Scratch, scratch, scratch… Tap, tap, tap.

Scratch, scratch, scratch… Tap, tap, tap.

She knew if she moved away from Ben the noise would stop, but she couldn't let them win. She found her AirPods on the nightstand, shoved them in, put some gentle music on her phone and hugged Ben again.

Scratch, scratch, scratch… Tap, tap, tap.

Scratch, scratch, scratch… Tap, tap, tap.

The sound was coming through her AirPods. She yanked them from her ears and lay there fuming. Then, she remembered. She reached under the bed to where all the old newspapers and letters were and fished out Ben's copy of *The Daily Celeb News* newspaper with the front-page story about Tia bumping off Greg. But it wasn't Tia's story she was looking for. She frantically flipped through to the back pages where she found the ad that had previously caught her eye.

GOLDIE PEACEHAVEN
Expert in spiritual house cleansing.
If spirit entities are causing you
stress at home,
Goldie can help.

Akashic Connection courses, Akashic Readings,
Space Clearing and Earth Energy Dowsing.
Call Goldie NOW!

'Goldie Peacehaven? Sounds like a porn star. Or a celebrity's dog,' Tia giggled to herself as she lay on the sofa, which she had done pretty much day and night for the last three days.

'You're in a good mood,' Patsy smiled as she took the newspaper back from Tia.

Tia suddenly looked guilty.

'No, no,' Patsy said, 'it's nice to see. I'm just saying.'

'Well, the paps think I'm in the Caribbean, so I haven't felt this relaxed in years.'

'Ah! You're welcome!' Patsy grinned almost hopping with delight as she stood in the middle of the living room.

'What did you do?' Tia said with a look of excited curiosity on her flawless face.

'Posted images everywhere of you in the Caribbean. Images taken a couple of years ago of course when you went to Barbados, but a bit of fancy editing from me and they were, officially anyway, taken yesterday in Jamaica.'

'Jamaica?' Tia frowned.

'Yep. Half these paps are so ignorant they think the whole of the Caribbean is the same. They'd never notice. Patsy laughed. 'Hopefully they're all winging their way there now at great expense to their employers at the tabloids, so you can slip off to your cousin's place in Scotland whenever you like.

'Amazing. Thanks, Patsy,' Tia said.

But to Patsy she didn't look too happy, so she asked, 'What's up?'

'No, no, it's amazing, really, but… it's been good for me, being here. Even with the ghosts,' Tia giggled. 'I haven't had that family feeling in a while.'

Patsy smiled. 'I'm so happy you felt at home.'

Tia winked. 'You're going to make a good mother, you know.'

Patsy waved the newspaper as if she was swatting the compliment away. 'Stop!'

'I might just stay one more night though… if that's OK.'

'Sure… of course. Now, excuse me I've got to call a woman about a clearance.'

Goldie's voice was exactly as Patsy expected it to be. Warm, breathy, soft and deep. Like Oprah with a Somerset accent.

'I'd like to meet you away from the flat,' Goldie said after Patsy had explained everything to her. 'Just at first. To get a sense of you without interruption from those entities, if that's all right with you, my dear.'

It was hard to refuse anything requested by Goldie Peacehaven's soothing voice.

'Sure. Where would you prefer to meet?' Patsy asked, eager to get started.

'Well, I happen to be not too far from you this afternoon in the countryside near the village of Ashwell. Can you make it?'

'Um,' she looked up at Tia who was listening in. Tia nodded enthusiastically. So, Patsy said, 'Yes.'

'Great. I'll send the location on Google Maps.'

Patsy realised why she would need a Maps location when she parked by the village green, after a drive up the A1M. The village was tiny. Like something from a postcard, which the low wintery sun helped light in a flattering way. Patsy pulled her black full length puffer coat around her a little tighter – everywhere outside London always seemed to be colder – and began walking to the meeting point. She was glad she had worn her fur lined boots as she walked across the green and out onto open fields which seemed to stretch for miles uninterrupted by anything but one giant gnarled tree in the distance. The land here was so flat. After five minutes walking Patsy doubted, she'd ever been so far away from another human or another building in her twenty-nine years on this planet.

She kept an eye on her phone to make sure she was going in the right direction. She started to feel a little nervous. Why would Goldie want to meet in the middle of nowhere? And why the hell had she come here alone? Tia had been up for coming along, but they both agreed when they'd thought about it sensibly, that Tia needed to lay low until she slipped off to Scotland – no point in giving the paps an opportunity to spot she wasn't in Jamaica.

As she got closer to the tree, which was devoid of leaves, but adorned with crows, she saw Goldie. Long golden hair (of course!) flowing in the chill breeze as she stooped over a pile of stones she was building, not far from the tree. As Patsy got closer, she could see that the stones were all smaller than the palm of her hand but balanced impossibly on top of each other about two or three feet from the ground. This little tower was at the centre of a circle of similar stones laid out around it about three or four feet in radius and Pasty stopped short of it not daring to step inside.

'Goldie?' she asked, as if it could be anyone else.

'Ah!' Goldie exhaled as she looked up taking in Patsy with piercing green eyes, that seemed constantly about to cry, but never did. 'Patsy, my dear. So nice to meet you.' She made the groaning sound, which Patsy reckoned all people over forty made as they got up from a chair or from the floor and smiled broadly showing a gold tooth (of course!) where one of her incisors should be and a black hole where one of her premolars should have been. The rest of the teeth were yellowing, but the smile was as comforting as her voice. Her white skin creased heavily around her eyes and Patsy could tell that she spent a lot of her day smiling, which kept this sixty something looking reasonably youthful, apart from the downy hair on her top lip and her chin, which the low sun illuminated unforgivingly.

Goldie shook Patsy's hand – or rather, took it and held it for a moment. In fact, she held it for quite a while, looking deeply into Patsy's eyes and saying nothing. Her touch felt so soothing that Patsy didn't become uncomfortable for at least thirty seconds and thankfully before a minute was up, Golde said:

'Sorry to drag you out here, but I felt the need to come here today and help.'

'Help with what?' Patsy asked.

'Healing the planet,' Goldie said as if it was obvious without making Patsy feel stupid somehow.

'This is a medicine wheel,' Goldie explained as she saw Patsy eyeing up the stone cairn and the circle. 'It represents the alignment and continuous interaction of the physical, emotional, mental, and spiritual realities. The circle shape represents the interconnectivity of all aspects of our being, including the connection with the natural world. On my travels I've visited many sacred sites around the world, and I saw that many countries have traditions that relate back in history to shamanic practises, which are all about guiding the souls and working with Mother Earth.'

Patsy nodded politely, not really understanding what this woman was talking about.

And as if Goldie knew that she elaborated for Patsy. 'When the energy of the land is traumatised, it can affect the homes we live in and spaces we work in. This trauma is also known as geopathic stress.'

Patsy was glazing over. She felt like she was in school again – and not the performing arts one that she had attended as a youngster, where she had such a memorable time.

'Geopathic stress is caused by many things,' Goldie said before breaking off and inhaling deeply as she clutched at the crystal hanging around her neck.

'Are you OK?' Patsy asked fearing the senior citizen was about to have a funny turn.

'Yes, excuse me, my dear. It was just my guide. She wants me to get on with the medicine wheel.'

'Your guide?' Patsy said looking around to see if they were not alone and suddenly worrying again that she was stupid to come here without Tia.

'My spirit guide.' Goldie smiled. 'But as I was saying, geopathic stress can be caused by past renovations, roadworks, crime scenes, war, mining… and that negative energy can affect the people who are living on that land. It can cause things to fall apart in their lives, divorce, ill health, trouble at work…'

Now you're talking, Patsy thought.

'And that negative energy can attract spirit entities to enter our homes where they can cause all manner of mischief or even something more sinister. I think the girls you spoke of are some such entities.' Goldie said putting a hand on Patsy's arm in such a tender way it made Patsy want to cry. 'Let me finish here and then perhaps we can go together to your home and take a look.'

Patsy nodded and smiled. She'd never felt so sure that she was in the right hands in her life. That was until, Goldie began moving her arms about energetically, so that her shawl of many colours flapped about like wings, as she danced and made strange sounds which reminded Patsy of a native American healing chant which she'd seen in films. But this aging white lady doing it under a tree in Hertfordshire, just seemed outlandish. Pasty still felt the need to cry, but this time with laughter. She didn't know where to look. She tried to dart her eyes around from the tree to the sky to the ground, everywhere but Goldie, but then she was transfixed, what was Goldie doing?

If Ben could see me now, she thought. *He'd poke fun at me so badly. And what about Kim? She would cuss me for believing in this stuff.*

But no matter how embarrassed Patsy was, she knew she had to take Goldie back to her flat. She wanted to believe this woman could help her. And, frankly, she didn't really have much choice.

Goldie parked her car next to Patsy's in Factory Way. As they both got out of their vehicles, Patsy noticed Goldie focus on the brook.

'What a lovely little river.' she gasped. 'And the ducks!'

'Yes,' Patsy smiled. 'That was one of the things that made me want this place.'

Goldie took herself to the riverbank and carefully walked along it, round the back of the block to the large well-maintained garden. She looked up and down the river for a moment as if she were searching for something, then made a beeline for the flower bed where Nelson was buried. She stood looking down at the earth. Patsy caught up with her and saw that her face was full of anguish.

'I forgot to tell you,' Patsy said. 'My cat. I buried him there. Then the entities brought the body back to the flat to haunt me, I think.'

'Awful,' Goldie said quietly. 'Just awful.' She pondered for a moment then added. 'Is it just the cat buried here?'

Patsy took a moment to absorb the question. She couldn't imagine what else Goldie might mean, so she said, 'Yes. I had to bury him a second time, right there.'

Goldie's brow smoothed out again and her face returned almost to its default tranquil demeanour when she said, 'Shall we go up?'

Patsy showed Goldie to the front door and up the stairs. As they passed Loz's door Goldie stopped and that anguished look came over her again. She shook her head and reached out a hand to the door, stopping short before closing her eyes and touching it.

'So much pain. So much loss in there. Do you know the resident?'

'Yes. I do. They're lovely. Her name's Lauren, a young mum with a lovely handful of a daughter…'

'Mindy,' Goldie stated.

Patsy's jaw dropped. 'Yes,' she whispered. 'That's… how did you…?'

'Poor Mindy,' Goldie breathed the words, almost inaudibly and carried on up the stairs, leading the way this time.

'Her mother is in a dark place at the moment. I think she's drinking a lot,' Patsy whispered as they went up to the top floor.

'Hmmm,' was Goldie's only response.

When they came to the landing Goldie stopped and turned to the neighbour's door. She didn't need to be told it wasn't Patsy's.

'And who lives here?'

Patsy shrugged. 'Actually, I'm not sure. I knocked once to introduce myself, but they didn't answer. I know they were there, but I don't think they're very… sociable.'

Goldie stared at the door for a moment, let out a dissatisfied huff and turned to Patsy's door. 'Beautiful colour you've painted this.'

'Ah thanks,' Patsy said admiring the eggshell blue.

'Very calming,' Goldie said smiling as if the colour had indeed restored her tranquillity again. 'Shall we?'

'Only me!' Patsy called out as she let herself in, so that Tia didn't freak and think a pap was breaking in.

'Hiya,' Tia called out brightly from the living room.

'I've got someone staying with me for a bit. Just a few nights on the sofa. She's very open to spiritual stuff, she knows everything I've told you.' Patsy said quietly as they went through the hallway and into the living room. 'Tia?'

'Yo!'

'This is Goldie. Goldie this is Tia.'

Tia switched off the TV, jumped up grinning and shook Goldie's hand. 'Nice to meet you.'

'Oh,' Goldie said still holding onto Tia's hand.

Tia and Patsy swapped a look, assuming Goldie was starstruck, like Vernon and everyone else Tia ever met.

'Treat me right,' Goldie whispered.

'Yes,' Tia smiled. 'That's me.'

'What's you?' Goldie asked exploring Tia's eyes with her own.

'*Treat Me Right*. My latest single.'

'Your what, dear?'

'My latest song,' Tia frowned.

Goldie pulled a quizzical face and it suddenly occurred to Patsy that Goldie had no idea who Tia was. 'Tia's a singer,' Patsy interjected. 'And *Treat Me Right* is the name of her latest track.'

'Oh,' Goldie smiled. 'I'm sorry I'm not up with all the rock n roll music or whatever it is the kids listen to these days.'

'Rock n roll?' Tia snorted.

'But you said *Treat Me Right* when you saw Tia,' Patsy probed.

'Oh, yes,' Goldie said, 'because that's all you want, isn't it, dear? It's become a bit of mantra for you.'

Tia's eyes welled up in an instant.

'But it's OK,' Goldie said stroking her hand. 'Things will be fine soon. You'll see. Very soon.'

Tia nodded and slumped on the sofa again, as if in relief.

'But as for you…' Goldie said turning to Patsy. She took hold of the Lapis Lazuli crystal hanging round her neck and inhaled deeply with intensity. She went to the window and did the same. She went out of the room and went into Patsy's bedroom. Patsy followed her and wished she'd tidied up a bit more before she went out this morning. Goldie looked around. She sat at the desk and closed her eyes for a minute. When she opened them again, she picked up a pen and drew on a piece of paper.

Patsy looked over her shoulder and felt queasy as Goldie drew a building on fire, with sad faces in the window and a pregnant woman with flames coming from her womb, all in the style of a child. Patsy felt ill because, although she had talked about the girls sitting at her desk playing and drawing, she had never mentioned the details of the picture to Goldie.

When she had finished, Goldie dropped the pen and looked up at Patsy.

'That negative energy, that geopathic stress I mentioned…'

Patsy nodded.

'There has been some great trauma to the land here. And it has opened a portal.'

'A what?'

'A portal is a spirit doorway, if you like, that opens because of the trauma. This lets the spirits enter. Has there been some kind of fire here in the past?' she said gesturing to the picture.

'Not recently,' Patsy said.

'No, no, it could be a long time ago. It would be good to know more about the history of this land, if you can find out anything. At the local library or on the internet. It might help me when I come to rebalance the energies of the place.'

'Oh,' Patsy said, not entirely following.

'Let's do a little research,' Goldie said gently, though Patsy couldn't help feeling like she was in school again being given a homework assignment. 'Then I will come and perform the clearing.'

Patsy couldn't bear the thought of sitting in a library. She hadn't done so since she was in primary school. By secondary school if she needed to do some research for a school assignment, she, like all her digital baby contemporaries, just googled it. So, to find out about Factory Way and the history of the land her block of flats now stood on, she did what she was best at: she went online and did her research, come on this was 2023 not the 1800s.

However, it wasn't as easy as she had anticipated. It took a long time to find anything about Factory Way and then it was just estate agents trying to sell more flats.

'It probably wasn't called Factory Way before these flats were built, idiot,' she scolded herself.

She remembered back to her school days. Learning about the fire of London which started on Pudding Lane. She used to love the name Pudding Lane. It made her reminisce of the delicious bread pudding her mother used to make, until she found out the origins of the name, it is associated with transportation of offal down to the wharf at the end of the lane to the River Thames. Pudding Lane was named by the butchers of Eastcheap Market who would take the offal down to be collected on waste barges. Offal was gross to Patsy, but at least it helped the lesson to stick in her head.

As she got in her car the morning after Goldie had visited, she looked across the brook at the flats on the other side. It looked like a very gentrified place. Clearly the huge, blackened building was once an old warehouse or mill that had been converted into trendy expensive apartments, no doubt with exposed brickwork and spiral staircases up to mezzanines where commuters slept on futons. It was similar to some of the places she had grown up in when her parents had purchased various old warehouse docklands-based do-er up-er apartments when they were dabbling in property investment throughout her childhood and had eventually settled on a leafy side of north London. She left her car and walked down to the main road, turning left over the bridge to the apartment block. She looked at the name of the road the block stood on: Rye Place.

'There you go!' she said to the air, quite pleased with herself, as cars and vans sped by. 'It was Rye back in the day, I bet.'

She pulled out her phone and a bit of googling confirmed it:

The Rye building was once used to store Yorkshire rye and wheat for the bakers of the area, and sheds to transfer freight from back and forth to rail carts, Cranes powered by horses then mid 1800s hydraulic power...

And by that reasoning she reckoned Factory Way was the site of a factory at a similar point in history – luckily, whoever named the streets round here was not very imaginative.

She sat in her car googling. Factory fire Silverton, she typed. She thought of the royal game the little girl had been playing. She took a guess and added a date: 191… she thought for a minute then just punched the first number that came into her head: 8.

It wasn't the right number, but google was not too picky about that, luckily for Patsy. Instead, it served up this:

A First World War National Government Cartridge Factory was established at Silverton in June 1916. Messrs. Goldstein Brothers agreed to manage the factory, built on 13 acres adjoining the company's own works. The munitions factory was called Goldstein's and was in Foley Lane, just behind Telford's Yard Street School. The factory produced bombs and mines. These caught fire on the 11th October 1918 at about 6AM. The resulting explosion and further fires were regarded as a major incident. Firefighting crews were brought in from nearby towns to support the local fire brigade, and roads in the vicinity were closed. The loss of life was considerable. One traumatised local firefighter was quoted as saying: "you couldn't tell whether the bodies were men or women because their hair, clothes had been blown off."

'Jeezzz,' Patsy said before noticing how late she was for the office. But there was one more thing at the bottom of the page.

Compilers note - the location of this factory, using historic OS maps, must be approximately TQ 32853 92841.

She started the car while texting Ben.

-Babe. What's an OS map?

-Ordnance Survey map. Didn't you go to scouts?

-LOL Of course not.

-How do I find out where TQ 32853 9284 is on that map?

-TQ is the name of one of the grids the country is divided into. The numbers after it describe the position in that grid.

Patsy looked at the screen blankly for a moment. What on earth was he going on about? Thankfully, he texted again:

-Shall I try and find it for you?

She sighed with relief and slammed the car into gear.

-Yes please. Love you!

-It'll have to wait until lunch.

-Sure

-Why do you need it?

She thought for a moment.

-Research. For work.

-OK. Laters xx

She dumped the phone in the passenger seat and sped off out of Factory Way.

'Look!' JJ said nodding over her skinny latte at the construction worker reading *The Daily Celeb News*. 'They reckon Tia's in Jamaica now. Did you know?'

Patsy took a long sip of her Mochaccino, so only her eyes were visible to JJ, and she danced her eyebrows up and down enigmatically.

JJ put her own cup down and sat forward. 'You do, innit? Is this your doing?' JJ grinned. 'She's not even in Jamaica, is she?'

Patsy shushed her and looked around Faye's Pantry coffeeshop. 'Keep it down!'

'Where is she then? Do you know?'

Patsy nodded and grinned back at her friend. She desperately wanted to keep schtum, but she was too proud of her success misleading the press and proud that Tia had chosen her place to lay low. She was struggling to keep it all in.

'Where?' JJ insisted.

'That's on a need-to-know basis,' Patsy winked.

'Right and I *need* to know, so tell me!' JJ was not going to let up.

'I can't.'

'You have to. You can't leave me hanging like this.'

'JJ!'

'Pats!'

Patsy tutted and shook her head slowly. She wished she hadn't opened her mouth now. JJ was like a dog with a bone. 'Let's just say,' she whispered. 'She's somewhere I can keep an eye on her.'

Patsy watched the cogs turn in JJ's brain. It was as if she was doing a crossword and she'd just been given a cryptic clue. 'Somewhere you can keep an eye on her. Eye…' JJ said to herself. 'Something to do with eyes?'

Patsy snorted. She was quite enjoying watching JJ fumble in the dark.

'Eyes. Optician?'

Patsy shook her head.

'The eye hospital? Moorfields Eye Hospital?'

'Why the hell would she be in an eye hospital?' Patsy chuckled.

'That's in Old Street,' JJ went on. 'She's in Old Street?'

This was painful to listen too. Patsy wanted to put her out of her misery. 'I said, somewhere *I* can keep an eye on her.'

JJ pouted like a child who couldn't win at Eye Spy. 'Well... Where can you keep an eye on...' JJ's face dropped. She nearly knocked her coffee over as she leant into Patsy and hissed. 'She's at your place?'

Patsy tried in vain to stifle a smile.

'Izzit! Oh, my dayz! She is, innit?'

Patsy shushed her again. 'JJ, don't you tell a soul!'

'Cross my heart and hope to die!' JJ said.

'Don't say that,' Patsy groaned.

'Why not?'

'Coz, I don't want you tempting fate.'

'I ain't going to say nothing,' JJ said slapping the air between them.

'That's a double negative!'

'Huh?'

'Oh... never mind, don't worry.'

'It doesn't matter if you do really,' Patsy sighed. 'She's moving on tonight.'

'Tonight?' JJ looked irritated.

'What's wrong with that?'

'Let me pop round after work. Before she goes.'

'JJ,' Patsy warned.

'Just like for a quick drink, like as if I was popping in for a cuppa.'

Patsy opened her mouth to protest, but JJ wasn't finished.

'I've never met her up close. You can't keep her all to yourself.'

Patsy laughed, but JJ was deadly serious.

'Call yourself a friend?'

'Just a quick cup of tea and then you have to leave her in peace,' Patsy growled as they went upstairs to the flat.

JJ was so excited she was dancing up the stairs singing *Treat Me Right.*

'Shh!' Patsy said, rolling her eyes and hoping she hadn't made a big mistake by giving in to JJ's emotional blackmail.

JJ just stuck her tongue out at Patsy like a dog waiting for a stick to be thrown. Patsy had to smile back. She knew this was going to make JJ's day, her week, her year. As she turned to take the final flight of stairs up to the third floor, she caught a glimpse of someone on her landing. Whoever it was must have been leaning over the banister looking down at them as JJ and Patsy came up. In a flash they pulled themselves out of sight and Patsy thought she saw something yellow, something purple too perhaps. And she was sure the person in question was white – pale, ghostly white. Patsy took the stairs carefully, but quickly, wondering who she would find at the top, but when she got there all that was left was a whiff of cigarette smoke and the sound of the neighbour's door being slammed. She watched as the figure behind the glass leant against it for a moment as if it was recovering from a near miss.

'Hello?' Patsy said.

The figure startled, realised it could still be seen and ducked further into the flat.

'Who's that?' JJ said coming up behind Patsy.

Patsy shrugged. 'The neighbour. Seems very reclusive.' She stared at the glass door for a moment longer until JJ snapped her out of it, by shoving her towards her own front door.

'Come on! Let's go!' JJ said like a child at Christmas.

'OK! OK!' Patsy said, fishing her keys from her bag.

'Should I call her Ms Sash?' JJ whispered, suddenly overcome with nerves.

'No!' Patsy snorted. 'She's not your maths teacher.'

'Thank God,' JJ grumbled. 'That old cow hated me. She thought I was making fun of her. But I genuinely thought it was called a hippopotamus.'

'What?' Patsy said as she opened the door.

'The long side of a triangle or whatever it is.'

Patsy frowned before the penny dropped. 'Oh…' she giggled. '…like in Geometry. *The hypotenuse* - the longest side of a right-angled triangle, the side opposite the right angle.' She ushered JJ inside. 'Only me!' she called out.

She followed the sound of Ben and Tia chatting in the kitchen. Ben was still in his work gear and busy making himself a tea. Tia was eating a packet of champagne chocolates. Her favourite. Patsy always had to make sure they were on Tia's rider when she did a gig.

'All right, babe?' Ben chirped kissing Patsy as she entered.

'Yeah. All right, T?' she said turning to Tia.

'Hey babe,' Ben said grabbing her attention again. 'That OS map position. Do you know what it is?'

'No.'

'It's this place.'

'Oh,' Patsy said, not really surprised, but she felt a heaviness in her heart at what had happened here all those years ago.

'Is it about…?' Ben flashed his eyes surreptitiously in Tia's direction.

'Kind of,' Pasty bluffed, then seeing the tea things she deftly changed the subject. 'Ah, the kettle's boiling. That's handy coz JJ's just popped round for a quick cuppa on her way home.'

'Oh, all right, JJ?' Ben said looking up. 'Didn't notice you there. Not usually this quiet.'

'Don't worry,' Patsy said quietly to Tia, 'she works for Fliproc Media too. She won't say a word.'

Tia and Patsy turned to JJ who hadn't made a sound since they came in. She was framed in the doorway like a waxwork. Paralysed. Her mouth hanging open. Her eyes moist as if she might cry any second.

'JJ?' Patsy said. 'This is…'

JJ suddenly sprang into life again, an avalanche of sounds and words coming from her mouth. She grabbed Tia's hand. 'Ms Sash, I mean, um, er, Tia, T, can I call you T or is that too familiar. I mean, I don't know, you tell me because you… you're her aren't you. You're actually standing here and I'm shaking your um…'

Tia and Patsy swapped a knowing look.

'Nice to meet you, JJ,' Tia said.

'Is it? Really?'

Tia nodded.

'Nice to meet you too coz I'm a big fan, like, proper big. I've been to loads of your gigs. I always get free tickets from work, not that I wouldn't pay of course, it's just you know…'

'I know. And thanks,' Tia smiled.

JJ stood for a moment breathlessly staring at Tia. Then just before it got too awkward, Tia broke the silence.

'Well, I better pack my stuff. Catch you all in a bit. Want the rest of these?' she said handing JJ the bag of champagne chocolates.

'Thanks,' JJ squeaked, gobsmacked. Then, after she was sure Tia was in the living room out of earshot, she hissed, 'Did you see that? *Did you see that?* She gave them to me. To me! I'm never going to eat them. I'm going to put them in a box, preserve them forever.'

'Here,' Ben said handing her a mug of tea. 'You look like you need it.'

She put the chocolates down on the counter as if it were a Fabergé egg and took the mug. 'A shot of whiskey in that wouldn't go a miss.'

Patsy laughed. 'Seriously?'

'If you can.'

Patsy nodded and opened the cupboard where she stashed the booze. As soon as JJ had taken a gulp of her tea cocktail, she seemed to snap back to her old self.

'So, how's it going Ben? No more hassle with intruders?'

Ben seemed thrown by the question for a moment, but quickly recovered. 'Oh, no. I guess it was a one off.'

'She sounded like a right headcase.'

'She?' Ben said, narrowing his eyes.

'Yeah, this woman, who wanted the flat.'

Ben looked blank so JJ turned to Patsy.

'That's what you said, innit?'

Patsy stuttered, 'No, no, I just said I *thought* it was that.'

'Really? I thought you said the police got her and that.'

Ben frowned at Patsy.

'No,' Patsy sung the word awkwardly. 'Just… I thought they might have picked someone up coz we haven't had any more trouble.'

'Well,' JJ crashed on obliviously, 'I was sure it was that Zack bloke.'

'Who?' Ben asked.

Patsy blanched and tried to cut JJ off. 'Another shot in there?'

'Nah, I've got to drive, innit.'

'Who's Zack?' Ben asked again.

Patsy cut in before JJ could answer, 'Some homeless bloke I've seen hanging around here. Looked like he had some issues. But perhaps I was just being prejudice coz of the way he looked. No, I bet it was someone who wanted the flat for themselves. We were so lucky to get it, you know.' She looked daggers at JJ. She was furious with her. She had told JJ that Ben didn't know about Zack; that she was worried what he would think if Patsy told her some bloke had become infatuated with her. Ben was the jealous type, although he always tried to hide his insecurities, Patsy could see through this.

Ben nodded and slurped on his tea as the front door opened and Vernon bounded in, providing a welcome distraction for Patsy.

'What's happening, roomies? Oh, all right, JJ? Long time.' Vernon's eyes lit up as he spotted the champagne chocolates. 'Oh, what? I love these,' and he'd shoved most of them in his mouth before JJ could stop him.

Patsy couldn't help feeling it was JJ's karma for opening her big gob in front of Ben, but he seemed to have forgotten about it already. He was too busy cracking up as JJ dived at a shocked Vernon, trying to wrestle the bag from his grasp and prise the chocolates from his mouth, but managed to drop most of what was left of the packet, on the floor, she was fuming.

Patsy told her boss that Tia was laying low at her flat for a few more days, a slight modification of the facts, so that she could 'work from home' the day Goldie had asked to come to do the clearance. It needed to be on a weekday so that Ben, Vernon, and Nina would be out of the house. She didn't want to freak them all out if it could be avoided. And, after today, there would be no need to worry about any of this anymore.

She booked Goldie to come at 10AM, that way she could be sure everyone would have left the house at least a couple of hours before. Vernon and Nina had gone before eight and Ben left just before nine – much later than usual, just typical! As soon as he left, Patsy began tidying up the place. Vernon and Nina's room looked like an explosion in Primani. She was just about to deal with this when her phone rang. It was Goldie.

'Patsy, dear,' the voice like a comfortable pair of slippers came down the line. 'How's the research coming on?'

'I found out what was here before. In the early 1900s there was a munitions factory right on this spot and there was a fire in 1918. The place exploded. So many people died horrifically.'

'That's the geopathic stress we were looking for. It makes total sense. The burned faces of the girls. The picture they drew. Perhaps they worked in the factory.'

'There was a school behind the factory too.'

'Ah, well, they could have even been schoolchildren then.'

'The fire started around 6AM according to the records and the things I've seen in the house often begin at 5:55AM.'

There was silence on the line. Patsy wondered if Goldie had hung up, but then: 'Are you married?'

'No,' Patsy frowned wondering what her marital status had to do with any of this. 'I told you I live with my boyfriend. My fiancé actually. Feels like we've been engaged forever,' she said oversharing a bit, but Goldie had a tendency to make you do that. Patsy couldn't wait to be married to Ben and start a family.

'But have you ever been married before?'

'No never.'

'Hmm,' was all Goldie said.

'Why do you ask?'

'Let's discuss more when I get there. Are you happy to go ahead today?'

'Well, it's all a bit strange. But yes, let's do it.'

Ben was halfway down Factory Way when he realised he'd left his phone by the front door. He berated himself as he trudged back. 'What is wrong with me today?'

As he let himself into the flat, he heard Patsy on a call. He would have just grabbed his phone and disappeared again had it not been for hearing her say:

'No. I told you I live with my boyfriend. My fiancé, actually. Feels like we've been engaged forever… No never… Why do you ask?… Well, it's all a bit strange. But yes, let's do it.'

Before Patsy hung up, Ben slipped out again unheard. As he went downstairs, he felt nauseous, his head started to pound, and his cheeks became enflamed, he could barely breath. He couldn't be sure, but he felt as if he may have just overheard Patsy setting up some kind of *hook-up*. It sounded as if she was sick of being engaged to him. How could she be? Being engaged had been all she had wanted; time and time again, she had dropped hints that she wanted a ring, and after getting married she wanted a baby. Women - they were an anomaly to Ben. He had never professed to understanding them. He found them to be a mass of confusion. And now, how was he supposed to go back to the building site and act 'normal'? He was used to passing the day having stomach-hurting-banter with his builder friends. But today was not a normal day, he felt as if his world had come to an end. Patsy was everything to him, his life, his future. Before her, he had coasted meaninglessly through life with no real direction. She was not only the most beautiful girl he had seen, but she was also clever, and funny, and she was like a banker with money; managing to clear his overdraft several times. He secretly admired her ambition and purposefulness, which he found to be far beyond her years. If he was right about this, this would alter the very infrastructure of his life. But he couldn't believe she would have an affair. After all that seemed so out of character for his beautiful Patsy. This was just so not like her. His head was in a spin.

So, he shook these tormenting thoughts from his mind and hurried off to work. A morning next to a pneumatic drill should blitz the paranoia from his mind.

Goldie brought a big red bag bulging with paraphernalia. Out came what looked like two L shaped Copper Dowsing Rods about 135in long with Copper Handles. She took out some clay pots and put them on the coffee table in the living room. She lined one with foil.

'It's just easier to clean after,' she said as she saw Patsy's quizzical look. 'There'll be a lot of soot you see.'

Patsy wasn't sure she wanted Goldie setting any fires in her living room, but she trusted that this maternal figure knew what she was doing.

Goldie poured a generous pile of Epsom salts into the bowl followed by a large splash of liquid from a bottle, the label on which said 99% ethanol. As she did so she held her free hand over the bowl and murmured some kind of chant, the words of which Patsy could not understand.

'Just applying some healing powers of reiki to the mixture as I go,' Goldie said looking up as if it were the most everyday thing in the world.

Patsy nodded as if she knew what that meant. She watched as Goldie finished her chant and reached into her bag for a lighter – the long kind that you use to light a stove or oven. She clicked it and held the flame to the mixture in the bowl. It ignited in a gentle explosion, but it startled Patsy, nonetheless.

Goldie said softly, 'Let's go!'

She picked up the bowl and started wondering around the room with her two copper dowsing rods and the bowl, but before she'd taken a few steps she stopped and gasped.

'So many energies in here, so many negative ones. So many trapped. The trauma has opened a portal and the spirits have flooded in. Many of them are confused. But one…' Her voice trailed off.

'Yes?' Patsy whispered.

'One of them. A male energy. He is in charge. He knows exactly where he is. He's not confused. He wants to be here.'

'Why?'

Goldie shook her head. Patsy didn't know if that meant she didn't know or if it meant *shut up*. She decided to do the latter.

She didn't want to annoy the person who could possibly release her from all this negativity.

Goldie carried on walking while wafting the fumes from the bowl about. 'I hear languages. Many languages. And stories. Many stories. Don't you?'

Patsy listened and gradually her ears began to fill with chatter. The chatter of children, of little girls, but also of adult voices. 'Tell him I'm all right, darling, will you? Why won't you tell him?' came a woman's voice in Patsy's ear.

'Because he's not here anymore. He passed over many years ago. And you should go too,' Goldie said softly, clearly hearing the same thing.

'Bitch!' screeched the woman, making Patsy startled.

Another voice took over the foreground of the cacophony now. It was also a woman's voice, but she had an accent. A French accent. 'That awful man told everyone I was a witch and they had me tried and burned alive.'

'This land has seen more trauma than just the munitions factory fire, my dear,' Goldie told Patsy, apologetically.

And then the voice Patsy knew too well. The angry malevolent male voice in a language she didn't know roared through the room and made even unflappable Goldie flinch.

'There!' she said with a glimmer of excitement. 'That's the entity that thinks he rules this roost.'

'Yes,' Patsy said breathlessly. 'I've heard it before, very scary… it wants me out.'

'Hmm,' Goldie said. 'I'm not sure it wants you out.'

Patsy was dying to know what she meant by that, but Goldie was already moving to her bedroom.

Goldie wafted the bowl around Patsy's bed, chanting, 'Let us clear and cleanse this space. Let's invite love in, happiness, solution, stability, creativity, beauty…' She put down the bowl and waved around the copper rods.

The entities here did not like that one bit. The windows began to shake so violently Patsy feared they may break at any moment. A cloud of envelopes and papers exploded from under the bed and rained down on them as if they were in a snow globe. It was bizarrely beautiful for a moment, until the screams began and the items from her desk began shooting across the room. Pens and pencils became dangerous missiles; Patsy and Goldie had to duck to avoid them.

'Let us clear and cleanse this space. Let's invite love in, happiness, solution, stability, creativity, beauty…' Goldie repeated looking into Patsy's eyes so she knew she should join in.

'Let us clear and cleanse this space. Let's invite love in, happiness, solution, stability, creativity, beauty,' they both shouted now over the roar of angry voices and the flinging of stationery.

A cup which had held all Patsy's pens was now empty and it too was flung across the room, smashing on the wall.

'Let us clear and cleanse this space. Let's invite love in, happiness, solution, stability, creativity, beauty…' she said with Goldie, although she was worried the flat would be anything but beautiful when they'd finished.

With a fizz of electricity her laptop screen switched itself on and opened a new document. Patsy watched as the cursor flashed ominously for a moment before a word typed itself across the screen in a large bold font.

HELL

She felt ill.

'Come!' Goldie demanded over the noise of windows shaking and voices screeching.

Patsy followed her into the spare room.

'Let us clear and cleanse this space. Let's invite love in, happiness, solution, stability, creativity, beauty…' they chanted.

The room erupted as Patsy's had. Windows shaking, objects flying.

'Stand firm!' Goldie told Patsy, even though Goldie herself looked more than a little frightened. 'It will all be over soon.'

They went to the bathroom and the kitchen, but when the knives in the rack began to rise into the air, Goldie backed out of the room and led Patsy back to the living room. This was like a scene from a horror film. Patsy thought, shrinkingly.

She set the bowl down on the coffee table and continued to chant. The voices raged around them as if they were trying to drown out the positive words. Patsy felt like she was on the worst kind of rollercoaster, and she couldn't get off. The sofa they sat on jolted about as if it was trying to buck them off. The armchair slid across the floor to the wall time and time again as if it wanted to knock itself senseless like a caged animal. But the voices that startled Patsy the most were the familiar ones of her brother swearing and Nina crying out in fright behind her.

'What the hell? sis!'

As soon as Patsy and Goldie registered their presence, the room fell silent, everything was still, except for the timorous heaving chests of the four humans present.

'What are you doing here?' Patsy asked, panting.

'What am *I* doing here? What are *you* doing?' Vernon gasped his eyes like saucers.

'Oh my God, this is insane,' Nina bawled. 'I knew there was something messed up about this place. The things I saw in bed, and you told me it was just my imagination. No… no… more. No more!' she stuttered, hurriedly off to the bedroom.

Vernon bolted after her and Patsy followed them both.

'What happened in here?' Nina screamed.

'Calm down!' Patsy told her. She wanted to add that it looked tidier after the poltergeists had ransacked the place, than it did when Vernon and Nina had left it this morning, but she thought, as funny as this was, it wasn't the time for sarcasm.

'Don't tell me to calm down!' Nina wailed as she started shoving things into her oversized, overpriced suitcase.

'It's fine now,' Patsy said, reassuringly. 'Look, there was an issue, yes, with some negative energies…'

'Negative energies?' Vernon laughed mirthlessly. 'The place is bloody haunted, Pats. I thought you and mum were just chatting rubbish. I didn't think it was actually real.'

'Well, it is. But I'm sorting it.'

'Come on!' Nina cried. 'I'm not staying here another minute.'

Patsy watched helplessly as they packed for a minute, then a thought occurred to her. 'Why were you here in the middle of the day anyway?' she asked her little brother.

Vernon blushed. 'Oh, we, wanted a bit of… lunch.'

Patsy would have laughed in a different situation. She knew from her brother's face that they had hoped to come back for some uninterrupted sex, but all she could think of now was losing her brother. She always knew he would move out eventually, but she didn't want it to be so soon, and not like this.

'You don't have to go,' she insisted.

Vernon nodded at Nina and shrugged at his sister. 'I think it's best. Damn, why do you even stay here?'

'This is my home. I love it and won't be driven out by anyone.'

'Not even a ghost?' he growled.

'No, not *even* a ghost.' She half smiled to try and reassure him. 'Anyway, it's sorted now. It's fine.' Patsy nodded toward the living room where Goldie was. 'She's a professional.'

'A professional what? Nah. Not for me, sis. Sorry, I've got to bounce.'

Patsy spent the rest of the day wandering around the flat as if she was grieving. She was harbouring a great sense of loss. Never had this flat felt so empty. Tia had gone. Vernon and Nina had gone. Even the angry and annoying ghosts had gone and occasionally through the day she felt a bizarre desire to have the meddling spirits back, just so she didn't feel so alone. She found herself longing to hear the ball thumping against the wall. She longed to hear the sound of the two little girls giggling. When she was tidying up her bedroom, she would look at the desk and find herself almost hoping the girls would be sitting there playing. But as the day wore on and she tried to do a bit of work on Tia's social media accounts, she realised that she was happy not to have that angry male entity bellowing in her ear or trying to force himself on her when she lay down for a nap.

Goldie texted her in the late afternoon:

Just checking in. Everything OK?

Patsy texted back:

Peaceful at last. Thanks.

And she meant it. By then she was adjusting to having her space back. She was looking forward to Ben coming home and it being just like it was in the beginning; when they first moved in; minus poor Nelson of course.

Good, Goldie texted back. Please remember to pay the rest of my fee today if you can.

Patsy was shocked by this seemingly cold and mercenary request at first, but she had to smile. Even ghostbusters needed paying, and gosh was it a fee, it set her back just under £300. But it was money well spent, as far as she was concerned.

When Ben came home, she was so happy to see him, she looked at him as if it were the first time, that she was seeing him. He was so the opposite to her normal type. She normally went for the stereotypical tall dark and handsome bad boys. Although, he was a striking looking English man standing at 5'10" with the typical builder physique and swag in the way he dressed and held himself. What really stood out was his personality although a deep complex character with dark moods that were extremely challenging at times; and they changed like the English weather, he had a heart of gold and a comical sense of humour that could leave any one in attendance with a pain in their side from laughing. What really struck Patsy was his deep love for her, he had the kind of love that makes someone lose all sense of reason. Leave everything behind, take a risk and build a future. He was holding a bunch of red roses, in his big builder's fists, they looked slightly odd, and his face was flushed with embarrassment. But Patsy loved all his romantic gestures, and boy was he romantic. After he'd given them to her, she held him tightly for so many reasons, feeling his unshaven bristles against her soft cheek, she tried not to ruin the tender moment with a shriek to say, 'oh your bloody bristles are stabbing my face', instead she kissed him gently coyly saying,

'What brought this on?', she hated herself for asking, but she couldn't think of anything else to say.

'Nothing', Ben grumbled. 'Just… you know… you're *my beautiful.'* This was Ben's way of saying she was special. He was a man of normally unembellished words, but this encapsulated all his love and warm thoughts towards her when he named her 'My Beautiful'. And Patsy understood succinctly what he meant.

Patsy told herself not to probe further and just be grateful.

'I was thinking,' Ben said as he washed up after dinner.

'Hmm?' Patsy said as she put the dried crockery away.

'Isn't it about time we got married?'

Patsy nearly dropped the earthenware bowl she was holding. It was exactly what she'd been thinking for a while now but didn't mention it. 'But what about saving up?' she said trying to steady the excitement in her voice, trying not to be too exuberant. 'We don't have enough cash yet, do we?' she said in a matter-of-fact way.

'We nearly do but, who cares. Your parents have a few bob to spare, I am sure they will help. And… we also have our credit cards, if all else fails. Life is short. And I love you and I want to have kids with you. And since your parents would go bonkers if we had a baby before we were married, we better get cracking, eh?'

Patsy put down the bowl and threw her arms around him. 'You read my mind,' she smiled kissing him again and again.

Ben rolled his eyes. 'Kind of,' he said to himself.

Patsy wasn't listening, she was too busy kissing him and hugging him. Eventually, he prised her off and went to the fridge.

'So, you're up for it then?' he said as if he was asking a mate to the pub.

'Up for it.' she giggled. 'Course I am.'

'Soon as possible?'

'Hmm a winter wedding?' she said pensively.

'Why not?' Ben shrugged. 'A summer wedding is bound to be ruined by the rain anyway.'

'True dat!' she laughed, pretending to tickle him.

'That's settled then,' Ben smiled and pulled out the bottle of champagne he'd secreted in the fridge. 'We can open this now.'

He popped the cork, and they sat on the sofa making enchanting plans for their future together. By the time the bottle was empty they were pulling each other's clothes off. Patsy loved having sex on the sofa – it felt so naughty – but she dragged Ben to the bed so they could finish off in comfort. The sex was some of the most passionate and athletic they'd had in a while, and it happened in a haze of alcohol and eye-rolling ecstasy. She thought they had a second steamy session in the early hours of the morning, but she couldn't be sure if she was dreaming or not. And she didn't care. It was all sensational – dream or not.

When she woke in the morning, she could feel a burning on her back, and she went to the full-length mirror propped up against the bedroom wall to check it. She had scratch marks across it. Long and deep. Her instant reaction was one of confusion, which quickly translated to one of amusement.

'Morning!' Ben said groggily from the bed. 'What are you up to?'

'Look what you did to me last night!' she grinned and threw herself on the bed face down so Ben could examine his handy work.

'Me?' Ben said lightly touching around the wounds.

'Well, who else?' Patsy rolled over. 'You naughty boy!'

She laughed. Ben didn't. Instead, he examined his nails. His short stumpy nails that couldn't have possibly caused such marks on her back. He was upset, that was evident, but he did his best to hide it. Patsy too felt a wave of nausea flow over her, they both looked at each other both indubitably knew that these claw marks on her back were not Ben's.

Who else? *Who else?*

She decided to keep laughing, to try and put Ben at ease.

'That was some hot sex last night,' she said. 'I'm surprised we didn't both get more injuries.'

'But…' Ben began.

Patsy cut him off. 'It's fine,' she said, jumping up. 'Doesn't hurt at all,' she lied and hurried out to the bathroom. 'I better show my face at the office today,' she called out as she examined the marks in the bathroom mirror now. 'I think I've milked this Tia thing long enough. And when I get there, I'll call mum about a date for the church, yeah?'

No response from Ben.

'Yeah, Ben?' she said loudly.

'All right.' His tone was weak, distracted.

As she examined her back, one of the occasions when the heavy-coated figure in the wide brimmed hat had pressed itself upon her in bed came to her mind. She hadn't registered it fully at the time, but she recalled its fingers now caressing her throat. The fingers had long jagged nails. Just the kind of nails that could have done this to her back.

Her mum was frustratingly, mute on the phone.

'Come here after work and we can discuss it,' was all she said when Patsy told Rose she and Ben wanted to marry as soon as possible. No *congratulations*, no *I'm so happy for you,* not even a *hallelujah.*

When Patsy got to her parents' house, her father Luca answered the door.

'Ciao, Bellissima!' he said warmly, grabbing her face and kissing her on each cheek as he always did whenever they met. Her dad was a Sicilian born man from the South-East of Sicily, who was a warm hearted, loving father who Patsy and her siblings adored. He loved big, and everyone loved him equally. Luca Conti was a good-looking man, standing at 6'0" tall, from a well-established wine-producing Sicilian family. His mother was Jewish Italian and his father French Roman Catholic, so the family was used to the extreme worlds coming together as one, and warmly welcomed the stunning young British Jamaican Rose into the family. Rose and Luca wed at 23 years old, after a chance meeting in Syracuse, Sicily. Rose had gone on a girl's trip for the week with her best friends and they had toured the family vineyard - the breathtaking Casa Conti, with a tour guide. The family-run winery was surrounded by old vineyards and beautiful, lush gardens, near the sea. Luca was an accomplished property developer and was always ahead of the curve with business deals. He had the Midas touch and Patsy felt the benefits of his success, being spoilt with all the latest designer gear in school that her friends could only dream about, she was a little conceited as a child having everything at her fingertips, but she had outgrown this during her teen years and learned to appreciate more of what she had. The whole family were, as people always felt it necessary to comment '*like something from a movie poster*'. But they never really spoke about looks, or material things, they all focused on much more intelligent and down to earth topics such as: education, career, political and existential debates. Rose had a capitalist mind with a socialist heart - a contradictory mêlé.

They spoke of ways to help mum Rose to improve her church community. 'Come in! Come in!' He ushered her into their palace-esque detached mansion-like house, which he had proudly project managed the build on – but complained that if it stood on Bishops Avenue – it would fetch more. In fact, it stood erect on Beech Hill within the leafiest part of the prestigious North London's, Hadley Wood and, as soon as he shut the dark bronze cast iron door, his face dropped. 'Are you pregnant?'

'Dad!'

'Your mother tells me you want to get married as soon as possible. Why else would you want to get married at this time of year?'

'Dad. I am not pregnant.' *Well, I might be after last night,* she thought with an inner grin as she recalled Ben groaning on top of her. Then, as if to chastise her for such naughty thoughts, the scratches on her back burned briefly. 'Ouch,' she winced.

'What is it?' Luca was concerned for his 'little one'.

'Nothing,' Patsy smiled. 'Just got my hair caught in this necklace I think,' she lied.

'Oh. So?' Luca was not to be distracted from the topic of the day as he led her through to the living room. 'Why now? Why get married now?'

'Because we want to, Dad. We're sick of just being engaged. We don't want to wait all the way until next summer. And it's so hard to find a date in summer anyway. We can have pretty much any day we like in winter.'

'Oh, so you think I do nothing in the winter?' Rose said from her bureau where she was working on her sermon for the weekend.

'I'll put the kettle on,' Luca said, and he slipped out.

'Hi, mum,' Patsy said, going over and kissing the top of her head, since she had her back to the room and didn't look up from her writing. Rose was everything to Patsy, she adored her, she was her best friend, she could hang out with her, go shopping and could always confide in her – Rose was always on Patsy's side, when life got tough, she could always turn to her. Although sometimes misunderstood by other people who could at times think she was brash, Patsy always understood her completely.

'December is the busiest time of the whole year for a pastor,' Rose added.

'I know, I know,' sighed Patsy. 'But I mean, for weddings summer is crazy, isn't it?

Rose cocked her head, not disagreeing. Then she spun round in her office chair and examined her daughter, looking her up and down. 'Are you sure you're not pregnant?' she said, her eyes narrowing as if she knew what Patsy and Ben had got up to last night.

Patsy tried to stop her face from flushing as she sat on the overly opulent green velvet sofa. 'No!'

'No, you're not sure?' Rose said mischievously.

Patsy tutted. 'I mean, yes, I'm sure I'm not pregnant. And anyway, I thought you'd be pleased we were finally tying the knot.'

Her mother cocked her head again. It was a habit that irritated Patsy especially in this case where it meant Rose wasn't prepared to say she was pleased Ben was marrying her daughter. Neither did she wholly dislike the idea. She liked Ben, but she came across as if she was neutral towards him and Patsy had often wondered why. She wondered if her mum could pick up the other side of Ben – his dark moods, especially when he'd had a beer. She knew it couldn't be because of race, after all Rose loved all races and she had married outside of her own race. Not that it matters. Patsy quickly dismissed these thoughts.

'We do want to have kids soon,' she added, 'and we know you'd want us to be married before I got pregnant.'

'And you can't keep your hands off each other until summer?' Rose said coldly.

'We couldn't keep our hands off each other when we were courting,' Luca said as he re-entered the room with a tray of teas. 'I'm still not entirely sure if Kim was conceived before our honeymoon.'

Rose kissed her teeth loudly. 'Of course, she was not.'

Patsy laughed, grateful for the ammunition from her dad.

'Will you have a honeymoon?' Luca asked. 'You must have a honeymoon.' His eyes sparkled with the memories of past travels. 'Where will you go?'

'Paris,' Patsy said without hesitation.

'Paris, I think we can afford somewhere a little further afield sweety', Rose said sarcastically.

'Ah!' Luca clapped his hands together. 'Of course. What could be more romantic!'

Patsy appreciated his enthusiasm, especially when Rose just rolled her eyes as if it were her job to be the antithesis of her husband.

'So, what do you think, mum. Would you officiate at our wedding? Can we do it at your church? Our church?'

Rose thought for a moment then spun back around to her desk and leafed through her diary. 'Hmm,' she sighed. 'I don't know. As I said, December is busy.'

Patsy sighed too, and as dramatically as her mother. 'Well, I can always ask Ben to sort a church out. I think his mum goes to one in Enfield sometimes.' She winked at her dad as she stoked the fire.

Her mum huffed derisively, '*Sometimes!*' and immediately found a date. 'Saturday December 2nd. That will have to do.'

Luca and Pasty shared a silent laugh and Patsy said, 'Ah, that's great, thanks, Mum.'

Rose spun back around to face her daughter. 'Has this rush to get married got anything to do with the entities still dwelling in your flat?'

'Why would it?'

'Because it sounds as if things are getting out of hand in that department again.'

'How do you…?' And then the penny dropped. 'Vernon's been blabbing, hasn't he?'

'Your brother has been informing me of the issues you're having, since you do not seem to think it proper to inform me yourself. He tells me you've had some witch doctor making things worse.'

'She's not a witch doctor nor is she making things worse. In fact, she seems to have helped actually.'

The scratches burnt momentarily on Patsy's back as if to mock her assertion that things were getting better at home. She flinched and Rose, noticing, examined her daughter like a hawk, yet again with her laser eyes.

'Did you not think to ask me?' Rose said trying her best not to sound like she was sulking.

'I did ask you,' Patsy snapped. 'And you said, and I quote, *such spirits are around all of us, all the time. It's just that you are able to see them. Like me. It's a gift.*'

'I said,' Rose corrected her daughter, 'if they are causing no harm there is little to be done. But what Vernon described to me, didn't sound like the work of harmless entities. So, if you are feeling threatened, I suggest you let me come and take another look.'

'No, no, it's fine,' Patsy said feeling offended on Goldie's behalf, angry at her brother for grassing her up and irritated at her mother for not coming to her rescue sooner. 'The person who did the clearance was successful,' she sniped. 'It's all done now.'

The front door slammed, and Vernon called out, 'Hey, roomies!'

Patsy looked at her dad. 'He's staying here?'

Luca nodded as Vernon bounded into the living room and stopped in his tracks when he saw Patsy.

'Oh.' He tried to recover himself quickly with some swag. 'Wagwan, sis?'

'You'll speak properly if you're living under this roof,' Rose said curtly. Although born and raised in England, Rose was quite used to family members speaking Jamaican Patois around her when they came to visit for months on end, as they had the tendency to do. However, Rose spoke English in a heightened received pronunciation style that sometimes had her children in fits of giggles, Rose would not be out of place at Buckingham Palace.

Vernon rolled his eyes and grinned to try and illicit some sibling solidarity from Patsy, but she just glared at him. The atmosphere was thick with unaired grievances, so Luca piped up:

'Guess what, Vernon?'

'What, Dad?'

'Your sister is getting married.'

Invitations had to go out quickly. There wasn't much time. Patsy insisted on keeping it small at around 100 people, as she sat with her parents after Rose had agreed to officiate and they made a list of family that it would be heinous not to invite. Although Rose was one of 8 children, they all lived abroad, the family was spliced across Jamaica and the USA. Yet all remained remarkably close, and they were competitive over Rose's affection, she was the youngest. Rose was the only one of her siblings that was born in England, after her mum and dad had visited friends in London and ended up staying for quite some time. All her siblings were Jamaican born. She was a natural over achiever, excelling in school and university graduating with a first-class degree in Philosophy. Rose had said that the guest list wasn't anything to do with her and yet somehow, she was the person who managed to get the most suggestions onto the '*definite* list'. Rose also said what Patsy wore on her big day was up to Patsy and yet, as Patsy scrolled through some suggestions on Instagram and Pintrest, Rose managed to pooh-pooh all of them. Patsy eventually decided on a couture lace A-Line, Princess ballgown with beautiful appliqués exquisite beading and low back – after a dress fitting and Rose and the girlie party all welled up when she put on the dress.

When she got home that night the list of guests was still forming and reforming in Patsy's mind over and over again. As she passed Loz's flat, she had an overwhelming desire to invite her and Mindy to the wedding. She didn't know Loz that well, but it would feel strange leaving the flat on the morning of the wedding and passing this door knowing Loz and her little one were inside uninvited. Despite the inevitable booze at the reception, an invitation to an event might be just what Loz needed – give her something to look forward to, something to get dressed up for.

She knocked on the door and waited. She heard the usual cussing from inside as Loz was disturbed from whatever she was doing. She heard Loz's feet sliding along the lino. She heard something being kicked out of the way. And finally, the door cracked open, and that stench seeped out.

'Hey, Loz,' Patsy smiled, trying not to grimace at the odour. She decided not to ask how she was and go straight in with, 'Guess what?'

'Cold potatoes ain't hot,' Loz rhymed, her eyes half closed, her voice lethargic.

'Pardon?' Patsy smiled awkwardly.

Loz shook her head, 'Just something my mum used to say.'

'Oh, how is she?'

'Who?' Loz said a little defensively.

'Your mum. Have you been down to Southend recently to see her?'

Loz shook her head slowly pressing it against the door as she did so; Patsy was worried she'd graze the skin, but the sensation seemed to bring Loz some kind of comfort, as if she had an itch deep under her skin she was trying to reach.

Mindy appeared between her mum's legs so Patsy added, 'Ah, well I suppose the weather's so rubbish these days it would be no fun for this one, being so close to the beach but not being able to enjoy it.'

Loz followed Patsy's gaze and then she shifted about nervously. 'What are you talking about?'

'Mindy,' Patsy said only slightly aware of Loz's reaction. 'I bet you can't wait until summer so you can go back to the beach, darling?' she asked Mindy, who nodded with the usual impish grin on her dirty face. Patsy was aware now just how dirty her face was, as if she had been playing in the flower bed again – playing for a very long time. And she had a sore looking mark around her neck.

When Patsy looked back to Loz, she saw that her mouth hung open and her lips quivered. Her eyes were just like Vernon's had been when he'd walked in on Goldie doing the clearance. Patsy thought the best thing to do was not to pry into Loz's business, but deliver her good news to try and get Loz out of this strange zombie-like state she was recently in.

'So anyway, my news. Ben and I are getting married. On December 2nd. And I want you to come. Will you come?'

'To your wedding?' Loz said as if her mouth was desert dry.

'Yes. I'd love you both to come.'

'Both?' Loz said distractedly.

'You and this little munchkin,' Patsy said reaching down to press Mindy's nose, but the girl jumped back startled, with a giggle before Patsy could make contact.

'What the…' Loz began, straightening up and shaking her head quicker now. In fact, every part of her seemed to be trembling. 'What the… what the heck are trying to do to me?'

'Loz?' Patsy was puzzled.

Loz looked down to where Mindy had been, but the little one had scampered off and Patsy could hear her making a mess in the living room. Loz looked back at Patsy and down at the floor again a few times. 'Don't try and mess with my head! Don't…' Loz was rambling now. 'Why would you say that? Why the hell would you?'

She shut the door and left Patsy on the landing wondering what she'd done wrong.

As she tramped up the stairs to her flat, she pondered Loz's reaction and by the time she got to her own front door, Patsy had decided that the whole idea of going to a wedding had in fact been triggering for Loz. She'd told Patsy she'd been abused by her husband. Goodness knows what Mindy had seen during those days too. Patsy berated herself. 'You idiot. You didn't think, did you. Flaunting your happiness in her face.'

The smell of smoke on the landing irritated her more than ever in that moment. She glared over her shoulder at her neighbour's door. She thought about knocking on it, but she'd done enough damage with the neighbours for one day. And besides she had a wedding to prepare for.

In bed that night, Ben and Patsy went over the list and Ben added his definites – the ones who he couldn't not invite otherwise he would never hear the last if it. They looked at online for outfit ideas and Patsy was happy to see Ben was completely focused. Patsy wanted to see him a pale blue suit – him and his brother Dave who would be best man. Ben wasn't too fussed about the colour as long as he was allowed to have skinny fit trousers. He would have had his mate Wayne as best man, but his mum would have made his life hell. She had no doubt Dave would be the best man, even though he and Ben hardly ever saw each other – they got on OK when they had to, but Dave was cut from a different cloth, so much so that, if they didn't both have the family nose, same height with the same striking features, Ben would wonder if they really did share the same parents. They both liked sport, but that was where the similarities ended. Dave was obsessed with money in a way Ben wasn't. Dave worked in the city for an American Investment Bank, and he only ever associated with people who looked just like him – young, middle-class white, soulless men. Ben was poles apart from him politically and poles apart emotionally, and Patsy was thankful for that every day.

Despite Dave being conscripted by his mother to the post of best man, Ben was excited. 'It's going to be a great day,' Ben said as they finally put down their phones and switched off the laptop.

'I hope so,' Patsy said biting her lip.

'Of course, it is. Stop worrying!' He kissed her and turned off the light, turned himself onto his side and she snuggled into him laying her head on his warm back.

She started to doze off but was woken again by Ben's voice in her ear.

'I cannot wait for our wedding day.'

She tapped his chest lightly as if to say, *I know, you said that, now go to sleep!* But she couldn't help grin as she dozed again.

'At last, we will be bound together forever. Finally, you can take me from this hell realm and together we will live in heavenly paradise for eternity.'

She thought he was taking the mickey. He wasn't religious, he wouldn't be saying, 'heavenly paradise for eternity'. He was just going along with the whole church thing to please her, and she was always grateful for that, but what was all this bound together stuff? These were not the kind of words to usually come out of Ben's mouth. And as he went on:

'My bride. My love. The servant of my heart.'

She realised that not only the vocabulary was not Ben's, but the voice was not his either. So, she threw her hand out to click the bedside light on and looked around her and at Ben, who was snoring away. There was no one else in the room. No one with a physical body anyway, but Pasty knew that didn't mean a thing. She reached under her nightshirt and felt the scratches which were hard and crusty now. She picked up her phone and scrolled down her contacts list to Goldie. Her finger hovered over the call button for a while, then she changed her mind. Instead, she wrapped herself tightly around Ben again, squeezed her eyes shut and whispered:

'Let us clear and cleanse this space. Let's invite love in, happiness, solution, stability, creativity, and beauty.'

She pondered those words for a moment as if she was working on a press release then, fearing Goldie had been too free with the word love, she wondered if a little editing was in order.

'Let us clear and cleanse this space. Let's invite… happiness in, solution, stability, creativity, beauty… for Ben and for me.'

'Friends, family and loved ones, we have come together in the presence of God to witness and bless the joining of this man…'

Patsy couldn't help feeling her mother said *this man* with a certain degree of disdain. She wondered for a split second why she didn't say *Ben* until she realised that was the way the ceremony script went and, if there was one thing Rose was certain to do in life, it was stick to the script.

'… and this woman in the sacred bond of marriage.'

Bond. The archaic language stung Patsy a little as she recalled the voice which had whispered in her ear the night, she and Ben had first made wedding plans. It wasn't the last time she had heard it. As the wedding got closer the voice would be there, just a few words every night, soothing and seductive even. She had a feeling the voice came from the entity which had been so angry and violent when she first moved into the flat, the voice which had spoken in a language which she didn't understand, but now it spoke English in a tone that was familiar with a hint of a Caribbean accent, she thought; soft, calm English, as if every day closer to the wedding brought the speaker more and more solace.

'The bond and covenant of marriage,' Rose went on, 'was established by God in creation, and sanctified by his presence…'

Pasty turned to look at Kim, her maid of honour. Despite all the times they fell out – the most recent being over their mother's clearance of Patsy's flat – it was never more than a day or two before one of them would share an Instagram reel with the other and that would signify the end of the battle. However, asking Kim to be her maid of honour was the greatest olive branch Patsy could ever offer her big sister – better even than anything the algorithms of TikTok or the Gram could serve up. Patsy thought Kim looked beautiful in her peach ankle length dress. She was smaller than Patsy and looked more European in complexion with more European hair, but Patsy found Kim to be more cultural and when she flung down some dance moves in a club all the girls rolled their eyes at Kim as they thought *who does this Italian girl think she is dancing to bashment like that?* Kim was also ecstatic when the Spanish woman in the supermarket made a racist remark at her, not knowing that Kim was fluent in Spanish from studying Spanish major at university, she smiled at the woman with glee when ushered along at the cashier till '*sigue adelante chica negra'*. Kim smiled thankfully and replied '*me daré prisa, gracias'*. Likewise, Kim was not used to being included in black hair cultivation frustrations with friends, she often felt left out, as she found her soft long bouncy curls a doddle to wash and blow dry.

She admired Kim and loved her dearly, most sisters would've been a little envious of her as a sister, but Patsy was not, and especially not on today. Pasty was happy with how Kim looked, but even more happy with how her own dress, hair and make-up looked. She felt like a scene stealer, in her beautiful lace princess couture gown. Patsy expected to see Kim raising a cynical eyebrow at their mother's speech, but Kim looked surprisingly serious, her eyes focused over Patsy's shoulder. Patsy followed her sister's gaze assuming it was Ben she was looking at, or even their mother, but it wasn't. Kim was staring into the space between them all as if she could see something there that she didn't like. But there was no time to dwell on this as her mother's voice demanded Patsy's attention again.

'It is this fruit of the vine that is a symbol of creation and the life that we celebrate today. Blessed are you O God ruler of the universe, creator of the fruit of the vine,' Rose continued, as an ode to Luca's Jewish ancestry, with a blessing over the wine. 'The union of husband and wife in heart…' She cleared her throat briefly to get the next word out, '…body, and in mind is intended by God for their mutual joy, for the help and comfort given one another in prosperity and adversity and…' She looked over the top of her reading glasses now and gave a reproachful look to her daughter and son-in-law to be, '*…when it's God's will*, for the procreation of children and their nurture in the knowledge and love of the Lord.'

Patsy had a burning desire to stop her mother and shout out, 'I told you, I'm not pregnant!' But she thought better of it of course.

'Therefore,' the pastor went on, 'marriage is not to be entered into unadvisedly or lightly, but deliberately, intentionally, thoughtfully…'

Patsy could've sworn Rose was loading each of those words with an unnecessarily heavy emphasis, but that's what you get for having your mother marry you!

'…and joyously,' Rose said, beaming proudly.

But nevertheless, Patsy looked at Ben and they shared a huge grin, like naughty schoolkids finally being allowed to get what they want.

'Into this holy union, Benjamin and Patricia now come to be joined.'

Both bride and groom winced as their full names were announced. Neither of them had ever liked being called by the names on their birth certificates and they both giggled their embarrassment away until the part Patsy always hated in a wedding ceremony sobered her up:

'If any of you can show just cause why they may not be lawfully married, speak now or else forever hold your peace.'

This moment always made Patsy's heart race. As if anyone was ever going to stand up and screw up a wedding ceremony right in the middle of it like this! That kind of stuff only happened in the movies. But, even so, it always made Patsy wonder. The next few seconds were excruciating at other people's weddings. Now, at her own, it was unbearable.

Patsy looked at her mother, hoping she would end the pause soon, but Rose seemed to be distracted. She was shaking her head almost imperceptibly at Kim. Patsy darted a look at her maid of honour, who seemed to be having a conversation with their mother only by means of anxious facial expressions.

However, the moment Kim noticed Patsy looking at her, her face relaxed and she smiled. Patsy instinctively smiled back and was relieved to hear her mother carrying on:

'I require and charge you both,' she said to Ben and Patsy, 'here in the presence of God and these people, that if either of you know any reason why you may not be united in marriage, you do now confess it.'

Patsy looked confidently at Ben, a little smugly even. Unlike the previous call to the congregation, she was sure that she and Ben would not hold up proceedings here – although, as she looked into Ben's eyes, which had been so shiny with excitement and love all morning, she saw a cloud scud across them; the shine disappeared for just a moment, so brief a moment that she hardly registered it. And then Ben was back, his eyes moist with emotion, but for the rest of the ceremony whenever she looked at him Patsy thought she was looking at Ben through a window, or through glasses that were in need of a clean, as if there was something standing between them, something transparent, but in the way, nonetheless.

Despite the oddities – which to Patsy were par for the course with all her family gathered in one place – the rest of the ceremony went without a hitch and then finally Patsy and Ben could kick back and enjoy the reception.

It would have been at the community centre on Factory Way if Ben had, had his way. But Rose insisted it was held in a more glamourous venue; a beautiful 5-star hotel suite with rambling grounds, a helipad, swimming pool for guests who were staying over. There were acres of surrounding shrubs and woodland. In true Rose designer fashion, the wedding was kitted out like something from Vogue magazine, with a peach and gold colour scheme, with gold plated table candelabras with an array of exotic flower centrepieces including bird of paradise and white cymbidium orchids. Patsy was not complaining, after all she had her mother's taste for luxury, something that Ben had had, to learn to accept. They had compromised with Rose in terms of location - it was not as far out as she would have liked. It was nearer to their home - not a particular part of town that Rose held dear, but near the high street so that they stagger home, as they had to be at the airport in the morning. They had stressed out about this wedding for weeks, and now they told themselves that they deserved to get messier than anyone else. Although Ben's brother Dave seemed determined to compete with them, drinking faster than he could even choose his next drink.

'Want another?' he slurred at the radiant newlyweds.

'No, you're all right, bruv,' Ben said shrewdly. 'I'll get them in.' He got up intending to get his brother a very weak single whiskey instead of the doubles he'd been knocking back all evening.

'Nah, nah, nah!' Dave said pushing Ben back down a bit too aggressively for Patsy's liking. 'My treat. You're going to need it.'

'What do you mean?' Ben said, his face showing he hoped it was some dirty joke about stamina on his wedding night.

But it wasn't. 'This lot'll have you doing the limbo to Calypso sipping on some overproof rum or something in a minute,' Dave said without even trying to sound like he was joking as he staggered off to the bar.

Ben put a hand on his wife's knee apologetically. 'Sorry, my beautiful.'

Patsy smiled at Ben. She knew Dave well enough by now to know that he was more than casually racist. In fact, he was not just inherently prejudice and racist he had a dark sinister side that nonchalantly presented itself after three beers, she had witnessed it countless times and had come to the point of naming his alter ego '*Davido*' who she saw as Dave's evil twin that lived inside him. When Davido appeared, Dave would instantly start shouting at the top of his voice until his face was red with a demonic rage, for no reason at all. The slightest thing could set him off and whoever was in the room at the time, found it hard to believe that this was the same human being who had been calm only moments before. Patsy had witnessed him smash his mum's crystal glass, and he screamed at his uncle and nearly got into a physical fight with this female cousin he was about to hit her when Patsy had jumped in and parted them like the red sea. Davido was an unbearable, despicable alter ego that needed to be exorcised just like the spirits in her flat, Patsy thought. He had verbally attacked Patsy on several occasions and once even lunged at her screaming in her face, calling her a failure for not being a successful popstar. He berated her and screamed 'you are nothing without Ben you half-breed! YOU ARE A FAILURE! You should have bought a house by now and had kids – you're nearly 30. What a waste of space you are. All that money your parents have and look where you choose to live. You are pathetic! You have nothing. Everyone pounces around you because you're beautiful – well you're not even all that. You ugly cow! Mulatto cow!' he giggled throwing back another beer.

Davido was the worst kind of bully. Patsy knew that bullying normally comes from a place of jealousy and his own lack of confidence projected onto the victim – she had witnessed pupils being bullied at school. The truth was Davido did not know anything about what Patsy had achieved in life, and she could not be bothered to educate him on her array of achievements. It was pointless justifying herself to him. She brushed it off and quite often did not share it with Ben or anyone. On her wedding day she told herself, she was marrying Ben, not his family – *thank the Lord!* – and she wasn't going to let Dave, Davido or anyone else ruin their big day. She went off to find some of her own family members, ones that were happy for them, before Dave got back.

'All right, sis?' Vernon beamed as she approached him and Kim, who was knocking back the G&Ts quicker than usual. 'Great party, ey!'

Patsy accepted a kiss from her little brother. 'Where did Nina go?' she asked, looking around the reception room.

Vernon grimaced. 'She…' He was about to lie, but Patsy saw it in his eye, and he knew it, so he told her quietly, 'She went home after the church. She didn't want to come this close to your flat, you know, after…'

Patsy stopped Vernon. She didn't want to get into it in front of Kim and risk more arguments. 'Well, there's plenty of girls here who want to dance with you instead,' she grinned mischievously. Kim and Patsy secretly thought that Vernon could do better. They suspected Nina of being one of those girls who could not share their man with his family, it was the intensity of her love and possession that scared them, they both adored their little brother and would be devastated if he turned *weird* on them and only wanted to see Nina and her side of the family, and then if they had kids they might never get to see their nieces and nephews, the quicker he finished with her the better, they contemplated.

'Yeah, bro,' Kim joined in. 'What about Flo. She can't take her eyes off you. Look!'

They all turned to see their friend Flo trying not to look from the other side of the room.

'But she is ten years older than me!' he winced.

'You're dancing, you dickhead, not having a baby,' Kim said, slapping his arm. 'Why does everything have to be about sex with men!'

Vernon sized up their friend for a moment more, then bounced across the room towards her.

'Talking of babies,' Kim said, turning to her little sister. 'Is there one in your oven yet?' She prodded Patsy's stomach, which was flatter than ever given that she'd nearly starved herself for the past month to make sure she looked great in her wedding dress.

'No!' Patsy moaned. 'Why do you lot all think I'm pregnant. We just wanted to get married, that's all.'

'Just like her mother. I told her nothing good would come of marrying a white boy.' Their grandmother was sitting at a table near them with her back to the sisters, so she was oblivious as they tuned into her gibbering away at another elderly relative.

'You told Patsy?' her contemporary croaked.

'No,' Gran kissed her teeth – what was left of them anyway. 'I told Rose. When she came round with that Italian mafia boy. Don't go marrying outside your own kind. Nothing good will come of it. But she ignored me. Thought she knew better.'

'I've heard enough of this bigotry…' Kim was about to steam over and shut her Gran up, but Patsy stopped her and carried on listening.

'Then she spent her whole life being shunned by racialists.' Gran shook her head. 'Stick to your own kind, I told her. This world is hard enough as it is. Why make trouble for yourself?'

'Mum,' Patsy whispered. 'It makes sense now. Her being so lukewarm with Ben. Obviously after Dad, she would never want me not to be with Ben, but she's scared I'll go through the same crap she had to suffer.'

Kim stared off into the middle distance and nodded. 'That's why he manifests as a black man,' she muttered.

'Who?' Patsy frowned. 'Manifests? Kim, what are you talking about?'

Kim snapped out of her trance. 'Oh, nothing. I mean…' She took another huge gulp of her gin.

'Kim?'

'Yeah?'

'Were you OK in the ceremony today?'

'Yeah, why?'

'You were looking at something. I felt like you were looking at something between Ben and I… you looked distracted.'

Patsy studied Kim closely and was sure she saw her eyes flash with the memory of something from that moment in the ceremony.

'What do you mean?' she stuttered.

'I don't know. I'm not sure. You tell me,' Pasty said goading her sister.

Kim puffed as if she didn't have a clue what Patsy was talking about and said, 'I need another one of these.'

She shot off across to the bar and Patsy was about to follow, but she was stopped by a tugging on her sleeve and Loz's voice behind her:

'Congratulations.'

'Loz! You came!'

Patsy threw her arms around her and felt Loz reciprocate weakly. She smelt of booze yet again, but then so did everyone in this room tonight. Patsy stood back and smiled at her neighbour, who'd made some effort. She was wearing a floral-patterned dress and heels. She'd put on some make-up and put her hair up. And yet all Patsy could see beneath the façade was pain. 'Let's get a drink!' she said and dragged Loz to the bar.

'I'm so glad you came. Where's Mindy?'

Loz's face clouded over. 'That's kind of what I wanted to talk to you about,' she said as they downed their glasses of fizz. 'I know it's your wedding day and that, but I've been horrible to you recently and I need to explain, but…'

Patsy put her hand on Loz's arm. 'It's OK. Take your time.'

And then Loz started to unload. 'I didn't know what to do. I didn't do anything wrong. Not really. I just knew if I called the police or the ambulance, then they'd say it was me. And it wasn't. It really wasn't, I promise you, Pats.'

'OK, OK, I know,' Patsy said, not really having a clue what Loz was talking about.

'But I didn't know what to do with her, so… you're going to think I'm a total freak…'

'No, no,' Patsy said, sensing Loz was on the edge of revealing something huge.

'I…' Loz began, but was stopped by the sound of a glass smashing and a shout from the other side of the room:

'You're a racist bastard!' It was Ben.

He was grabbing Dave by the collar and dragging him out of the room.

'Ben!' Patsy called out and hurried after him.

'Carry on, everyone!' Ben called out over his shoulder. 'Don't mind us!'

Patsy caught up with her husband as he threw Dave into the street. 'Ben!'

'Sorry, baby,' Ben said brushing his hands off. 'But I will not let him bad mouth you or your family anymore. Your family is my family now, and they have been nothing but good to me.'

Dave had landed in a heap in the road and was scrambling around on the frosty tarmac trying to get up.

'Benjamin!'

Patsy turned to see Ben's mother standing in the doorway, every bit the female version of Greg Yale, even down to the facial hair – almost. She was such a boulder of a woman that she blocked anyone else from coming to gawp at the drama.

'Stop it, you two!' she boomed. 'His suit will look all messed up in the photos.'

'Umm really? That's what you're worried about, mum?' Ben said, exasperated. 'Go inside now! Or you can go home with him.'

Ben's mum considered this for a moment, then lumbered inside, as Ben dug Dave's phone from his pocket and ordered a taxi for him.

'Your Uber's on its way,' he said chucking Dave's phone at him where he sat in the gutter. 'Come on, Pat,' he said softly leading Patsy inside.

'I didn't do anything wrong,' Dave called out after them. 'They're just brainwashing you, like they are the entire country.

Black lives matter! What about us, ey? What about the people that actually come from here, don't *all* lives matter?'

Ben stepped back, turned around angrily, 'Oh just typical of you Dave, ignorant! When they say *Black lives matter* – they're not implying that other lives don't matter. They know that all lives matter, you idiot! It is a social and political movement, highlighting discrimination, and racial inequality experienced by black people, they promote anti-racism. It started following the killings in the USA of Trayvon Martin, and others. Oh, my words are wasted on you. Just go home!' and he walked back into the reception to join his wife.

Dave finally got to his feet and shoved his phone into his pocket.

'Bastards,' he hissed and shook the wet mud from his hands. He looked down at his pale blue suit. It was scuffed with muddy streaks and ripped over one knee. 'Crappy suit anyway. Looked like a poof in it.'

'I come from this country,' someone said softly in his ear.

He swung around to see who was there.

No one. The street was empty. Dead. Even the sound of the party inside the hotel seemed far away now to Dave's booze-addled brain.

'This is my home,' the voice said.

Dave spun around again. 'Who the hell said that?'

'And it has been long before you were ever spewed into this world.'

'Who the…?' Dave spat.

'Me, that is who,' the voice said.

Dave turned again. He was getting dizzy. Dizzier than he already was. But this time he saw the voice came from a tall man in a heavy overcoat and a wide-brimmed hat. A black man with a pencil moustache over his top lip and eyes that shone like the frost in the streetlights. He was standing inches away and just as Dave was about to shout some expletives in his face the man's hand shot forward and his long fingernails pierced Dave's abdomen as if they were five sharp knives.

Dave's eyes bulged with untold pain as the man's claw latched onto his ribcage and dragged him by it off the street until Dave's legs gave out and he collapsed. But the man didn't let go. He just carried Dave, still holding him by the ribs, like a heavy bag, up the bank to the train tracks which ran behind Factory Way.

'It hurts when you burn,' he said as Dave gurgled and squealed in horror at his own entrails spilling out of his upturned body and flopping over his face. 'They burned me for being a warlock. I wasn't. I just knew things they didn't. It's fear you see, fear that makes people persecute others. You feared them, didn't you? You feared people who look like me – I mean, people who look like I do now,' he smirked. 'I didn't always look like this of course.' He scoffed. 'Well, now you can fear no longer.'

The fast train to Cambridge screamed past them and off into the night.

And shortly after it had passed the man tossed Dave as if he was no heavier than a handbag up onto the overhead cables.

The crackling and popping and sizzling was so loud that birds fled from the nearby trees where they'd been sleeping. The flash lit up the darkness momentarily like a meteor, after which Dave's mutilated body was left blackened and hanging like a charred piece of meat.

'You will not ruin my wedding day, nor speak ill of my wife,' the man said.

He turned from the scene and saw the Uber arrive. The driver wound down his window as the man in the overcoat moved towards his car.

'Dave?' he asked.

'No. Dave had to cancel. Sorry.'

'Well, Dave should've told me, I'll still charge the journey to his card, the idiot!' said the driver and sped off.

The man watched the car go then turned to look at the little girl sitting on the wall by the riverbank watching him. He smiled at her. She didn't smile back. She was distracted by Lauren hurrying from the hotel, rubbing at the mascara running down her face.

Loz headed for home at the end of Factory Way. She was so upset she barely noticed the smell of cooking flesh in the air. She was just glad the drama with Ben and his brother had happened when it did and stopped her from blabbing any further to Patsy. She didn't know what had come over her. She couldn't tell a soul about what had happened, especially not some neighbour she barely knew.

She fled back to the safety of her neglected flat.

'Going to keep your mummy company?' the man said to the little girl.

Mindy stared blankly at the man for a moment, then slid down from the wall and followed her mother down the road.

The man watched her go and as she neared the flats his attention was caught by someone looking out at him from the top floor. It wasn't Patsy's flat of course – no one was in tonight. It was her neighbour. He was holding back a dirty net curtain so he could see down into the street, his wizened face framed with matted grey hair illuminated by the streetlights. He was wearing the same thing he wore every day – a moth eaten purple suit jacket over frayed red trousers. He'd taken his yellow hat off, as he always did when he was home.

He locked eyes with the man in the street, who seemed momentarily knocked off kilter by his onlooker. For more than a minute they stared at each other, and it would have been clear to anyone passing by that they knew each other; that they'd known each other for a long time; for ages, literally.

Finally, with a snarl, the man in the street tore his eyes away from the window, turned and went back to the hotel. Back to his wedding reception.

They had booked a luxury Airbnb in the *le septième* 7th Arrondissment of Paris, with majestic panoramic views of the Eiffel tower and the river Seine. The Eiffel tower was a stone's throw away. Well, it kind of overlooked the Eiffel tower. In the photos on the website the views were perfect, but when they arrived, they realised you had to lean over the balcony precariously to see the tower in full and getting a selfie with the tower in the background was taking your life in your hands. Luckily the balcony was made of strong stuff. The flat was part of a centuries old building made of smooth ivory coloured stone, which Patsy found out was in fact, limestone after a bit of googling, she couldn't help herself she always needed to know details. The rooms had high ceilings with ornate stucco embellishments, a grand four poster bed in the bedroom and a well-equipped rustic looking kitchen, which they had no intention of using as they wanted to try as many restaurants as possible during the few full days they had here. They had already lost some time when Ben was detained at the airport. He had put his hand luggage through the machine at security and been pulled aside by the guards.

'What's going on?' Patsy said when she caught up with him.

'Stand aside, madam!' said one of the security guards, a skinny runt who didn't look like he could secure anything.

'He's my husband,' Patsy said. 'I'm not going anywhere.' She felt a rush of pride at being able to describe Ben as her husband; it was the first time she had used that phrase since the wedding yesterday.

But the words seemed to ignite an unexpected fire in the security guard's eyes, and he demanded, 'déplace-toi sur le côté!' Patsy was so shocked at the combustible energy coming from him she did as she was told.

The guard, who also seemed momentarily shocked at his authoritative tone, searched the bag, and pulled out a bottle of hydrogen peroxide.

'What's this?' he said like a school ma'am.

Ben grumbled, 'What it says on the label. Mouthwash.'

'Really?' the guard raised an eyebrow.

'Can you read?' Ben sniped.

'Yes, I can read, but it's also highly explosive,' the guard informed Ben. 'So, we'll be confiscating that. And you'll be coming with us.'

They kept Ben in a room until he'd convinced them that he really did use hydrogen peroxide as a mouthwash. He was obsessed with getting white teeth because his always looked so yellow next to Patsy's in photos, her teeth were sparkling white in comparison. But when he was free, they had missed their flight and had to get the next one, which, thankfully, since it was only a single to Paris, didn't cost the earth.

'I thought you were going to leave that at home,' Patsy hissed as they waited for their new tickets. 'You knew it wasn't allowed in the hand-luggage; you know we are not allowed more than 100ml containers.'

'I know,' Ben said with a baffled look on his face. 'That's why I *did* leave it at home. I swear. I have no idea how that got in there.'

Patsy was so peeved that their honeymoon was being jeopardised, she didn't even consider that Ben might be telling the truth.

The beauty of the apartment in Paris obliterated any negativity from Patsy's mind and, after freshening up, they hurried out to the tower while the sun was still shining. They snapped themselves under the 'crotch' of the tower, as Ben called it, and then began the ascent to the top.

'You know, I don't really like heights,' Ben said as they waited on the second floor for the lift to the summit, 'and that lift looks tiny.'

'Don't worry sweetheart, we can't reach the summit by stairs. I'll look after you.' Patsy grinned as the lift arrived and tourists poured out.

They shuffled in and the attendant inside asked them to move further in.

'We can't,' Patsy said feeling the pressure of people all around her. Ben didn't like heights, but in fact, Patsy detested lifts but put that aside the best she could; 'It's full.'

'No, it's not,' the attendant said brusquely. 'There's a space right next to you.'

Patsy turned to where she felt Ben pressed against her but saw that there was a space between herself and him. He beckoned her closer and she thought no more about it as he grabbed hold of her for security. The lift was indeed tiny and there was nothing but a few inches of puddle iron around it all the way up to make Ben feel any safer. So, Patsy cuddled him back and could feel his hands holding her tighter than ever. She hated the idea of him feeling scared, but she loved the idea of being needed by him. She saw the lift attendant glaring at them, no doubt because she challenged him in his little empire, and instead decided to focus on the city getting smaller and smaller as they rose through the neck of the tower, as the lift elevator shot up powered by high pressured hydraulic motor.

Despite a cage of thick wire enclosing the narrow observation deck at the summit, Ben kept his back to the wall while Patsy drank in the spectacular views of Paris, golden in the low sunshine, yet a gentle frost wind made her take a quick breath.

'They're serving champagne,' Patsy said, seeing the champagne bar.

'*How* much?' Ben said frugally when he saw the price for two glasses.

'But it's our honeymoon!' Patsy sighed.

'Course, babes,' he smiled, 'I'm only joking. Get it. I need it.'

They clinked glasses – well, tapped them; they were plastic – and took a sunset selfie near the edge. Then immediately after, Ben scrambled back to the safety of the wall. He smiled at Patsy as she enjoyed the views a little more, then they made their way back to the lift.

'Wow, how many people is it safe to have up here at one time,' Ben muttered as a flood of people arrived on the deck.

In their big winter coats and scarves and hats, the people seemed to take up much more room and Ben was anxious to get into the lift, which was fast filling up. As soon as Patsy got in, the doors closed before Ben could enter. She looked around for an attendant, but this lift seemed not to be staffed, which she found strange. She momentarily panicked on Ben's behalf but told herself to wait on the second floor. He would be down in the next lift.

While she waited, she wandered back out onto the deck to watch the city come alive with lights in the growing darkness. She recalled the excitement of her wedding yesterday and she felt giddy with happiness, it was the fairytale she'd always dreamt it would be. Then she got a lump in her throat, when she had a flash back of the moment when Ben angrily threw Dave out of the reception, how embarrassing? But then, she thought with a smirk, it wouldn't be a wedding without some kind of family drama, would it? She was just surprised the drama hadn't emanated from her family. In fact, when Patsy's parents had said their goodbyes last night, Rose looked tearful and pensive.

'Take care. Send me a text. Go safely,' she'd said.

'It's only Paris, Mum. It's not the other side of the world.'

'I'm not talking about Paris.'

'Then what are you talking about?' Patsy insisted.

'Your uninvited guest.'

Patsy felt her face flush.

'I think a holiday is just what you need,' Rose had whispered out of Luca's earshot. 'Hopefully everything will be settled by the time you return.'

Patsy was surrounded by well-wishers by then, it wasn't the time to continue this sinister conversation, so she just nodded and kissed her mum before she and Ben went home.

As she continued to drink in the sight of Paris by night, she felt a tourist standing uncomfortably close to her. He was tall in a large overcoat with a wide-brimmed hat. He looked down at her and smiled warmly. Above his smile she was surprised to see a pencil moustache – it looked very old fashioned, as did his clothes. As she took in his garb, she felt her heart quicken, but she wasn't sure why – it was as if she didn't know if she was afraid or feeling aroused.

But then she noticed a smell and thought for a moment that the man was smoking. But he wasn't. He smelt of smoke, strangely of charred meat, made her think of Brazilian Picanha steak with Chimichurri. If she ever had been, she was definitely not turned on anymore. She kept her eyes on the view hoping he would move on, but he didn't.

'Divine, is it not?'

'Mmm,' she said trying not to engage without being rude.

'As are you, my love,' he sighed and slipped his arm through hers.

Patsy stood, frozen.

Ben was swept away from the lift in a tsunami of tourists, which seemed to come from nowhere, like some kind of perverted flash mob with the goal of keeping him from getting down from the summit. He found himself back out on the deck and the flood of people kept coming, nudging him further away from his comfort zone until he found himself near the edge, pressed up against the cage and he suddenly felt like he was at a football match on the terraces when a crowd surge occurred. Except now there wasn't a grassy pitch before him, but a thousand-foot drop. He felt himself being squeezed against the thick wire; he felt it start to imprint itself on his body.

'Stop!' he called out. 'Stop pushing!'

No one seemed to notice him. No one else was shouting. No one seemed worried at all by the situation. They were like a herd off zombies. He felt the wire start to buckle, felt it jerk outwards as a few of the rivets popped out of the holes they'd securely fitted for so many years. He pushed against the tide of people with all his considerable strength, but he couldn't make them move, he roared in one last ditch effort, but his own bear-like body made the wire give way quicker than that of some puny bloke might. And his stomach turned as he sensed himself falling. He grabbed at the wire with palms so soaked with sweat he couldn't get a grip. He cried out as his limbs flailed around trying to find something solid.

She disengaged from the man and felt long nails scrape her wrist as she did so.

'Do you mind?' she said in a bizarrely British way, trying not to make scene, while fearing she was about to be sexually assaulted.

The man did not respond but kept staring out over Parisian skyline. She hurried back to the lift, which she hoped Ben would be coming out of any second.

The lift doors opened bringing the next lot of tourists down.

Ben was not among them.

'Are you OK, sir?'

Ben saw it was the bolshie French attendant who had asked them to cram into the lift on the way up here. He looked around and saw he was on his knees, gripping the wire and there were hardly any tourists about, just a few onlookers wondering what the English bloke was crying about.

'I think you had a panic attack,' the attendant said, leading a trembling Ben inside. 'I noticed you in the lift on the way up. You do not like high things, I think.'

'No,' Ben panted. 'No, I really don't. But there was a crush. I mean, loads of people. Too many on the deck. And it…' he looked out to the fence, but it was intact. 'I thought it gave way.'

'Do not worry, sir. It is very safe. But let's get you down to the ground level?'

Ben nodded enthusiastically, yet trying to regain his idea of masculinity as the attendant led him to the front of the crowd waiting for the lift, while other tourists grumbled, wondering why he should get to jump the queue, '*Personne malpolie*' muttered an old lady rolling her eyes at Ben.

'Oh babes,' Patsy said, trying her best to keep a straight face. 'I didn't know you were that scared.'

'I'm not,' he sulked. 'I mean, I don't like heights, I told you that, but this was weird. This was like... I could've sworn there were people pushing me out over the edge and it gave way. I saw it.'

Patsy rubbed his arm as they took their seats. 'A panic attack, the man said?'

'I suppose. But I've never had one before.'

'But you've never been up to the top of the Eiffel tower before either.'

'True,' he said, almost smiling.

Patsy took in the ambience of the theatre. The red velvet seats they sat on, the red velvet curtains which adorned the stage, it was every bit the Moulin Rouge she'd loved in the Baz Luhrmann movie. The show was not quite as engaging as the movie, the tables cramped quite closely together, and full of tourists, not locals; however – she liked the memorable spirited energy of the renowned French Cancan, the feathers and rhinestones epitomised this famous Parisen show– it was all part of the Paris experience, yet some would say, a little tacky. They made the most of the champagne that was included with the astronomical ticket price. But when Patsy became aware of a man sitting closely at the table cramped next to them on the left - who looked remarkably like the man who'd linked arms with her on the Eiffel Tower, she unexpectedly encouraged Ben to leave early, which he found unusual.

'What's the rush?' Ben asked inquisitively, having trouble keeping his eyes off the dancers on stage as they stood up.

'Nothing,' Patsy said as cooly as she could. 'I think we've seen enough.'

They found a bar nearby and continued drinking, laughing at the tackiness of the show and gazing at each other across the table between interludes of looking at the Parisienne buzz around them.

'Thanks for making this happen,' she beamed at him.

'Team effort,' he smiled. 'Paris baby!' He clinked his glass on hers. 'To us!'

'To us!' she echoed, but her face fell as someone in a large overcoat and wide-brimmed hat walked into the bar. However, as soon as she saw it was a white man, she regained her composure.

'You OK, babe?' Ben asked, noticing her wobble.

'Yeah,' she said shrugging it off.

'Did something freak you out in the show, when we left early, I mean?'

Patsy thought about saying no, but she'd had too much wine by now and the truth was flowing. 'Well, I don't know. When I was waiting for you in the Eiffel Tower, this man came up and tried to put his arm around me.'

'Really?' Ben snarled, instantly protective.

'Yeah. I didn't let him, of course, but then I thought he was sitting next to us in the Moulin Rouge. That's why I wanted to leave.'

'And was he?'

'What?'

'Sitting next to you.'

'I don't think so. It was just a weird feeling.'

'Sure?' Ben probed. 'You can tell me anything you know.'

'I'm sure,' she smiled.

She saw Ben begin to brood on this, so she deftly changed the subject and ordered more wine.

When they got back to the flat, they went out on the balcony to look at the tower in all its luminous glory.

'It's so romantic,' she smiled between kissing Ben.

'If I wasn't worried about having another panic attack, I'd be on the other side of that balcony now saying, 'Juliet! Juliet! Wherefore art thou?'

'It's *Romeo, Romeo, wherefore art thou*, silly!' Patsy laughed.

Patsy slapped him playfully and they kissed again and again. But Ben's words had triggered a memory, and she just couldn't shake it from her boozy brain.

They had sex in every room in the apartment and on just about every surface – the kitchen came in handy for something after all – but as they lay in bed after, the memory persisted.

It was that summer evening when she was looking out of her second-floor bedroom window over the gardens of Cricklewood and she heard, 'Oh, Juliet! Juliet!'

She looked down to see Zack in the alleyway between the gardens.

'This is where you sigh and go *Romeo, Romeo, wherefore art thou, Romeo?*' he called up at her with a grin. 'Here I am, Juliet!'

She didn't know what to do or say, so she laughed awkwardly and pretended her phone was ringing, gesturing at it, and ducking inside to take the phantom call.

Now, as she lay with her head on Ben's broad chest listening to the relaxed rhythm of his heart, she felt an overwhelming desire to tell Ben about Zack. She knew the booze in her veins was making her bolder, but there was also a voice in her ear, a familiar voice, encouraging her:

'Tell him! Tell him! It's time to be honest.'

So, she took a deep breath and without looking up she said, 'Babes?'

He grunted, 'Mmm?' as he dozed.

'I'm so happy to be your wife and I think we have the best relationship, better than so many people I know. And I love the way we're always honest with each other. And I want it to stay that way forever, OK?'

'Yeah, course,' he muttered

'That's why I've never lied to you about anything… except on one occasion.'

She felt his breathing stop for a moment.

She waited.

'Oh yeah? When was that?' His voice was more alert now.

'Just when JJ came round to see Tia and she said that I told her some woman had wanted our flat and that's why all that weird stuff happened with Nelson and that.'

'Oh yeah.'

'And JJ talked about someone called Zack and I said it was some homeless bloke who was hanging round the flat.'

'Yeah.'

'Well, he wasn't.'

'What?'

'Some homeless bloke and he wasn't hanging around the flat. Zack used to live opposite me in Cricklewood and I moved out because he became infatuated with me. He started stalking me basically.'

'Infatuated?' Ben asked shifting in the bed, so Patsy had to move her head and look at him now. 'Why would he become infatuated with you?'

Patsy saw Ben putting two and two together and getting five. 'See, this is why I didn't tell you!'

'Were we together at the time?' Ben growled.

'Yeah, near the end of it, yeah. Not at the beginning.'

'So, you were with him when you were with me?' He sat up pulling himself away from Patsy.

'No! He *wanted* to be with me,' Patsy insisted, sitting up too and putting her hands on Ben's legs as if she could stop him moving away.

Ben looked disgusted. 'But why did you let him think he could be with you?'

'I did not!'

'But he was the one who was harassing us in the flat?' Ben's eyes flicked from side to side as if he was reading a book of the past, as he tried to make sense of everything.

'I thought so at first, but then I realised it was something else… Something more spiritual, more sinister.'

Ben wasn't listening anymore. 'And you never thought to tell me every night when I was taking a baseball bat to bed?'

'It wasn't him.'

'I can't believe I've been so stupid!' Ben said quickly trying to piece together all the events. 'It all makes sense now. The phone calls, the scratches on your back. I knew it. I knew something was going on.'

'What phone calls?'

'You can't deny it, Pats. I came home one day when I forgot my keys and I heard you on the phone,' he said stabbing a finger at her, 'talking about me and organising some kind of hook up. Is that why Vernon left too? Coz, he found out?'

Patsy couldn't believe what she was hearing. 'No, no, no, no. I don't know what calls you're talking about.'

'Tell the truth!' Ben demanded. 'You just said you wanted us to be honest with each other. Now's your chance.'

Patsy was racking her brain. 'What did you hear on the phone?'

'I'll never forget it,' Ben said getting up and pacing about the room, getting flustered. 'You said, *I live with my fiancé*. And you said you were getting bored of it, of me, and then you said, *so let's do it*.'

The words were all skewed and out of context but now she realised which call he was talking about. 'Oh, sweetheart, that was Goldie.'

'Oh, I see, like the drum'n'bass DJ… ermmm… another one you got on the go, eh?'

'No, a clairvoyant. I called her up to come and cleanse the flat of the negative entities.'

'Of the what?'

'Like when I asked mum round. You see, Zack wasn't doing anything to us. It was these ghosts. The flat was… haunted.'

'Come on Patsy! Do you really expect me to believe this crap?' he said to the ceiling.

Ben was the complete opposite to spiritual, or religious. He didn't really believe in anything that wasn't in front of him. He never had any existential questions about life, never thought about God or angels or any other spiritual forms of life.

He was the quintessential builder who loved drinking beer and watching football with his mates, he was from a small town in Eastbourne who grew up by the sea in a little family run Bed and Breakfast, who had a hardworking dad and a perfidious mum that was friendly on the outside but deep down would have preferred him to marry a blue eyed blonde, and definitely didn't want brown curly haired grandkids, which she alluded to in passing to Patsy. He was a Simple man, with a simple outlook on life.

'Ask Vernon! That's why he left. Coz, he came back and saw what the poltergeist did when Goldie came to cleanse the flat.'

'Oh, this is ridiculous! I've heard some excuses in my time…'

'It was not Zack. I never did anything with Zack.'

Ben looked like he wanted to vomit. 'Stop using his name. It makes me want to puke.'

'Why?'

'Because you were sleeping with him behind my back. And you have been all this time because you're bored of me.'

'I wasn't bored of you; I was tired of being just your fiancée. I wanted to be your wife. And this is our honeymoon, babe, so what are we fighting for?' Slamming her hands on the duvet in frustration.

'I'm not fighting,' Ben said, yanking on his pants and trousers. 'I don't need to.' He started shoving things into his bag.

'What are you doing?' Patsy said, but she knew exactly what he was doing, and she burst into tears.

'I'm out of here. Enjoy your honeymoon! You can invite Zack if you want.' Then another irrational thought struck him. 'Or is he already here? Was that him on the Eiffel Tower. Is that what you were trying to tell me? 'Oh, how could I be so naive!'

He went to the bathroom and grabbed his washbag. Patsy got up and followed. 'Dave was right. I should never've got involved with you lot!'

'What?' Patsy was stunned.

'What are you saying? This isn't you, Ben. Listen to yourself, you sound like your racist brother!' she cried.

He spun round violently brandishing his toothbrush like a knife, 'So how did you get those scratches eh? Coz it wasn't me, was it?'

She stammered for a moment as she tried to find the words. 'Look, I think there's still an entity hanging around and I think he's trying to come between us.'

'Entity? oh stop with this entity – mumbo jumbo!'

He spat the words pushing past her. 'His name's Zack, mate. And if I bump into him, I'll be punching his lights out. Bloody, entity!'

Ben yanked open the apartment door and hurried down the stairs.

'Where are you going?' Patsy cried out and her voice echoed loudly around the old stone stairwell compelling her to quieten down. ‘Don’t go now!’ she hissed. ‘Not like this. It’s too late anyway. Where will you go?’

Ben’s only answer was the door to the street clanging like a guillotine behind him.

She lay on the four poster bed, which now felt just absurdly big, not grand. She looked out of the window at Paris, which now seemed foreign and unfriendly, no longer something from a fairy tale. She looked at her phone with eyes wide with worry, longing for sleep that would never come. She messaged Ben again and again. None of the messages were received on his WhatsApp. He must have turned his phone off. She opened Instagram instinctively – but she had no desire to look at her feed and everyone living their best lives. When she thought how she had intended to saturate her grid with posts from Paris she burst into tears again. She was desperate to call someone – JJ, Kim, her mum even – she needed a shoulder to cry on, but she couldn't bring herself to do so. She was so embarrassed. Left all alone in the most romantic city in the world on the first night of your honeymoon – could it get any sadder?

'Well done, my love. You did what you had to do.'

Her eyes snapped open. She thought the voice came from behind her. She looked over her shoulder to see the bed empty where Ben should have been, and her guts lurched. She grabbed at her phone. 6:55AM. It was still dark outside. Her mind raced. Where was Ben? Had he gone back to England? Should she go back too? Or should she wait here in case he comes back? She sent him a message asking him to contact her just so she knew he was safe and flopped back onto the bed exhausted from the distress.

She must have dozed off. She only realised she had when she felt an arm around her waist. She put her own hand on Ben's, pulling it closer, as she always did. But this hand was thin and bony, not thick, and strong like Ben's.

She threw back the covers and jumped up. The bed looked empty, but she knew it wasn't. Keeping her eyes focused on it, she threw on some mish mashed clothes ordering an Uber she hurried from the flat, leaving her luggage behind. Even as the car took her north on Pont d'Iéna through Paris, onto Place. de Varsovie she looked at the seat next to her. She knew she wasn't alone. She sneered at the space in the back seat then caught the driver's eyes in the rearview mirror wondering what she was sneering at.

The driver dropped her on Rue du Chevalier de la Barre by Sacré Coeur. She jumped out and hurried towards the Basilica. This had been on her bucket list of things to see on the honeymoon. But now she didn't take time to admire the beauty of this prominent opulent white exterior of what they call the Taj Mahal of the West; she didn't sit on the steps looking out from the summit of Montmartre over the entire city glistening in the frosty sunshine; she didn't eat a croissant and take a selfie – all the things she had planned to do and post about with Ben. She headed straight inside, not to admire the great yawning arches, nor the ethereal colours of the stained-glass windows, nor the intricate mosaics. She simply went inside to feel safe from whatever evil had followed her from her home and tried to destroy her marriage; she was seeking protection.

She sat on a pew as close to the altar as she could get without intruding on the service going on. It was still early, so apart from the few devoted locals participating in the mass there were not many tourists. She breathed deeply imbibing the words of the priest, even though she didn't understand them. She soaked up the sense of peace and the sense of awe in the heavenly, which the church instilled in every visitor, and she prayed.

'Beautiful piece of architecture, is it not?'

Her prayers were interrupted by the whisper in her ear.

'Neo-Byzantine Romanesque. Forty years in the making.'

She daren't look to see where the voice came from. Her skin tightened; her mouth dried instantly. She kept her eyes fixed firmly on the priest. She knew who she would see if she turned to her right.

'I came for the formal consecration. It was just after the First World War. If I was such a warlock, why would I be such a lover of churches?' he chuckled. 'I must say, this is a superlative basilica, but our little church where we got married, my love, will always be the most special to me.'

Now she turned. The absurdity of his words compelled her to. He held his wide-brimmed hat in his bony hands now. And she noticed his hair was cut tightly and neatly. His eyes sparkled in the light from the rose window and Patsy was horrified that she found him so handsome.

'What are you talking about? Our church?' she whispered, her voice trembling.

'Your mother did us proud. And as for your sister… well, all I can say is that beauty runs in the family.'

Patsy's stomach turned as she recalled the wedding ceremony; the moment when Rose seemed to be distracted; when she shook her head almost imperceptibly at Kim; and how Patsy darted a look at her maid of honour, who seemed to be having a conversation with their mother only by means of anxious facial expressions. And suddenly Patsy knew that not only had her mother seen this man standing next to her, between Patsy and Ben, but somehow her sister had seen him too.

Patsy ran from the church, as fast as she could. The morning light was blinding after the gloom of the church. She squinted as she looked about, searching for an escape. She decided to head towards the centre of Montmartre, to the square, where she knew she would find hundreds of artists, all vying for the opportunity to make a buck by painting portraits of tourists. She thought it would be the busiest place nearby and she felt the need to be around people, as many people as possible. As she entered the square, she realised it was still too early to be busy with tourists. She glanced behind her to see if he was following her. She couldn't see him, but she knew that didn't mean much. She weaved through the stalls ignoring offers from artists and eventually found a bar that looked different from the typical tourist traps. It wasn't all gingham table clothes and brightly painted window frames. It was cracked plaster and an aging sign you could barely read. But importantly it was busy at this early hour. It was furnished with spartan wooden furniture inside, like a scene from a Toulouse Lautrec painting. Clearly the clientele comprised of locals, artists, she thought, steeling themselves with a stiff drink for the day ahead in the market. She sat down on the only free table inside.

'Coffee? Please?' she asked a waitress.

The waitress looked at her from beneath heavy eyelids and didn't respond. Patsy and Ben had already experienced the Parisienne's intolerance for those who didn't speak French, so she tried again.

'Je voudrais un café, s'il vous plait,' she said, remembering her GCSE French.

'Non,' the waitress muttered, her face unchanged.

'They only sell booze,' a voice said over her shoulder.

She turned to see a young woman with a cap pulled low over her brow and a scarf obscuring her mouth. But to Patsy, Tia was unmistakeable. Patsy stopped herself from blurting Tia's name out loud, while Tia ordered two drinks from the waitress in solid French with a great accent. Patsy slid over to join Tia, who was drinking alone.

'What are you doing here?' Patsy whispered, almost laughing with relief at seeing a friendly face.

'I'm still in hiding.'

'I thought you went to Scotland.'

'I did, but you've got to keep moving to shake off the paps, innit?'

'Things are cooling down now in England, finally!' Patsy reassured her. 'Some TV presenter is being accused of sleeping with their married co-star, so the media have got their teeth into that. They've almost forgotten about Greg.'

Tia nodded into her empty glass.

'No need to worry anymore. Come back to England. Get back to work.'

The waitress brought the drinks and Tia nodded at hers. 'I'm kind of enjoying the holiday, she said pouring a little water in her Pastis, it went all cloudy, and looked delicious like cloudy lemonade.

Patsy frowned. Even though she'd ended up working in PR, Patsy had always wanted to be a performer ever since she was a little girl, so she couldn't believe anyone would ever want to holiday from it.

'But enough about me,' Tia said brightly, 'What are you doing here?'

Pasty shrivelled. 'Oh. Well, I'm on my honeymoon, believe it or not.'

'Oh? So, where's Ben?'

Patsy shrugged. 'Long story…'

'Well?' asked Tia intrusively.

Patsy did not want to talk about the honeymoon debacle; but it was Tia after all, so she relented.

'He walked out on me last night. Thinks I'm having an affair.'

'Really?' Tia said, clearly finding the idea utterly unlikely.

'It's the spirits in the flat. Well, one of them. Goldie got rid of the rest. There's a real ominous male entity. He is convinced that he's, my husband. He is deluded and believes that he got married to me the other day, not Ben. And he's managed to drive me and Ben apart.'

'Sounds like a dickhead,' Tia said sipping her drink, nonchalantly.

'You could say that,' Patsy said looking around the room. 'And he followed us here to Paris. I think he's been trying to sabotage the honeymoon ever since we arrived at the airport. And he just appeared to me in the Sacre Coeur.'

'Wait a minute… you can see him?' Tia asked, putting her drink down and looking panicked.

What does he look like?' Tia said following Patsy's gaze around the bar. 'Is he in here?'

'He's black. Big coat, wide hat. Pencil moustache. Tall and…'

'And what?'

'Kind of hot.'

Tia scoffed. 'Nah Pats! You don't fancy your poltergeist! You're jokes, man.'

Patsy managed a giggle. 'Well, Ben left me in the middle of our honeymoon, I have half a mind to make the most of Paris and if a hot young man wants to sweep me off my feet, then perhaps I should let him.'

'Maybe. But it would be better if he wasn't dead right?' Tia sniggered.

'Well, yeah you've got a point there,' Patsy smiled. 'My gosh, it's so bloody good to see you. Just what the doctor ordered.' She raised her glass.

'Cheers!' Tia said.

'Cheers!' Patsy said with relief and downed the first of many.

The next morning Patsy was throwing her guts up in the toilet of the Airbnb while Tia held her hair back.

'Thanks,' Patsy said, gasping from the violence of vomiting.

'Safe,' Tia smiled despite her own hangover, 'Can't have that stuff getting in your hair. Nightmare to get out.'

When the toilet and Patsy were clean, the two women both flopped back into the big bed where they'd spent the night. Patsy was so glad to have someone to share the bed with, even if it was just a friend.

'I didn't think I drank that much. We were in bed by midnight, weren't we?' Patsy grimaced as her head pounded.

'Yeah, but we started drinking at breakfast,' Tia giggled.

'Oh yeah,' Patsy sighed before downing a glass of water. She looked up at the stucco ceiling for a moment and listened to her stomach growling. 'Now, breakfast. That's what I need. And none of your continental stuff. I want grease. Full on English breakfast.'

'Is it? Well, you might struggle, girl, we're in France,' Tia laughed.

Patsy laughed too and, apart from the way it exacerbated her headache, it felt so good to be happy. She had to keep laughing. Because if she had enough time to think about the reality of her situation, she would surely curl up in a blubbering ball.

They found a café that served something close to an English breakfast and, after they'd had their fill, walked it off along the river.

'So, anything else on the bucket list while you're here?' Tia said.

'A couple of things,' Patsy sighed, 'But… no offence, I really wanted to do them with Ben.'

'Course,' Tia smiled. 'I get it. So, you should get your butt back to London then.'

'Do you think that's where Ben is?' Patsy said with a childish innocence.

'Only one way to find out,' Tia shrugged.

Patsy hugged Tia. 'You should come back too. Come with me!'

Tia pondered this for a second then: 'Nah, not yet. I'm kind of hoping Greg's body will turn up first.'

No sooner had Tia spoken than Patsy's phone pinged. She yanked it from her pocket in the hope that it was Ben. But it wasn't. It was her news app telling her:

> The body of Tia Sash's manager has washed up on a beach near Folkestone.

She gasped.

Tia grabbed the phone and read. 'What the…?'

'You're welcome,' said a voice.

They both looked up to see the man in the wide-brimmed hat striding off down the promenade. He spun round, twirling his large overcoat, and winked at them, before disappearing into thin air.

'Did you see…?' Patsy begun.

'Yeah,' Tia squeaked. 'And you're right.'

'About what?'

'He is hot.'

When she got back to the flat in Factory Way her heart sank, as it had every morning on waking since Ben left her in Paris, but this time her heart seemed to sink all the way to the ground floor of the building and beyond. Ben was not there and there was no sign he had been.

She felt sick – and not just emotionally. She bolted to the toilet and threw up. And as she stood at the sink after, brushing her teeth, she noticed how much her body ached. She touched her ribs assuming the pain was from all the crying and vomiting. But her fingers moved up to her breasts. They were tender to the touch, and they looked bigger than usual. So, she took her top off and her bra and examined them more closely. She looked at her stomach and felt the need to suck it in.

'That's what a few days of stress eating and getting drunk does for your figure,' she sighed.

Despite this revelation, she lay on the sofa most of the day watching TV and stress eating some more. The discovery of Greg Yale's body was all over the news channels. A cause of death had already been determined: drowning by suicide. Tia was off the hook. It was some comfort to Pasty, but it didn't stop her eating. However, she couldn't find exactly what she needed in the kitchen. She had to get on an app and get it delivered. She was gagging for some Marmite on hot toast, and liquorice, two things her father loved and always ate when she was growing up. She wasn't a fan of either… until now.

Tia messaged her as she was ordering:

`How's it going?`

Patsy messaged back immediately:

`Ben's not here. I'm on the sofa comfort eating. Have a weird craving for…`

She stopped typing. That word. Craving. That's the kind of word you use when you're…

She checked the calendar on her phone where she kept a record of her periods. She was late. Very late. She got up and rushed to the bathroom and stripped off examining her body again – the swollen breasts, the stomach that seemed to be growing every time she looked. The vomiting.

'No way,' she whispered.

She put a long coat over her sofa-day comfies and shoved on some trainers. As she opened her front door the neighbour's one clicked shut.

Patsy shook her head at the shadow standing behind the door and the stench of smoke they had left behind, but she didn't have time to fuss about the unsociable neighbours now. She rushed out to the chemist on the main road and bought a pregnancy test.

'Ben!' she cried, as she sat on the toilet back in the flat cradling the test kit. 'How could you? How could you? Come home! Come home! We're having a baby!'

She couldn't put it off any longer. She called Kim. She didn't care anymore about how sad she looked. She needed that shoulder to cry on and Kim was the most pragmatic person she knew. It was Kim that sorted out the housing situation when Zack turned into a stalker and Patsy was sure Kim would drag her out of the doldrums now and initiate some positive action, into this listlessness.

'Oh gosh!' Kim said as she found Patsy lying on the sofa surrounded by sweet wrappers and an empty jar of Marmite.

'It looks like a world war in here,' Kim said drily starting to tidy up, 'at least you haven't lost your sense of humour.'

'What am I going to do, Kim?' Patsy moaned a little dramatically.

Kim stopped tidying and slapped Patsy's legs out of the way, so she had to sit up and let Kim sit next to her. 'First, you have to decide.'

'Decide what?'

'Whether you want to keep this baby or not.'

Patsy tutted. 'Of course, I'm going to keep it. This is everything I ever wanted.'

'But do you want it alone?'

Patsy thought for a brief moment then said, 'No, I want it with Ben.'

'Right, so you need to find Ben and let him know.'

'But I've tried. None of his texts are getting through.' Patsy showed her phone to Kim.

'Weird,' she said. 'That means he hasn't turned his phone on since he walked out on you.'

'I guess he doesn't want to hear from me.'

'Maybe, but he'd use his phone for other stuff. We all use our phones every day.'

'So?' She anxiously searched for a clue in Kim's expression.

'Well, I suppose we should find out if he's all right first and if his phone's not off because he can't turn it on.'

'Kim! What are you… Do you think he might have done something to… hurt himself?'

'Where would he go if he didn't want to be here?'

‘He was living at his mum’s before.’
‘So, we start there.’

'Well, that explains a lot,' Emma growled sucking on her teeth as if there was a piece of meat stuck between them, which, knowing Emma, there probably was.

Kim and Patsy stood in the living room waiting to be invited to sit while Emma dumped herself back in her PVC armchair, which seemed to screech with horror as she sat into position, from the weight.

'What do you mean?' Patsy asked as gently as she could. She'd told Ben's mum they'd had a disagreement, but nothing more.

'Well,' Emma said, 'Dave hasn't been back since the wedding either. So, I imagine they're off somewhere having a boy's jolly, drowning Ben's sorrows.'

'But they had a fight at the wedding,' Patsy reminded her.

'They're brothers,' Emma scowled at Patsy as if she was stupid. 'They fight all the time. They soon make up.'

Patsy was dying to point out that Ben and Dave had never liked each other, but she didn't think the timing was appropriate.

'So, what was the argument about?' Emma asked, 'Sit down, you're making the place look untidy.'

Kim and Patsy did as they were told, feeling like two schoolgirls again.

'Just a lover's tiff,' Kim said covering for Patsy.

'Were you there?' Emma asked Kim.

Kim shook her head, 'No, but…'

'So, what do you know? I'd rather hear it from her,' Emma jabbed a finger at Patsy. 'Coz, you don't walk out on your honeymoon over a lover's tiff I can tell you that for nothing.'

Patsy thought about lying but knew it would be a tangled web to weave in front of Emma, who had spent her whole life being suspicious of people. That was her survival mechanism. She would probe and probe until she found out the truth – or at least the truth that she wanted to hear.

Patsy took a deep breath then came out with it: 'He thought I was having an affair.'

Emma groaned, as if she'd been expecting that. 'And what made him think that?'

'Nothing,' Patsy began.

'Nothing?' Emma scoffed. 'My Ben doesn't walk out over nothing. Try again!'

Patsy wanted to slap her mother-in-law. She found her to be the least endearing individual, and she was so angry with herself for coming here. 'He heard me on the phone and thought I was talking to some other bloke, but he got it wrong. I was talking to… a friend… and he got it all mixed up and anyway I told him I used to have a stalker and he thought the stalker was a bloke I was having an affair with… which I wasn't.'

'Why would you tell him you had a stalker, and especially on your honeymoon?'

'Because I was trying to be honest with him.'

'Or trying to make him jealous,' Emma said grimacing with disgust.

'Why would…' Patsy cussed under her breath.

'Touched a nerve, have I?' Emma looked pleased with herself; pleased that her suspicious mind was once again vindicated.

'No!' Patsy said getting up.

'So why are you getting up?'

'Because, Emma, I'm going to go before I say something I might regret.'

'Oh, I think you already have said something you'll regret,' Emma sneered.

As Patsy headed for the door, Kim remained sitting for a moment and shook her head at the middle-aged misanthrope.

'What's *your* problem?' Emma said to Kim as she picked dog hair from her jeans.

'Believe in life after death?' Kim asked.

'Yeah, what's it to you?'

Kim was hoping for that answer. 'Ever asked yourself why your husband has never tried to contact you from the other side?'

'What you on about?' Emma snapped.

'Because he never looked back, that's why,' Kim smirked as she got up and followed Patsy to the door.

As they marched to the car, Patsy grumbled, 'Ben wouldn't spend half an hour with his brother, let alone go on a *jolly,* as she put it.'

'You can see where Dave gets it from, can't you?' Kim nodded.

'Yeah exactly, awful woman. He gets his bigotry from her too. But she hides her prejudice under a veiled smile – the worst, so disingenuous. I can see where Ben got his paranoia from too,' Pasty said. 'But I'm convinced now something's happened to him. He would've contacted me one way or the other. He's not staying away by choice. We need to find him.'

'Then we call the police,' Kim said.

Patsy nodded and immediately her phone pinged. She fished it from her pocket. A text from Ben. Her thumb moved like lightning to open it. She read it in an instant and showed it to Kim:

`I am fine. Put me from your mind.`

No sooner had Kim read it than Patsy grabbed the phone and texted Ben back:

`I'm pregnant. With your child.`

Her phone pinged with a quick response. She read it and handed the phone to Kim, slumping against her Beetle, the sobs coming quickly. Kim read:

`No matter. It is time to move on to pastures new.`

'Pastures new?' Kim kissed her teeth. 'What a dickhead.'

For the next couple of weeks, Kim only left Patsy to go to work. Patsy watched her body change and endured the sickness and constant need to go to the toilet along with the pain of knowing Ben didn't care. But the fact that he wasn't laying somewhere in the bottom of a ditch, still gave her a glimmer of hope that he would realise he was wrong and come back. She read his texts over and over again. She sent a few too, but none of them reached him. The idea that he might've blocked her sent her into fits of sobbing.

Christmas came too soon, and it was, of course, excruciating; the TV was saturated with images of happy families, happy couples, children opening presents; rubbing it in that Pasty was alone. She spent Christmas day with her family. Her dad was so sad for her, but put on the Christmas cheer, cooked up an amazing dinner as always, and treated her like a princess in a bid to make her forget her sorrows. Kim and Vernon managed to make her giggle on a few occasions with some family in-jokes which Nina just found irritating because they excluded her. Rose smiled at some of the ribbing, but she spent most of the time examining her youngest daughter over the top of the wine glass she drank from. Patsy would have loved to have got drunk, but she wasn't going to do anything to jeopardise her pregnancy.

After dinner she sat with her dad, Nina, and Vernon watching TV, but there were only so many romantic magical cliches she could stomach, so she wandered into the kitchen to see if Rose and Kim needed help with the washing up.

'…anything to do with the entity?' Rose was saying as she dried up.

It made Patsy stop at the doorway and eavesdrop.

Kim shook her head, her hands in the sink. 'I don't know. *I* didn't see it. Not at the flat. Not since the wedding. And the text from Ben was pretty conclusive.'

Patsy couldn't believe what she was hearing. 'Kim!' she squealed, making her mum and sister jump. 'You're a seer?! What the hell Kim?!' Patsy screeched.

'Patsy!' Rose gasped.

'No, don't try and distract me,' Patsy said continuing to lay into Kim. 'Why wouldn't you tell me something like that?

You're always saying you don't believe in that stuff. You're the science buff for goodness' sake! If you can't measure it, it doesn't exist, isn't that what you always say?'

'I know I know,' Kim said shaking her soapy hands and grabbing the tea towel from her mother. 'I don't want to be a seer. I hate it.'

Rose looked offended that her daughters didn't seem to be as proud of the family trait as she was.

'It doesn't make any sense,' Kim went on in frustration. 'So, I…'

'You saw something at the wedding ceremony, didn't you? Both of you.'

Rose and Kim swapped a look. Then Rose nodded.

'A man, right? A man standing between Ben and I.'

Kim paused for a moment then admitted, 'Yes.'

'Why didn't you tell me!'

'It was your wedding day, we didn't want to spoil it,' Rose offered.

'Well, that… thing followed us to Paris. He is the reason Ben is not here now. He's been trying to sabotage everything all along.'

'I didn't know that,' Rose said defensively. 'You didn't tell me. I went to your flat while you were away and tried to clear the place again.'

'But he wasn't there, was he? He was with me.'

Rose looked embarrassed.

'You knew it wasn't Zack that was messing with me, with Nelson, didn't you Kim,' Patsy said recalling her words when they argued all those months ago:

'The clearance. It's sorted now. There's no more trouble, no more weird goings-on.'

'It's not sorted,' Kim stated with a sense of sadness that Patsy wasn't used to seeing in her big sister.

'It is, I'm telling you. I know, I live here,' Patsy insisted, 'So you see it wasn't Zack at all. Lucky, we didn't get him in trouble unnecessarily, wasn't it.'

'And I thought you were talking about Zack, but you knew there was still a presence in the flat, didn't you?'

'It was my first time seeing too,' Kim pouted. 'I didn't want to see it. You must understand how it messed with my head.'

'And what you said to Ben's mum. Did you see the spirit of Ben's dad?'

'No,' Kim scoffed. 'I just wanted to torment her a little… it's only what she deserves.'

Patsy glared at Kim, and it seemed like they would both burst out laughing for a moment at the thought of Emma believing her husband had abandoned her for heaven. But the moment was lost when Patsy doubled over in pain. She cried out.

Luca came rushing from the living room. 'What is it?'

Patsy collapsed on the floor clutching her womb. 'Daddy!' she cried.

'Rose, call an ambulance!' Luca bellowed.

Rose hurried to the landline, while Kim got down on the floor with Luca and hugged her sister.

'It's the baby,' Patsy gasped.

'No, no, no. Don't think like that,' Luca pleaded. 'Everything will be fine.'

'No ambulances for hours,' Rose said frantically as she returned.

'Forget the ambulances!' Kim said. 'We'll drive.'

'Who will drive?' Luca hissed. 'We've all been drinking.'

'I haven't,' Pasty gasped.

'Yeah, but you can't drive like this,' Kim said, half-laughing at the thought.

A shadow fell over them as something huge blocked the light. They all looked up.

'I'll drive.' It was Nina. 'It takes a lot to get me drunk. I'm still sober… unfortunately.'

Nina bombed through the streets of North London in her BMW 1 series, while Kim held Patsy in the back.

'Are you sure, you're not drunk?' Kim called out.

'Sure,' Nina said swerving around a cyclist who wobbled frantically in the BMW's slipstream.

'She always drives like this,' Patsy said with a wry chuckle, before gasping in pain again.

'Where are you going?' Kim asked.

'North Midd. It's the closest, innit?' Nina said.

'OK, good,' Kim huffed.

Nina added, 'My gran went there with a broken hip, caught COVID in there and died.'

'This is not the time to tell her stories like that Nina… sorry to hear about your nan… but can you shut up and drive please?!' Kim yelled, trying to calm Patsy down.

As they neared the hospital Nina screeched to a halt.

'What the…? Kim shouted.

'Bloody tree in the road.'

Patsy and Kim looked up to see the streetlights illuminating an enormous old oak fallen across the street and blocking their path.

'Don't worry,' Nina said, throwing an impressive three-point turn. 'This is my 'hood. I know the back streets like the back of my hand.'

As she turned into one of those back streets a black cat, almost invisible in the darkness, darted across the road making Nina swerve wildly.

'Gosh, anyone would think someone's trying to stop us from getting there,' Nina muttered.

However, in just another minute she was pulling up outside the A&E department.

'Hang on! I'll get a wheelchair or something.'

She jumped out of the car and went inside.

'Come on!' Kim said. 'Let's not wait. I'll help you inside.'

Just as Kim was helping Patsy from the car, Nina was ushered out by a hospital porter.

'Don't bother,' she growled jumping back in the driving seat.

'What?' Kim was exasperated.

'They reckon they're full. Said if we want to be seen quicker than eight hours we should go elsewhere?'

'Elsewhere? How informative!' Kim snarled, helping Patsy back onto the towel, which Nina had put over her leather seats to protect them.

Patsy and Kim both saw the blood on the towel. Kim could see Patsy's terror and hid her own. 'You'll be all right,' she said, 'Both of you,' she smiled.

'Finchley Memorial's not far along the A406. I'll get you there in no time,' Nina said speeding off.

The hospital porter watched them go. He smoothed his pencil moustache with his long fingernails and then seemed to disappear into the evening mist.

At Finchley Memorial, Kim didn't wait for Nina to go in. She bundled Patsy out of the car and supported her into the reception where a woman sat behind the desk typing, her long fingernails tapping irritatingly on the keyboard.

'We need to see a doctor right now!' Kim demanded.

The receptionist looked up, her eyes a sparkling brown, but her face jarringly masculine. Kim even thought she detected a moustache above the woman's pursed lips. 'I'm sorry, you'll need to go elsewhere. We are full.'

'Elsewhere?' Kim spat. 'What is it with you lot and elsewhere? No, we are not going elsewhere because this woman is bleeding from her womb.' She gestured at Patsy who was clutching the towel between her legs. 'And the last time I looked that would put her in an urgent category of triage, so I'm taking her through. Feel free to try and stop me.'

The receptionist looked stunned for a moment, then her lip curled in anger. She hadn't bargained for someone as well informed or strong willed as Kim. But she didn't move or try to stop them. She just looked over her shoulder as she heard Yasmin the receptionist – the real receptionist – coming back.

'I'm going to slap them when I find out who it was,' Yasmin grumbled as she took her seat again. 'Wasting my time. Making me go all the way down to the back entrance for a delivery that didn't exist.'

She stopped muttering to herself abruptly as she looked at her computer screen and saw the words typed across the document:

HELL HELL HELL HELL
HELL HELL HELL HELL

It was a miscarriage.

Patsy's world came crumbling down as the final brick of joy was removed from the life she was building. Kim stayed with her for a few days after Christmas, Rose and Luca visited with surplus food from the tonnes they'd bought for Christmas, but eventually life had to go on for everyone. Even Patsy had to go back to work after New Year, but she didn't know how she would do it. She would stand at the living room window sometimes looking out over Factory Way and the whole city beyond. And it was like standing on the tallest mountain where the wind is howling, screaming through you and you try to scream yourself, but nothing is coming out. And then you look down and you can see the whole world going about their business as usual, as if nothing happened. But something had happened. To Patsy. She had lost the life inside of her, she had lost her baby and so she screamed for real. She screamed and screamed until there was a knock on the door. She cracked the door open. It was Loz.

'You alright?' she asked.

'Mmm,' Patsy lied.

They both looked at each other for a moment, both looking like a mirror image of each other – rung out, hollow.

'If he's beating you…'

'No. He's not. Thanks for coming though.' She put on her best smile. She hadn't told Loz what had happened in Paris or what had happened after. She had barely seen her since the wedding and Patsy wasn't used to being the one in need in their relationship.

Loz turned and went back downstairs. Then Patsy closed the door and slid down it, crumbling to the floor where she sobbed silently, her body convulsing with the stifled wailing.

She lay on the sofa watching TV, but not seeing anything. She picked up her phone every five minutes and looked at her chat with Ben. Still nothing. It twisted the knife in her. Not only had she lost their baby. She had lost him too.

She would often wake up on the sofa at three in the morning and drag herself to bed. She would sometimes dream of Ben's arms around her and, when she awoke to reality, her guts would flood with the hot sense of grief all over again. She wondered if it would ever end. How could she possibly '*get over it'*, as some friends thoughtlessly said she would? How could she 'move on', as others hoped she would? She still loved Ben deeply, and she still loved the baby that had been growing inside her.

It was New Year's Day when there was some period movie on TV jabbering away to itself as she looked at her phone for the umpteenth time. Instagram kept bombarding her with images of Paris because she had searched it before the honeymoon. The very algorithm which she was master of exploiting in her work, which had saved Tia from the paps, was now taunting her. She flicked the app closed and opened WhatsApp instead, for more masochistic scrolling. She looked at the last messages Ben had sent yet again.

-I am fine. Put me from your mind.

-I'm pregnant. With your child.

-No matter. It is time to move on to pastures new.

Put me from your mind? No matter? Pastures new? He sounded more like one of these seventeenth century fops on the TV, than her normal builder husband from the South-East coast of England. She looked at the TV. Then back at her phone. Then at the TV again. She cussed long and hard as the penny dropped.

'That's because this is not him,' she whispered, sitting up.

She immediately dialled Kim.

'It's not him,' she said as soon as Kim answered.

'What's not him?' Kim tried to keep up.

'The text Ben sent. Pastures new and all that. Remember?'

Kim kissed her teeth. 'How could I forget?'

'Well, that's not the way he talks. And it's not the way he texts. Kim, he's been abducted.'

The line went dead.

'Kim? Hello? Can you hear me?'

She looked at WhatsApp. *Reconnecting.*

'Grrr this app,' she growled.

Then she felt the arm around her. Just as she had on the Eiffel Tower. The bony fingers and the long nails were unmistakable.

'Forget him,' the voice breathed in her ear.

She stiffened, petrified.

'He left you. And so did his baby. But that's a good thing. It is the way things are meant to be. Now we can get started on making our own life, our own child.'

She looked to her right and he was there, sitting next to her.

'You!' Her voice cracked and squeaked with horror and fear. 'You did this. You took Ben. And you took my baby.'

She lurched forward to get away, but he tightened his grip – and his grip was strong.

She remembered when Tia had described in court Greg Yale barging into her hotel room and assaulting her and she had a terrible sense that the same thing was about to happen to her. Instinctively, she let her body relax. She knew that the more she struggled the tighter he would hold her.

'That's it,' he cooed. 'You know it's the right thing to do. We are married now. You are my bride. My property to do with as I so choose. You know there is no point in fighting that.'

Although Patsy wanted to vomit, although she wanted to shout down his misogynistic crap, she stayed silent and nodded like a good wife. She glanced at him and saw he wasn't wearing the hat nor the coat this time. In fact, he wasn't wearing anything at all, except his old-fashioned Y front underpants. His body was fit, strong, sculpted and, Patsy couldn't believe she even thought about it, but it flashed through her mind how beautiful he was. She had to fight with every fibre of her rational mind not to be seduced by his touch, nor tempted by the words he dropped in her ear like poison.

She put her hand up and he stopped.

'Let me turn this TV off,' she said gently. 'It's such a distraction.' She smiled at him as seductively as she could stomach.

He returned the smile and reclined on the sofa watching her as she crossed the room and touching himself as she went. The remote was right next to them on the sofa, but this ancient soul wasn't up on technology. When Patsy reached the TV she unplugged it, picked it up and, with every last ounce of energy she had, she threw it at the window. It crashed through the glass and fell three flights into the garden below.

Now all she could do was pray.

The man was on her in a flash. 'Is this some attempt at escape?' he said standing between her and the smashed window, his claws sinking into her forearms.

'No,' she said calmly. 'TV. I've had enough of it. Bad news every day.'

He studied her for a moment, searching for the lie. Whether he found it or not, Patsy couldn't tell, but he suddenly let out a peal of laughter, throwing his head back. Patsy's blood ran cold at the sound.

'I agree,' he smiled. 'The worst invention of the twentieth century.' His face hardened. As did his grip. He pressed himself against her. 'Now…'

'Can we go to the bedroom?' Patsy said as shyly as possible, acting her heart out.

'Of course,' he said.

He released his grip and she saw blood seeping from the wounds he'd made in her arms. He led her by the hand, his palm icy cold in her sweating one. The bedroom door was right near the front door. As soon as he walked into the bedroom, she would unlatch the door so Loz could get in when she came to see what all the racket was about this time, why Patsy's TV had just been flung out of her window. At least, that was the plan. But as they came to the threshold of the bedroom, he stopped, blocking her way to the front door. He gestured gallantly.

'After you, my love.'

She tried to keep her face calm, but her insides were screaming out with despair. She looked over his shoulder at the front door. He cocked his head into her sightline.

'Everything all right?' he smiled.

She nodded meekly and after a painfully stretched out second, as she hoped for a different outcome, she stepped into the bedroom. The lights came on without anyone touching the switch and he made her face him at the foot of the bed. He dipped his claws into the top of her t-shirt. Then he ripped it from her body. She could barely contain the gasp of disgust that welled up inside her.

His face lit up, his eyes flashed at the sight off her body, then…

A frantic pounding of a fist on the door.

'Pats! Pats! I know you're not, OK? Open the door!'

It was Loz.

Pats shoved the man aside and lunged for the bedroom door screaming out, 'Loz, Loz, help me! Call my sister! Tell her…'

Patsy felt herself flying through the air until she hit the headboard and flopped onto the mattress.

'Ooh,' the man grinned towards the front door, 'it's this one, is it? Oh, she must come and join the party.' He wrenched open the door and yanked Loz inside, dragging her by the hair to the bed and dumping her at Patsy's feet. 'She has so much she wants to tell you.'

Loz was on her feet in an instant. 'What the hell? you piece of shit,' she began, but was silenced by the slap he gave her around the jaw, so hard she blacked out for a moment.

'Loz!' Pasty held her, partly to protect Loz and partly to protect herself. 'Loz, Loz, wake up!'

Loz came around and immediately snapped back into lioness mode. 'Who's this?' she said looking around for a weapon.

'He's trying to attack me,' Patsy blurted out the words.

Loz saw red. 'We'll see about that.'

The man looked on amused as Loz, finding no weapon, launched herself at him from the bed. She landed with her arms around his neck and her legs locked around his waist, but no sooner had she landed than he grabbed her throat and held her aloft by it. She choked and spluttered for what seemed like forever. Pasty screamed at him to release her.

He did. Throwing her to the floor.

She scrambled back against the wall and slumped there for a while trying to breathe. The man stood over her as Patsy's wardrobe door ripped itself open and things were flung out of it. Plastic bags full of old clothes waiting eternally to go to the charity shop were emptied until one hung in the air above Loz.

Loz watched, her eyes bulging in disbelief.

'She came to the wedding to confess,' said the man to Patsy. 'Confess what she'd done to her little girl.'

Loz was no longer the lioness now, but the gazelle in the grip of the predator.

'But that stupid ignoramus of a man caused a scene and distracted you, my love. So, she couldn't finish. But now you can finish,' he told Loz.

'No… what?' Loz mumbled.

The plastic bag floated down to where Loz sat and tied itself like a snake might around her neck. Loz grabbed at it to stop it cutting into her neck, just as her daughter Mindy had done with the shopping bag which had once been Nelson's coffin.

'Stop!' Patsy screamed.

'Finish!' the man demanded of Loz. 'Tell her!'

The plastic tightened so much now that it cut into Loz's fingers like a wire through cheese and forced them to press against her own windpipe. She started to panic.

She tried to scream, but by now the handle was so tight she couldn't make any noise, but a horrible rasp. The rasp became a gurgle. Her eyes glazed over.

'Stop! And I'll be your wife! I'll do whatever you want,' Pasty begged.

The plastic bag loosened, and Loz gasped, glaring at the man with bloodshot eyes. He crouched in front of her.

'Tell her what you wanted to tell her.'

Loz's chest was heaving, but she managed to get out the words. 'Mindy, she…' Loz said sheepishly to Patsy, but now she knew the truth, she modified the word. '*He*… choked her with a plastic bag.'

'She'd been told a thousand times by you,' the man scoffed. 'Don't play with plastic bags. But go on. Then what did you do?'

Loz looked at Patsy and back at the man.

'TELL HER!' he bellowed so loud Loz smacked her head against the wall as she flinched.

'I… panicked,' Loz wept. 'I knew I couldn't explain it. The bag was tied around her neck. I knew the police would come and accuse me of abuse. They'd already come too many times before when Trevor was beating me. So… I couldn't tell anyone she'd died.'

'Died?' Patsy said.

'I wasn't thinking straight. Or… I don't know, maybe I was thinking straighter than ever. People like me, you see, they don't give us a chance. The courts would lock me up and throw away the key. I couldn't explain it.' She glared at the man. 'And now I know why.'

'Finish it!' he growled.

Loz took a deep breath and then the words came tumbling out, 'So I buried her. In the garden,' she cried, pointing limply towards the window and the garden beyond.

'When?' Patsy said, not knowing why she asked.

'It was a few months back. October.'

'But I…' Patsy begun.

'You've seen her since then, my love, haven't you,' the man stated confidently. 'So, have I. She's a feisty one. She's not going away anytime soon.'

Loz looked at Patsy in utter bewilderment as Patsy recalled all the times, that she'd seen Mindy since autumn began:

Mindy pressed her lips to the glass and blew so her mouth inflated comically and made a farting sound. She looked up at Patsy and grinned. Patsy grinned back as Loz reached the ground floor.

'Did she have a friend over last night?' Patsy asked, turning to Loz.

'Ey?' Loz said groggily.

'Mindy. Did she have a friend over last night? I thought I heard two little gremlins running up and down the corridor and playing ball against your wall. Not just one, as usual,' she smiled down at the little gremlin in question.

Loz looked startled and stuttered. She looked as if she might vomit at any second, but eventually she managed, 'Yeah… yeah. A friend over last night. Keeping me up all night with their nonsense. That's why I feel so bloody rough. Yeah, that's it.'

'Ah, well, nice she has some playmates, though,' Patsy smiled.

'Yeah,' Loz said a little more brightly. 'I s'pose it is. She has playmates,' she added, almost to herself.

There was an awkward pause, which Patsy ended with, 'Right, well, I better get off to work. See you two later.' She opened the door and Mindy bolted. As usual Loz didn't seem that bothered. 'Last chance for a lift!' Patsy sang, trying to lighten the heavy atmosphere.

'I'm good. You go!' Loz said, her face still stony.

And it was clear now why every time she had seen Mindy since then, Loz didn't seem to be aware that Mindy was even present:

She watched Mindy standing on the riverbank, picking violet-blue Lobelia flowers, and tossing them into the stream. She smiled, even though her heart was in her mouth at how close Mindy was to the edge. She looked around to see that Loz was nearby, and did not seem disturbed by this at all, so she set off to work. She looked in the rearview mirror as she drove off. It looked as if Loz had forgotten Mindy as she slouched down the road alone, but after a long tense moment for Patsy, she saw Mindy race into view after her mother, so Patsy accelerated away.

Then there was the time that Mindy had asked to play with the two little girls in Patsy's flat. Patsy had thought it was because Mindy was a seer like her, but it was simply because Mindy now inhabited the same realm as those two dead little girls who'd died in the munitions factory fire.

And no wonder Loz had freaked out when Patsy had spoken to Mindy in front of her:

'So anyway, my news. Ben and I are getting married. On December 2nd. And I want you to come. Will you come?'

'To your wedding?' Loz said as if her mouth was desert dry.

'Yes. I'd love you both to come.'

'Both?' Loz said distractedly.

'You and this little munchkin,' Patsy said reaching down to press Mindy's nose, but the girl jumped back startled, with a giggle before Patsy could make contact.

'What the...' Loz began, straightening up and shaking her head quicker now. In fact, every part of her seemed to be trembling. 'What the... what the heck are trying to do to me?'

'Loz?' Patsy was puzzled.

Loz looked down to where Mindy had been, but the little one had scampered off and Patsy could hear her making a mess in the living room. Loz looked back at Patsy and down at the floor again a few times. 'Don't try and mess with my head! Don't...' Loz was rambling now. 'Why would you say that? Why the hell would you?'

She shut the door and left Patsy on the landing wondering what she'd done wrong.

Patsy looked at the man, her face riddled with questions.

'I thought the girl would be useful,' he shrugged. 'Like the other two. But she was quite the handful in death, as in life. The other two were obedient. They helped me for a while. But it wasn't enough. And they couldn't resist your witchy friend. They just were not strong enough.'

As if to demonstrate that he was strong enough, with a nod from him, the plastic bag, which was laying at Loz's feet, sprang up and became a noose around her neck again. As she squawked and flailed about, the man calmly climbed onto the bed and straddled Patsy, his claws curling inside her jogging bottoms.

She knew all her physical might could not stop this creature, this phantom made flesh, so she prayed. She prayed and she bargained with God, she screwed her eyes up in desperation, she felt were his claws against her thighs, ripping away her clothes.

He roared. A blood curdling roar.

Then she felt the weight of him lift.

She smelt stale cigarette smoke.

She opened her eyes.

And he was gone.

The furrow faced man, with the yellow hat on his greying hair stood before her in his frayed red trousers. And for the first time, with him this close as he wrapped her in a towel and ushered her out of the room, she recognised him.

'Zack?'

Patsy pulled away from her living stalker. 'Get off me!'

'You need to come with me!' If there was any doubt about who this man was, since he was even more dishevelled and craggy than he had been in Cricklewood, Zack's voice was unforgettable to her. 'He will be back very soon. There's only so long I can hold him off in here.'

Patsy saw Loz in a heap on the floor, her noose destroyed with the exit of the poltergeist.

'Loz!' she shouted, trying to scoop up her friend while keeping the towel around her in front of Zack.

'You both need to come with me,' Zack insisted. And when Patsy looked at him with confusion and disdain, he elaborated. 'If you want to survive, come now!'

Patsy weighed up her options and in that moment Zack, a living being, who had never yet done anything to harm her physically, seemed like a better option than the spirit of the dead man who had tried to assault her.

'Where?' Patsy said as she got Loz to her feet.

'Follow me,' he urged her as he beckoned her out of the flat.

'I need clothes,' she insisted.

'I've got clothes,' he said firmly.

Patsy had no idea where he was leading her and Loz, so she defiantly grabbed some more jogging bottoms and a top and cardigan and shoved them on before following Zack out of the flat and across the landing.

As he let himself into the opposite flat, Patsy stopped in her tracks.

'Come in!' he said.

Loz wasn't in the mood to argue and stumbled inside.

Patsy couldn't believe it. But the sound of something smashing in her flat propelled her forward.

Zack locked the front door behind them and shepherded the women through the gloomy, musty flat to the living room which was lined with lit candles and smelt strongly of sage.

'Come, come! Sit in the middle!'

Loz and Patsy sat on the floor as Zack poured salt on the carpet all around them.

'What the hell is all this, Zack?' Patsy said. 'If you don't tell me what you're doing right now…'

'Hang on!' he said as he finished the circle of salt.

But Patsy felt as if she might be going from frying pan to fire, so she got up.

'No, no, no, no, no. Please stay inside the circle,' Zack said and the fear on his face convinced Patsy to step back. 'I know what I'm doing, trust me! This is my religion, I'm well trained.'

'Religion?' Pasty scoffed.

'OK, it's not quite like yours, but in my belief system we understand deity to be manifest within nature. We believe that nature is sacred and that the natural cycles of birth, growth and death observed in the world around us carry profound spiritual meanings. Human beings are seen as part of nature, along with other animals, trees, stones, plants, and everything else that is of this earth and in the whole cosmos for that matter. We believe in some form of reincarnation, viewing death as a transition within a continuing process of existence and we recognise divinity as taking many forms. Finding expression in goddesses as well as gods; goddess worship is in fact central to my practice. The female form is vital. Women are strong, forces of nature. But you don't need me to tell you that, do you?' He knew as soon as he said it that it sounded a bit creepy coming from him, so he added. 'And I'm sorry. I did worship you in this way. And I overstepped the mark. But when I saw where the housing association had put you…'

'You followed me here?'

Zack put up his hand. 'Wait please! When I saw this place… Your flat, the negativity was overwhelming. The geopathic stress was off the charts. This land was so traumatised, I knew a portal had opened up because of it and it was opening out right in the middle of your home.'

The words he used echoed Goldie's and it instantly made Patsy feel like he knew what he was talking about, that he wasn't making this up just to be near her, that he just might have the abilities that Goldie had demonstrated.

'But I knew you wouldn't want to hear all this from me,' he said, bowing his head remorsefully. 'So, I knew the only thing I could do was be close and try to protect you from here.'

'But how did you get this flat?' Pasty said, bewildered by this avalanche of revelations.

'I made the tenant an offer they couldn't refuse,' he said proudly.

'What do you mean?' Patsy said, anxious that he meant something violent.

Zack sighed theatrically. 'Well, if you must know, I paid them a tonne of money.'

Patsy was even more confused by this. 'But…'

'What?'

'You don't have…'

'Money?' Zack smiled. 'Oh, Patsy. Don't judge a book by its cover! I thought you understood that from all your work on Instagram.'

Patsy almost smiled. 'But… you look a lot older. And it hasn't even been a year.'

'It's a full-time job trying to keep those entities back, you know. It takes its toll,' he smiled coyly.

'Sounds like you got yourself a guardian angel there,' Loz croaked.

Patsy studied Zack's wizened face for a moment longer, then sat down and put an arm round Loz. 'So, what do we do now?' she said looking up at Zack.

'Crystals,' he said, hanging one each around Patsy and Loz's neck.

'Mind if I hold mine,' Loz said, her neck still tender from the plastic noose.

'Sure. They're great for clearing negative energy and creating a feeling of peace,' Zack went on. 'I imagine Goldie told you that.'

'You know Goldie?'

Zack shrugged. 'The healing world is like the music business… you know – everyone knows everyone.'

Patsy had heard stranger things today.

Zack spoke enthusiastically now, like he used to about *Star Trek*. 'Kyanite, selenite, obsidian, hematite, and desert rose are the best. I keep a piece of kyanite on my windowsill under the full moon to charge it up every month,' he said as he hurried to the kitchen.

Patsy raised an eyebrow at Loz – if they hadn't seen what they had seen tonight, they would have laughed Zack out of Factory Way.

Zack returned immediately with a pan of charred sage. He dipped his fingers in the soot and smeared it on the women's faces.

'What's all this?' Loz asked, shrinking from his touch.

'Sage,' he said applying it like camouflage paint to soldiers. 'In Roman times, sage was sacred to Jove and was gathered with great ceremony. The genus name salvia is related to the Latin word salvere, meaning to heal, preserve or redeem. Sage was associated in European traditions with wisdom, long life, and even immortality. An Italian proverb states…'

'Why should a man die when he has sage in his garden?' Patsy joined in.

'You know it?' Zack smiled.

'My dad says it all the time when he's cooking,' she smiled back.

'Well, maybe he's one of us too,' Zack chuckled, before his face became quickly serious again. 'Now, there's only three of us, but five is the magic number.'

'That's not what De La Soul reckon,' Patsy giggled. She couldn't believe she was making a joke at a time like this, but there was something bizarrely soothing about Zack now, his sense of authority in this situation, like some kind of big brother.

'Eh?' Zack said.

Patsy shook her head and winked at Loz.

'So,' he got back to the matter in hand, 'we need to make a couple of calls.'

'Why don't we just stay here if we're safe. And, better still, why don't we just all move out?' Loz said, her voice trembling.

'Because he follows me,' Pasty said. 'He came to Paris. And he…' She turned to Zack. 'What did he do with Ben?'

'That's what I hope we'll find out. He thinks he's your husband. He thinks you're married. He's more of a stalker than I was,' Zack snorted.

Patsy and Loz looked blankly at each other and then at Zack.

'Too soon?' Zack asked meekly.

Patsy nodded.

'OK,' he said and opened the door to the landing.

Patsy's eggshell blue front door, which she had so proudly painted, was blackened as if by soot. And it was rumbling as if there were an earthquake on the other side.

'Oh,' Zack said, chewing his lip. 'He's really angry.'

'Men!' Loz sneered. 'Always throwing their toys out the pram when they don't get what they want.'

Zack didn't seem remotely offended. In fact, he nodded, but his attention was fixed on the door. 'We have to go in *now*. He's discombobulated from the last incantation I cast.'

'Bloody hell! Who swallowed the dictionary?' Loz said, using her irrepressible humour to cope with the insanity of this situation.

'And his anger is clouding his judgement,' Zack added. 'Stay behind me, but do not run away, whatever he tries. It's all smoke and mirrors, trust me.' He took a deep breath. 'Go!'

He launched himself at the door which gave way easily, but the heat coming from inside almost drove them back – it was so intense Patsy thought that the flat was on fire for a moment. However, she could see no flames as they shuffled in behind Zack. The lights in every room were flashing on and off. A raging cacophony filled the air, a sonic cocktail of roaring flames, of once human voices crying out and even a cat screeching, which made Patsy's heart leap.

'Nelson?' she said to herself.

Patsy could imagine just what it must have been like to be at the munitions factory the day it had burned down.

'Make it stop!' a woman's voice screamed in her ear.

'Help! Please help!' a man moaned.

'Mummy, mummy!' a child squealed, and Patsy almost burst into tears.

'Make it stop! Only you can make it stop. Do as he wants!' the woman cried out frantically and Patsy could sense that this spirit saw flames creeping towards her feet.

Zack poured salt all around the hallway as they moved through into the living room, where pictures, ornaments, coins left on the coffee table or lost down the back of the sofa, flew about like missiles. As Zack flung salt around this room, the furniture went from merely trembling to sliding across the floor, smashing into each other like dodgems at the fairground.

Zack bellowed against the tempest, 'I ask the universe to bless this home and fill it with light and love. Negativity and darkness are not welcome here. This is a positive sanctuary.'

A huge crash from the bedroom was the response and the sound of little girls screaming.

'Come on!' Zack shouted over the noise.

Patsy and Loz followed him into the bedroom where they were all stopped in their tracks by the sight of the two little girls, who had once sat at Patsy's desk playing happily, now.

Clutching each other on the bed as the man stood over them the first thing that Patsy noticed was their faces. The girls were no longer burnt beyond recognition. They had beautiful, smooth, youthful skin, which was only blemished by the expressions of fear as the man presented them with a ball of flames. He toyed with it in front of them and brought it ever closer. Patsy could tell the girls were reliving the way they had died that fateful day in 1918 and she was horrified for them.

The man glanced over his shoulder at Patsy and her friends, and his eyes flashed with mischief. He turned back to the girls and shoved the ball of flames in their faces. Patsy heard the hiss of skin being seared. The wail each girl let out was like nothing she'd ever heard.

It made her cry out, 'Stop! Stop it! Leave them alone!'

It was exactly what the man wanted. 'Then come with me!' he called out over the raging air.

'Smoke and mirrors, Patsy, smoke and mirrors,' Zack called out and it snapped her out of her trance of dread.

'Smoke and mirrors, eh?' the man snarled and threw the ball of flames at Zack which knocked him off his feet as it were a bowling ball, and he was a pin. He flew across the room, hitting the window so hard it smashed as he fell to the floor. Patsy feared for his spine. She instinctively ran to him.

'No, carry on!' he groaned.

'Pats!' Loz shouted, running over to the window too, trying to keep the troops together.

After a moment's hesitation, Patsy grabbed the salt from Zack and began flinging it around the room.

Loz shouted out the incantation Zack had taught them, 'I ask the universe to bless this home and fill it with light and love. Negativity and darkness are not welcome here. This is a positive sanctuary.'

Patsy joined in. 'I ask the universe to bless this home and fill it with light and love. Negativity and darkness are not welcome here. This is a positive sanctuary.'

The man watched them from the other side of the bed with something like curiosity at first, then his expression became one of a man betrayed as he looked at his 'wife' with her sage covered face, throwing salt and incantations at him. Then his face registered anger, then vengeance, callous vengeance.

And suddenly everything went silent.

So silent, so quickly that Patsy and Loz stopped chanting and tossing the salt about.

'Mummy!' came a muffled sound from outside, down in the garden.

Loz recognised the voice instantly, as any mother recognises the sound of their own child. She looked out of the broken window and, in the light spilling from the train tracks, she saw Mindy clawing her way from the flower bed, spitting mud from her mouth, and wrenching her limbs from their tomb, just as she used to pull herself out of the sand on Southend beach when Loz had buried her up to her neck on a summer's day and put the bucket and spade on top of her sand-belly.

'Help me, Mummy!'

Loz's voice croaked as she tried to scream. Patsy had followed her gaze and instantly turned back to the man, who was grinning like a kid caught with their hand in the cookie jar.

'Loz!' Patsy grabbed her as she felt her friend about to bolt downstairs unable to resist a mother's instinct to protect her daughter.

'Smoke and mirrors, remember, smoke and mirrors,' Zack panted, getting to his feet.

'Mummy!' Mindy was tearful now.

It was too much for Loz to bear. She ran. Patsy was about to follow, but Zack's voice stopped her.

'I ask the universe to bless this home and fill it with light and love. Negativity and darkness are not welcome here. This is a positive sanctuary. Don't leave me hanging, Patsy!'

She tore her gaze from the door Loz had fled through and chanted too. 'I ask the universe to bless this home and fill it with light and love. Negativity and darkness are not welcome here. This is a positive sanctuary.'

The man simply rolled his eyes and lay on the bed, his hands behind his head as if he were completely unaffected by their words.

By the train tracks outside was a pile of charred remains, which had laid there for weeks now since it had fallen from the overhead cables. Some animals had gnawed at the barbequed flesh, pulling it into the bushes, some flies had laid eggs in the once warm entrails that spilled from Dave's ripped torso. But now, the disembowelled young man, unsteadily got to his feet and staggered towards the flats on Factory Way. Some of his intestine trailed behind him, but he didn't seem to notice. Nor did he mind the maggots twisting and pulsating in every orifice of his body.

As Loz came flying out of the flats turning left for the garden, Dave came from the other side of the building, catching the door before it closed and making his way upstairs to see his sister-in-law.

Loz skidded around the corner of the building and found Mindy standing by the riverbank, looking down at the water, sobbing.

'Baby!' she cried out. 'It's OK.'

Mindy was caked in mud, but Loz couldn't care less. She grabbed her, spun her around and went to hug her, comfort her, but the sight of Mindy's face arrested her.

The little girl's skin was a putrid shade of green. Her mouth still full of mud and maggots, her eye sockets empty. She held out her decomposing limbs to her mother and Loz fought the urge to vomit. As Mindy looked up with unseeing eyes, Loz could see a chasm in her daughter's neck where the plastic bag had once begun to cut through, but now it was a gaping wound through which Loz could see the little girl's spine.

'Mummy!' she grinned. And lunged at her mother.

'I ask the universe to bless this home and fill it with light and love. Negativity and darkness are not welcome here. This is a positive sanctuary.'

Zack and Patsy continued to chant, and the man continued to lay nonchalantly on the bed until there was a hammering at the front door.

'Patsy! Patsy!'

The voice was familiar but muffled. For a second, she thought it was Ben – brothers can often sound alike – and she, forgetting her own advice to Loz, ran for the door.

Zack closed his eyes in frustration and continued to chant. The man laughed and when.

Patsy threw open the door and Dave was standing there in what was left of his wedding suit, melted to his skin and, in some places, his bone. Pasty screamed as she took in the sight of his guts trailing down to his feet and stumbled back into the flat. She could barely tear her eyes away from the gruesome sight of her brother-in-law, but as soon as she managed to, she headed straight for the safety of Zack.

'I told you, Patsy, smoke and mirrors,' he said before continuing to chant.

'What did you do? What did you do?' she yelled at the man.

'He was a disgusting individual,' the man sighed, 'Don't tell me you're not happy about it. Call it my wedding gift to you,' he said gesturing to Dave as the corpse staggered into the bedroom and swayed in the doorway.

'Where's Ben?' Dave slurred through a dislocated jaw.

'David,' the man said cooly, 'look at yourself in the mirror! You look so nice in your wedding suit.'

Dave took in the sight of Zack chanting, the black man lying on his sister-in-law's bed, and, as if he was still in a haze of drunkenness, ignored such a bizarre scene, took the man up on his advice and went to the full-length mirror propped up against the wall. For a moment, with nothing but Zack's chanting in the background, Dave gawped at his mutilated body. Then his eye – the one that had not been completely fried – widened, slowly, as he tried to comprehend what he was seeing.

He moaned long and loud as his boiled brain registered what he saw. He grabbed at his intestine and tried to gather it up and push it back inside him. And while Patsy was suitably distracted by this, the spectre on her bed threw another ball of fire at Zack, which sent him hurtling against the wall a second time. The hurricane of noise, of pain and fire, ripped through the flat again. It brought Patsy to her senses, and she jumped back as the man tried to grab her with his talons.

'I ask the universe to bless this home and fill it with light and love. Negativity and darkness are not welcome here. This is a positive sanctuary,' she shouted at him, and he stayed on the bed as if the floor was no longer safe for him.

'I ask the universe to bless this home and fill it with light and love. Negativity and darkness are not welcome here. This is a positive sanctuary,' said her mother and Goldie as they hurried into the room, Rose brandishing a crucifix, Goldie brandishing a steaming bowl of Epsom salts and alcohol. Patsy was so relieved to see her mum, she wanted to cry, but for now at least, she knew she had to stay strong.

'Took your time,' Zack sniped between chants.

'Traffic was murder,' Goldie tutted.

Together the four of them chanted and the man now looked uncomfortable for the first time. He began to crawl about on all fours, like a caged animal. Then he reared up, thrusting himself into the air.

'Take it inside you!' he bellowed. 'Take my seed! Have my child!'

'I ask the universe to bless this home and fill it with light and love. Negativity and darkness are not welcome here. This is a positive sanctuary.' Loz's voice joined the chorus now.

Patsy grabbed at her like a life ring in the ocean as she ran back into the room and they hugged as they chanted, over and over again, the five of them. And since five, as Zack had told them, was a powerful number, the man on the bed ceased laughing and now thrashed about, curses spewing from his lips as a blast furnace wind tried to subdue the healing chant, while Dave, oblivious of it all, sank to the floor lamenting his reflection in the mirror and trying in vain to put himself back together again.

Rose led a change in the incantation. 'For we wrestle not against flesh and blood, but against principalities, against powers, against the rulers of the darkness of this world, against spiritual wickedness in high places. I drive all evil out of this place, we drive all evil out of this place. Be gone, be gone, be gone!' she yelled, tossing some water at the man. Judging by the way it seared his skin, Patsy knew it was holy water from the church. 'So, it is said, so it shall be,' Rose added. And they all repeated it, taking each other's hands.

Patsy felt something like electricity flowing through them all, but not in a shocking way; it was more of a pulse, massaging, soothing, empowering.

'So, it is said, so it shall be,' she said with more conviction than she had ever said anything in her life. 'So, it is said, so it shall be,' she cried out.

'So, it is said, so it shall be,' they all roared together.

And every single window in the flat – bar the two already smashed, of course – exploded outwards. A tsunami of air and wailing rushed through the place, taking their breath away and momentarily their sight before it hurled itself through every opening in the walls and out into the night.

As they blinked around the room in the ensuing silence, punctuated only with their heavy breathing, they could all see that the man was gone and so was Dave. Loz ran to the window and looked down to where she had left the monstrosity that purported to be Mindy, and she was both relieved and devastated to see that she too now had vanished.

'Patsy! Patsy!'

When she heard the voice, her skin shrank around her bones. For a second, she was sure it was Dave. That he hadn't left the flat at all. And if he hadn't left then, she presumed, her phantom stalker was still present.

But as she came to her senses and the voice called out, 'Babes!' she realised which sibling it was.

'Ben!' she gasped and ran into the living room where she found her husband standing bemused, dumbfounded, in the wreckage the poltergeist had left.

She threw her arms around him, and he held onto her tightly.

'What the f… what is going on?' he stammered, confused.

'You're safe, you're safe, you're safe,' she said as if she was going to chant everything she ever said from now on. 'I love you; I love you; I love you.' Tears of joy, pouring down her face.

'I love you too, babes. But… how did we get here? And what happened? Oh, don't cry Pats. What's wrong?' he said surveying the carnage. 'The last thing I remember we were standing on the balcony in Paris mucking about.' A thought occurred to him, and his face clouded over. 'Did I have another panic attack?'

'No, not exactly,' Patsy smiled as Rose, Goldie, Zack, and Loz came into the room.

'Rose. Loz,' Ben said, bewildered. 'And who's this?' he said nodding at the two healers.

'I think you better sit down,' Patsy smiled.

‘When this one comes along, we should probably move to a bigger place,’ Ben said as he sat next to Patsy in the ultrasound room.

‘Why?’ she frowned.

‘*Why?* I think you know why,’ he muttered.

‘We have two bedrooms. The place is plenty big enough,’ Patsy smirked, knowing exactly why Ben wanted to move out.

‘You know it’s not about the size of the place,’ Ben said, ‘What if…’

The nurse came back in, so Ben became cryptic. ‘What if it happens again.’

‘It hasn’t happened for a long time, has it. Besides, we have Zack across the hall and my mother on the end of the phone. And I told you I would never be driven out of that place. It’s gold dust. Housing Association places like that are few and far between.’

‘But Patsy, your parents are rich. They can buy us a house in a second! In any area we want…’ he pleaded.

‘But you know I don’t want to ask them for help.’ She answered defiantly.

‘Right shall we take a look then?’ the nurse cooed. ‘Let’s just pop your top up and we’ll squeeze some of this gel on. Now it might feel a little cold at first, but it’s perfectly harmless.’

Patsy had got pregnant again before January was out. She and Ben came to the hospital now full of trepidation, knowing how the chances of a smooth pregnancy were affected after a miscarriage. Although all the doctors and nurses they spoke to told them the risk of miscarriage in a future pregnancy was small, Pasty had read it was twenty percent after one miscarriage and that was a big enough percentage to cause her some anxiety.

‘Don’t worry,’ Ben smiled at her and squeezed her hand as the nurse rubbed the sensor around in the gel over her ballooning womb.

She had had morning sickness just as before; she’d had tender breasts and a constant need to pee. She’d even had cravings again, but this time it was, for some reason, for roasted beef and porridge.

'Our boy will be fine,' Ben smirked. 'He's strong like his old man.'

'Boy?' Patsy slapped him playfully. 'It's going to be a girl. I know it. I feel it.'

'Do you want to know the gender?' the nurse chirped.

'NO!' they both said in unison.

'OK! OK!' the nurse grinned for a moment. But her face began to fall with every glance at the screen. She moved the sensor around time and time again. 'Hmm,' she said.

Ben and Patsy watched her face.

'Everything all right?' Ben asked.

'Yes… um… but… um… just bear with me one moment, will you?' She hurried out.

'What is it? What's happening?' Patsy said, fear bubbling up inside of her. She put her hands on each side of the bump in an attempt to cradle the foetus, to soothe it.

Ben tried to look at the screen, but it had been turned off. When then nurse came in followed by a balding bespectacled doctor, Ben sat back in his seat quickly as if he was doing something wrong by trying to ascertain the health of his unborn child.

The nurse flicked the screen on and made sure it wasn't facing Patsy as the senior physician assessed the images. 'Hmm,' he said slowly.

Ben was starting to lose patience. 'Will everyone stop saying *hmm* and tell us what's going on!'

'Well,' the doctor cleared his old throat, 'you seem to be something of a marvel of medicine,' he said to Patsy with a conciliatory smile.

The words sounded positive, so Patsy looked up at him hopefully. 'Is my baby, OK?' she asked.

'Well, that's just it,' the doctor smiled with a sadness behind his eyes. 'There is no baby, I'm afraid.'

'What?' Ben growled.

'Your uterus is indeed enlarged, you have had all the symptoms of pregnancy without a doubt, but there is nothing in there,' he gestured to Patsy's bump. 'I think, I'm sorry to say, my dear, you might be having what is known as a... *phantom* pregnancy.'

The word was diabolically apt.

She recalled him cackling at her, 'Take it inside you! Take my seed! Have my child!'

And what made Patsy curl up on the examination table and shriek right then was not that there was nothing inside her, for she knew – just as she knew there had been someone sitting in the empty space next to her in the back of the taxi as she fled to the Sacré Coeur, and just as she knew there was someone in that grand four poster bed overlooking the Eiffel tower with her after Ben had gone and on goodness knows how many other nights after Paris – she knew now there *was* something in her womb, growing, gestating, pulsating. But the medical professionals would never see it.

She knew the doctor was talking, but she didn't hear a word of it. She knew Ben was trying to hold her, but she was numb to any touch.

After what could have been minutes or hours, the nurse found a porter with a wheelchair to take Patsy back out to the car. She was in no fit state to walk.

The porter put the brakes on and watched, stroking his pencil moustache as Ben helped Patsy into the chair. Then the man reached down and released the brakes, before putting a hand on Patsy's shoulder.

'Don't worry. We'll get you home in no time,' he said in her ear.

This was the first thing she had heard clearly since the doctor had said the words *phantom pregnancy.* And the porter's touch was the first thing she had truly felt since then, because his fingernails felt so sharp as they gripped her tightly, possessively.

About the author

Alison Naomi Porter (*née* Francis) BA (Hons) Assoc CIPD is a writer, singer, actress and songwriter from London, England. She is alumni of The St. Marylebone CofE School and performing arts institutions including Sylvia Young Theatre School, Italia Conti Theatre School, Anna Scher Theatre School, The Popular School of Dance (Balls Pond Road, Hackney; under Jean Taylor) and Identity School of Acting (London). She also has a bronze Shakespeare certification from RADA.

Alison graduated from Roehampton University with a BA (Hons) in Educational Studies with Dance Studies. On graduation she completed voluntary work experience at Media Village music PR company, where she was spotted working tirelessly (*for free*) by Paul Kennedy (Managing Director) of the record label Freakstreet Records/12One Management, who instantly gave her a paid job on the spot as a Personal Assistant to a Top Ten British pop star. He trained her as a PA, and she credits him with instilling in her a high standard of work ethic.

She has worked in the corporate world of Investment Banking, Oil and Gas, Cybersecurity, and HR & Recruitment. And has had a creative career in fashion, as a model, and in music, penning the song *Amazing Love*. She also featured on White label UK House and Garage singles by Skyworks (*featuring Alison – Naomi and MC Tweety*), *Why Should I cry* and *You're all I need* and toured with the revisioned Boney M.

Alison is married with two stepsons, and lives in London.

This is her first novel.

Acknowledgements

I would like to thank my dearest mother – Yvonne *'Faye'* Simms Foley – for being a woman of substance with a pioneering mindset, a great teacher and role model that has always believed in me, continues to inspire me, is always on my side, and helped to shape my positive outlook on life from childhood. You inspired me to believe that I can achieve anything that I set out to accomplish. You are a facilitator of dreams.

Beatrice Regina Wright – a most dearly beloved dedicated godmother who had an air of gravitas.

Carole West – for your unwavering support.

George West – for the help that you always extended.

Doris Adu – for your work ethic, positivity, and care.

Sharron Spice – for your encouraging words.

Cheleene Gordon – for your enthusiasm and support.

Eleanor Morgan – for your analytical visionary eye.

Danny Francis & Mark Francis – for helping to raise me, take me back and forth to dance classes, and auditions; and for helping to make childhood even more fun.

Francis Foley – for helping to save my life, and for introducing me to an eclectic taste in music and style.

Daddy C – for providing the best with the hand you were dealt.

Mr Dennis Aldersea (my music teacher) – for recognising my singing gift and helping me to flourish in The St. Marylebone School classical choir, where we sang Handel's Messiah annually at The Royal Festival Hall. We also sang for amongst others His Majesty HRH King Charles III (*who was then, the Prince of Wales*). It introduced me to classical music and helped build my confidence in musical sight reading and performance.

Ms Jean Taylor – for your dedication to your dance school which shaped my earliest steps. I will never forget that you graciously drove from Benfleet / Billericay to Hackney each Monday and Friday, sometimes only to teach me when no one else had turned up.

Norrie Carr – Norrie Carr Modelling agency – for my work experience and Modelling opportunities as a child.

Sylvia Young – for recognising me in dance class and giving me opportunities.

Paul Kennedy – for my introduction into the professional world.

Levi Roots – for windows of opportunities, and for years of friendship and support.

Keith Abbott (MTP) & Karolina Robinson Zammit (MTP) – for your creativity and assistance.

To all of you, I say thank you. X

Printed in Great Britain
by Amazon

40502020R00128